T0162133

QUEENS OF TRISTAINE

TRISTAINE BOOK FOUR

Acclaim for Culpepper's Fiction

"When Brenna begins work as a medic at a clinic where political prisoners are held and interrogated, she's not supposed to feel anything for the miscreants she doctors. Despite cultural and political expectations, however, Brenna can't help but feel for her patients. In particular, one named Jess piques her curiosity. …The first of what is so far a three-part series (*Battle For Tristaine: Book II, Tristaine Rises: Book III*), *The Clinic* sets the tone for what promises to be a terrific series. Culpepper's writing style is spare and evocative, her plotting precise. You can't help but feel strongly for the Amazon warrior women and their plight, and this book is a must-read for all those who enjoy light fantasy coupled with a powerful story of survival and adventure. Highly recommended." — *Midwest Book Review*

"… this smartly edited and tightly written 2nd edition [of *The Clinic*] takes hold of the reader immediately. It is engaging and thought provoking, and we are left pondering its lessons long after we read the last pages.…Culpepper is an exceptional storyteller who has taken on a very difficult subject, the subjugation of one people over another, and turned it into a spellbinding novel. As an author, she understands well that fiction can teach us our own history without the force and harshness of nonfiction. Yet *The Clinic* is just as powerful in its telling." — *L-Word.com literature*

Visit us at www.boldstrokesbooks.com

QUEENS OF TRISTAINE

TRISTAINE BOOK FOUR

by

Cate Culpepper

2007

QUEENS OF TRISTAINE

© 2007 BY CATE CULPEPPER. ALL RIGHTS RESERVED.

ISBN10: 1-933110-97-X
ISBN13: 978-1-933110-97-4

THIS TRADE PAPERBACK IS PUBLISHED BY
BOLD STROKES BOOKS, INC.
NEW YORK, USA

FIRST EDITION, NOVEMBER 2007

THIS IS A WORK OF FICTION. NAMES, CHARACTERS, PLACES, AND INCIDENTS ARE THE PRODUCT OF THE AUTHOR'S IMAGINATION OR ARE USED FICTITIOUSLY. ANY RESEMBLANCE TO ACTUAL PERSONS, LIVING OR DEAD, BUSINESS ESTABLISHMENTS, EVENTS, OR LOCALES IS ENTIRELY COINCIDENTAL.

THIS BOOK, OR PARTS THEREOF, MAY NOT BE REPRODUCED IN ANY FORM WITHOUT PERMISSION.

CREDITS
EDITORS: CINDY CRESAP AND J. B. GREYSTONE
PRODUCTION DESIGN: J. B. GREYSTONE
COVER ART: BARB KIWAK (www.kiwak.com)
COVER GRAPHIC: SHERI (graphicartist2020@hotmail.com)

By the Author

Acknowledgments

I remain grateful for the stamina, expertise, and unending good humor of Cindy Cresap, who has edited every book in the *Tristaine* series. My thanks also to J. B. Greystone for her excellent copy editing.

Warm appreciation to my good friend Connie Ward, who provided invaluable medical advice for *Queens* and priceless personal support throughout its writing.

The talented artist Barbara Kiwak painted *Queens'* cover image, and Sheri produced a wonderful cover design. I'd also like to give a shout-out to my sister bard at Bold Strokes Books, Merry Shannon, for serving as our cover's model for Brenna.

My love and thanks to Jay Csokmay for her first readings, and to all the members of the Tristaine discussion list for their many years of loyalty and inspiration.

And as always, my warm appreciation to Radclyffe, and all the women at Bold Strokes Books, for their professionalism and true dedication to making all our books the very best they can be. Rad—I thump fist to chest.

DEDICATION

For Mac
Who bettered the lives of hundreds of kids
Loved her dogs and Dan Fogelberg
And helped me catch my first fish
Rest well

CHAPTER ONE

Jess ran with the mustangs, her stride long and smooth and effortless. Her powerful legs churned through the high grass of the pasture, her dark hair a snapping wildness at her neck. A smile tugged irresistibly at Brenna's lips as she watched her lover. Every line of Jess's body radiated strength and joy.

Brenna stood with several other Amazons on a low ridge overlooking the meadow. Jess and a dozen of her warriors raced among the horses cantering through the field, their cries answering the trumpeting of the beasts. They darted in and out between the loping mustangs, some leaping aboard their broad backs, others avoiding their flashing hooves in a teasing dance. Brenna's pulse spiked higher in an exhilarated rush.

Well, half exhilarated and half appalled. This would be Brenna's fourth year in Tristaine, and the third time she'd witnessed the drawing of prime horses from the clan's herd. This annual selection was eagerly anticipated, a highlight in a season rich with festivals and celebrations. The women watching with Brenna were having a high old time, yelling encouragement to the warriors below. For most Amazons, this summer rite was jubilant fun. For Brenna, it was still a bit more harrowing than thrilling. In that way, if no other, she remained a City girl.

"They look like kids down there," Kyla said beside her. "Tomboys running with big friendly dogs."

"Dogs who weigh at least a thousand pounds each, on the hoof." Brenna let her fingers coast across the base of her throat. She often stroked the gem-bright glyph etched there when she needed reassurance and Jess's strong arms weren't immediately available.

"What was that?" Kyla's arm slid through Brenna's, her dancing brown eyes still fixed on the chase below. "You're talking to yourself again, Br—*sheesh!*"

"What?" Brenna jumped and stared wildly into the running herd, searching for Jess.

"Dana." Kyla grinned and pointed. "She's trying, but she still hasn't got the hang of the whole getting on thing."

Finding Dana in the milling crowd of women and horses was easy enough. She was picking herself up out of the grass, slapping dirt off her butt and scowling. She glared at a large roan, then skipped into a fast run straight toward him. Dana launched herself into the air, a dive of impressive height and distance— unfortunately, so high and distant she catapulted right over the trotting horse's back and crashed gracelessly to the grass on its other side.

"Ouch," Brenna and Kyla gasped in tandem.

Dana rolled immediately to her feet, bellowing obscenities loudly enough to reach the cheering section on the ridge.

"Mustang, two," one of the other Amazons sang, "City soldier, zilch!"

Laughter met this remark, but the merriment was sparse and faltered quickly. Brenna glanced at Kyla and saw the muscles in her delicate jaw standing out. She pressed Kyla's arm gently.

"How many of Tristaine's battles does she have to fight?" Kyla murmured, "How many glyphs does Dana have to earn before she stops being a City soldier and becomes an Amazon?"

"You know Dana is Amazon to the core, Ky, City-born or not." Brenna nodded to acknowledge the apologetic looks a few of the women offered them. "I thought that kind of idiotic remark stopped after our last battle with Botesh. No one denied Dana's bravery and loyalty that night."

"Yes, but that was two years ago." Kyla drew in a deep breath and waved encouragingly at Dana. "Eight seasons of peace, and

Tristaine's warriors are itching for a fight. Amazons aren't above picking at each other if no new enemies present themselves."

Brenna studied Kyla silently and with some sadness. Her tone held a note of adult wryness that still seemed foreign to her. Brenna remembered the exuberant teenager Kyla had been when they met almost four years ago. That was before she lost her wife, Camryn, to a crossbow bolt intended for Jess. Kyla also lost some crucial youthful essence in those dark days of grief.

But she had healed a little since then. Two years earlier, when the clan battled a demon queen, Kyla had been given the most extraordinary gift granted any Amazon. For a few precious moments, she had been reunited with her lost lover across the veil of death. Camryn herself had wished Kyla a happy, peaceful life, rich with love beyond their marriage, and Kyla was working hard to be worthy of that blessing.

She was singing again, and that was a gift to the entire clan. Grief had silenced Kyla's ethereal voice after Camryn's death, but as she healed, music refilled her spirit and created moments of sheer beauty around the Amazons' storyfires. And Kyla was finding joy in her sisters again, thanks in part to the "City soldier" who had fought so bravely for Tristaine. The friendship between Kyla and Dana had grown strong these past seasons, and Brenna saw Kyla's expression soften again as she watched her.

"Hey, Miz Brenna!" Aria cocked a curvaceous hip and waved five perfectly tapered, berry-painted fingernails. "Looks like your brawny adonai down there has chosen her horse!"

Brenna shielded her eyes from the sun's glare and focused on Jess running in the meadow below. She was pacing a pretty little bay with a white mane, woman and horse matching stride for stride. With a burst of speed, Jess vaulted aboard the mustang's back, a motion so fluid she seemed to meld with the bay, her lithe body a natural extension of the horse's grace and strength.

The mare made a brief fight of it. She shied and skittered, as if trying to pitch Jess off like a stubborn horsefly. Jess rode her like one, through a twisting series of circles and a few sharp lunges, until the bay began to settle under her light touch.

A chorus of admiring whistles rose from the women on the ridge.

"That was *so* pretty." Kyla sighed. "Do you ever get tired of half the clan fawning over Jess after one of these public displays of macha?"

"Not as long as she remembers whose bed her macha butt warms at night." Brenna smiled at a private memory and then caught Jess's eye.

Jess reached down and patted the bay's neck, arched one brow at Brenna, and flashed a grin that was pure rogue, white teeth gleaming in her tanned face. Brenna fell in love all over again.

"Come on." She took Kyla's hand. "Let's go round up our tomboys."

❖

If Gaia intended Amazon queens to be remote, untouchable icons of virtue, Jess thought, she has to stop making Amazon queens who look like that.

She rested one ankle on the bay's neck and watched Brenna stroll into the meadow. If it had been blackest, moonless midnight, Jess would have been able to pick her adonai out of the group of Amazons with her. A pleasing sensuality flavored Brenna's movements now, a certain light, sultry confidence that had grown in her these last seasons as her roots in Tristaine ran deeper. Her blond hair was still short, but thicker and wilder than she'd worn it in the City. It drifted against her slender neck in gold waves. The clear green of Brenna's eyes could exude warmth or desire, or, as they did now, frank admiration. Jess soaked up the affection and pride in Brenna's gaze and fell in love all over again.

Jess took a hemp rope from her belt and slipped it over the bay's head, then lifted one leg across the horse's neck and dropped lightly to the ground.

"Hey, hotshot." Brenna rose on her toes to kiss Jess's cheek. "You did some fine horse-wrestling out there."

"Not much wrestling needed, lass." Jess straightened, letting her tall shadow shade Brenna from the sun. "Our herd's half tame. Hakan attends every birth, so Tristaine's foals know a woman's touch before their eyes open."

"Not that big old roan." Dana scowled, tipping her chin so Kyla could examine a bruise on her jaw. "Did you see that mangy mutt run out from under me? That horse is a damn bigot. It hates Amazons."

"We saw it, my little pookie." Kyla patted Dana's cheek.

"Hey, she looks familiar!" Brenna stepped closer to the mare and stroked the blaze of white on her forehead. "Jesstin, you found Bracken's twin!"

"Aye, she's of Bracken's line." Jess enjoyed the sparkle of pleasure in Brenna's eyes, and her obvious ease with this horse. Brenna's self-assurance had been a long time coming—she'd worked hard to overcome her fear of the big beasts. Jess coiled the hemp rope that encircled the bay's neck and offered it to Brenna.

Brenna looked at the rope, puzzled. "You want me to take her to the stables?"

"Up to you, Bren." Jess shrugged. "She's yours to stable if you wish."

"Mine?" Brenna smiled and laid her palm on the warm, firm swell of the mare's jaw. "Jesstin. You're giving me this horse?"

"Brenna, you've earned this horse." Jess patted the bay's side. "She's deep-chested, like my Bracken, so she'll have his endurance. She'll be gentle, once she's used to us, but fast as a—*mrrf*."

Laughing, Brenna surged against Jess, pulled her head down, and planted a kiss smack on her lips.

"Technically," Dana said, tapping Brenna's back, "this horse belongs to Tristaine, so she's not Jess's to give or yours to own, but—"

"Damn, girl, please shut up." Kyla rested an elbow dreamily on Dana's shoulder. "We're witnessing a real rite of passage here."

"Ah, I know that." Dana grinned at Brenna. "Congratulations, adanin."

Brenna still had her arms wound around Jess's neck. "Thank you, teacher," she murmured.

Jess smiled, touched by the honorific, and rested her forehead against Brenna's.

The bay mare chose that moment to break wind, genteelly rather than crudely, but Dana and Kyla were still reduced to fits of adolescent cackling.

❖

By the time the horses were gathered and tethered and the Amazons started back to the mesa, the sun had lost its bright sheen and was coasting toward the western peaks. Brenna walked beside Dana, greeting other women as they filtered past through the trees. Jess and Kyla were ahead of them, Jess's arm draped across the younger woman's shoulders.

Brenna craned her neck to try to spot her bay in the small herd being led toward Tristaine's stables. Her palms already itched to stroke her mount's velvet-soft nose again, and she couldn't seem to banish the grin wreathing her face.

She remembered buying her first car in the City—an exchange of mundane commerce and necessity. Nothing like this thrill. Horses were far more than transportation to mountain Amazons. They were a vital, natural link to their shared history. That pretty brown beast with the white mane was Brenna's four-legged diploma into an important aspect of clan life, as dearly won as any of her City medical certificates.

Brenna took in the blue glory of the mountain sky shading to indigo with the coming of twilight. The fresh, clear air was redolent of the pine, spruce, and fir that carpeted the hills around their mesa.

She noted Dana was scowling and rubbing her hip again. "I'm wondering if I should insist you drop your drawers so I can take a look at that."

"No way. I'm not gonna expose my naked buttock to you." Dana jerked her chin at Jess and Kyla, several yards up the trail. "Not with your goliath girlfriend up there, who would tear out my trachea in a fit of jealous rage."

Brenna grinned. "Somehow I think Jess would control her fury in the face of medical necessity."

"Eh, I'm the one who's jealous." Dana crammed her hands in the pockets of her trousers and kicked a pinecone off the path. "Look at her, Brenna. Not a mark on her. She's not even dusty. Jess lands the first horse she targets, and I fall on my butt three times in a row."

"We've both seen Jess take her share of falls on other days, honey." Brenna wound her arm through Dana's. "Even Hakan's taken a few dives off horses at a dead run. You're being a little hard on yourself."

"I just wanted to show her I could do it." Dana's brown eyes weren't on Jess any longer; she was watching Kyla. "It sure would have been sweet to see Ky's face when I landed one of the stupid runts."

"Yeah, it would have." Brenna studied her friend. Dana was growing into one of Jess's most able warriors. Fearless in battle, cool-headed and smart, she sometimes even mastered the stoic mask that marked a blood-tested Amazon fighter. Except when she looked at Kyla. "She loves you, Dana."

"I know she does." Dana nodded toward Kyla and Jess. "See that?"

Brenna glanced at the pair walking ahead of them and smiled. Kyla's arm was draped with friendly warmth around Jess's waist. She bumped the much taller warrior playfully with her hip as they laughed together, the affection between them palpable and deep.

"Kyla walks with me like that now," Dana said. There was something stiff in her smile. "She paws me like that, all the time. We're good friends. We're adanin."

"But?" Brenna tried to see her.

"But she doesn't walk with me the way you walk with Jess."

"What do you mean?"

"Well..." Dana colored. "Think about it."

Brenna's sense memory had no trouble recalling Jess's muscular body against hers, heating the length of her side as they strolled down Tristaine's shaded paths. Their matched steps were more often a relaxed, sensuous dance than mere walking, as different from the platonic friendliness evident between Kyla and Jess as night and day. Brenna remembered the combined strength and gentleness of Jess's arm around her, and that led inevitably to more intimate memories, of arching beneath the strong hands holding her down...

Brenna shivered.

"That's what I mean." Dana smiled at her sadly. "Kyla doesn't walk with me like that. She doesn't look at me the way you look at Jess. I'm thinking she never will."

"Maybe." Brenna watched Kyla thoughtfully. "But I hope you won't give up on her, Dana. Kyla and Camryn were friends for ten years before they became adonai, remember? She's always been careful with her heart."

Dana sighed, and Brenna watched her visibly shake off the topic. "Well, give me ten more years and maybe I'll learn to sit a damn horse, at least. Hey, your little sister learned to ride faster than either of us, Bren. Sammy's gonna be jealous of your new hooves."

"Yep, she will." Brenna smiled.

"Won't bother you a bit, huh?"

"Not me."

"Ah, sisters." Dana bent down and lifted a glossy black feather from the trail. "I thank my lucky butt I've got no blood-kin in the clan. Where is Sammy, anyway? She was looking forward to watching us slide around in horse poop."

"She still had a sore throat this morning, so I talked her into staying back."

Brenna had to admit she still mothered Samantha, even now, well into their twenties. Her younger sister tolerated it reasonably well. Sammy was smart enough to realize she might still need some maternal care after the losses she'd suffered.

Brenna noticed that the dark, elongated shadow beside her was bouncing oddly. She glanced at Dana, whose gaze was pinned again on Jess. Dana had stuck the black feather in her chestnut hair and was walking with an overly long stride, her jaw clenched, her shoulders swinging in slow, brawny arcs.

Brenna snickered. Dana had an uncommon gift for physical mimicry, and she had Jess's long-legged saunter down to a T. "You know she's going to catch you doing that someday."

"Doin' whut?" Dana might be able to imitate Jess's moves, but her rendition of her mild brogue was a miserable failure. "Doan worry, lassie. Yer warrior's too dang tall ta see me from way up thar."

"But she's got uncommon hearing." Jess turned and waited for them, her arms folded. Kyla stopped too, grinning.

Dana straightened quickly, and Brenna reached up to tousle her hair, almost dislodging the feather.

"How does she do that?" Dana muttered.

Brenna smiled at Jess. "Well...she's uncommon."

"Brenna, lady!" A husky Amazon, well past middle age, hustled up to them, beaming ear to ear. "Sorry to interrupt your council, sisters, but Brenna, Shann asks that you come to the healing lodge. Nothing urgent," she added quickly. "She just wants you to check out some new herbs she found."

"Thanks, adanin," Brenna said. "I'll be right there."

"I'll tell Shann, lady." The woman turned, but Brenna touched her wrist gently.

"Carelle," Brenna said kindly. "Tristaine has only one queen. We have only one lady."

"Oh, Brenna." The wrinkles bracketing Carelle's mouth deepened with her smile. "I know that, dear girl. I honor Shann as the only ruler of my clan, we all do. Just forgive your adanin if we want to honor Shann's daughter, and our next queen, as well!"

Brenna smiled and patted the big woman. Carelle waved a cheerful farewell and trotted back toward the mesa.

"Jesstin." Brenna forced the words through clenched teeth. "Am I still smiling?"

Jess tipped Brenna's chin up to check. "And a lovely grimace it is."

Brenna hissed out a long breath and worked her stiff jaw back and forth.

Kyla slipped her arm through Brenna's as they continued down the trail. "Carelle didn't mean any harm, Bren."

"Of course she didn't. She's a nice woman." Brenna pulled open her collar and pointed to the colorful tattoo at the base of her throat. "But where on this glyph do you see a royal insignia, Ky? Hmm? Anywhere?"

"Let's take a look." Dana turned and walked backward, peering at Brenna's throat. "I see some stars, a little hand with a whirlpool in it, and a pretty weed."

"A *weed,*" Kyla groaned. "You wear the sigils of a healer and a mystic, Bren."

"Nothing queenly," Dana added.

"Thank you." Brenna snapped her collar closed, mollified.

Jess draped her arm around Brenna's shoulders. "No queen can be forced to rule, Brenna. All you have to do is decline Shann's throne."

"Which I've done, Jess, every way I know how." Brenna

kicked another black feather off the path, irritated. "I'm a good medic, but I won't pretend to be anyone's leader. Shann seems to hear me, but the word sure hasn't filtered through the ranks yet. *Lady* they call me, for heaven's sake."

"Aye, you're a fine healer," Jess agreed. "And a talented seer."

Brenna mumbled grumpily.

"You are, Brenna, you're amazing!" Kyla squeezed her arm. "You see into the realm of spirit more clearly than any mystic Tristaine has ever known."

Brenna sighed.

Dana nudged Kyla. "See, she's learned not to argue with that."

"Being called a seer bothered you at first." Jess kissed Brenna's hair. "You used to snap at me like a harpy whenever I mentioned your sight."

"Well, stuff just kept happening." Brenna fingered the coarse fabric of Jess's vest. "You can only have so many visions, and so many out-of-body strolls, before denying that you're having them starts to sound psychotic."

"Confidence in your powers came to you slowly, but with certainty, over time." Jess's rough palm caressed Brenna's upper arm. "Just as all our gifts take root and grow."

"Jesstin." Brenna peered up at her suspiciously. "Please tell me you're not implying I'll simply *get used* to being an Amazon queen."

Jess chuckled. "I don't presume to know what our Grandmothers intend for you, adonai. I'm just enjoying the journey."

Jess stopped walking and trained her cobalt eyes on the sky, and then Brenna heard it—a dry, cawing sound overhead. She focused on its source just as the large bird made a clumsy landing on a thin branch high in a pine by the side of their trail.

"Crow?" Dana squinted up at the black creature as it pecked slowly at the branch.

"Not this far from the City," Jess said. "A raven."

The bird seemed unsteady, rocking slightly on its narrow perch.

"A drunk raven," Dana added.

Jess crouched, resting her elbows on her knees, and studied the ground. Brenna saw two more long black feathers in the grass, and another further along into the trees. She looked up and spotted a raven balancing awkwardly on a thin branch. It rose with an angry snap of wings and flew in a slow, ragged arc toward the east.

Jess rose. "Something's up."

Brenna noted they all stepped closer to Jess, an instinctive raising of their shields. Jess nodded toward the trees and started toward them, and they fell in behind her with the ease of long seasons of drills. They wove quickly and silently through a stand of aspen, following the bird's lurching progress overhead.

J'heika, rise.

Brenna came to a dead halt, and Kyla very nearly smacked into her back.

"What is it, Bren?" Kyla steadied herself against her.

"Nothing," Brenna murmured. She touched Kyla in reassurance, then turned and followed Jess.

She didn't recognize this new voice. In the past, the voices that had whispered those two words in Brenna's mind had all sounded elderly. Shann said it was the Grandmothers calling her. This voice was someone new, someone young. Brenna hadn't heard this particular command in years, and a thrill of misgiving went through her.

❖

Jess hadn't felt this kind of prickling at the back of her neck in many seasons. She had learned to respect this rising of her inner hackles, as Dyan had called Jess's keen instincts for danger. Shann's adonai and the leader of Tristaine's warriors, Dyan had died beneath a hail of City bullets shortly after naming Jess her second. Now Jess carried the burden of her clan's protection alone, and she relied on her gut. One addled bird didn't mean disaster, but any disruption in the natural world was worrisome.

She couldn't keep sight of the black bird's path through the canopy of green branches above them, but visual tracking wasn't necessary. Jess heard the discordant chorus of dying ravens before she saw them.

They emerged from the trees into a small, circular enclosure, a patch of sparse grass all but carpeted with dusty black feathers and droppings. Jess put out a hand to stop Brenna, a chill working up her back.

There were fifty or more birds milling in the clearing, staggering, flapping frayed wings without gaining flight. Mountain ravens were big creatures, with wingspans nearly four feet across, but these birds looked shrunken, diminished. Their cawing, usually a crisp, sharp cracking sound, was reduced to throaty rattles. Several were already dead, on their backs in the grass, their stick-like legs stiffened, their black eyes milky and vacant.

"Sweet Gaia." Kyla stepped carefully into the circle. "Jess, what's happening to them?"

"I don't know, lass."

"Could they be poisoned?" Dana nudged a dead bird cautiously with one foot. "What do these things eat?"

"Insects, carrion." Jess watched another bird convulse in the grass, then lie still, and an odd shiver coursed through her. "I can't see this many feeding off any one source."

"And they don't travel in big groups like this, do they?" Kyla hugged herself. "They're suffering, Jesstin. Is there anything we can—"

"Brenna?" Jess frowned and took her wife's arm. Brenna's posture was rigid, and she stared at the ravens intently. The color was draining from her face.

Brenna heard the sharpness in Jess's tone, but she couldn't

respond. Even if she hadn't been gripped by the paralysis of sudden trance, she was too filled with horror to summon any sound.

Dying Amazons, dropping in drifts at her feet. Young women, older ones, children, clothed in tattered gray shrouds, staggering, falling to their knees. Their faces were ghostly white, and contorted with the futile agony of trying to draw breath in vain. Other Amazons knelt at their sides, and the harsh cawing of the ravens sounded in Brenna's ears like the grief-filled shrieks of the bereaved. Then those who comforted the afflicted fell ill too, their hands clawing at their throats in terror.

"Kyla, back away!" Brenna's tone rang with command, and Jess started and reached for the dagger in her vest.

Kyla obeyed at once, stepping around the stumbling ravens until she reached clear grass.

Brenna went to Dana in three fast strides and snatched the black feather out of her hair. "Keep your hands away from your faces, all of you. Let's get out of here."

"Brenna, what the—" Dana began.

"*Move,*" Brenna ordered, and they moved.

Jess ushered Kyla quickly out of the circle. She took Brenna's arm as they weaved through the trees and felt her trembling.

"Head for the stream." The fingers Brenna wrapped around Jess's wrist were cold. "We need to wash our hands."

Jess swallowed, her mouth suddenly dry. "You're thinking plague, Bren?"

"Maybe I'm wrong. I pray I am." Brenna closed her eyes. "I have a sister with a sore throat."

CHAPTER TWO

The night was fragrant with the light scents of sandalwood and lavender.

Brenna asked Sammy to move from the cottage she shared with three other women to Tristaine's healing lodge until her symptoms cleared. It was a comfortable log cabin, scrupulously clean, but far more warm and friendly than any hospital unit in the City. Colorful arrangements of dried wildflowers brightened each corner, and the white pine walls were adorned with paintings from the artists' guild and drawings by the clan's children.

"This is overkill." Samantha sat propped up in bed against a thick sheaf of furs. Her arms were folded, but her gaze on Brenna was affectionate. "You used to do this at the Youth Home, Bree. You'd threaten bloody mayhem if they tried to make me go to school when you thought I was sick."

"I had to go by my instincts. You claimed to be sick every single Friday when you had a math test." Brenna frowned as she palpated the base of Samantha's jaw. "Does this hurt?"

"Yes, a cold claw digging into my throat hurts." Samantha gave Brenna's hand a playful slap. "Brenna, I have a head cold."

"Well, then you and your head need to stay under these blankets." Brenna pulled the furs up to her sister's waist. "I don't want you out spreading your phlegm all over the village."

"You're so uncouth. Hey." Sammy tapped Brenna's arm. "You look worried. Should I be?"

Brenna hesitated, studying Sammy's delicate features. Her color was good and her green eyes focused and alert. The circles beneath them might be a little more pronounced. Sammy, who used to hit their shared pillow in the Youth Home fast asleep, hadn't slept a night through in three years. Brenna wondered if any woman ever truly recovered from the deaths of her husband and child. But physically, Sammy seemed no worse than she'd been that morning. There was still no fever.

Brenna brushed Samantha's wrist with her thumb. "We don't know enough yet, Sam. But, yeah, this might be more than a cold. I'll want to watch you carefully for a while. I promise you'll know everything as soon as I do."

"Okay. That's fair." Samantha sighed. "So, am I quarantined? To keep my phlegm to myself?"

"I'm afraid so, honey. For now at least." Brenna bent and kissed her sister's forehead, then stood up. "Try to get some rest."

"This might help." Shanendra, daughter of Elaine and queen of the last great Amazon tribe, smiled at Samantha with a sweet maternity as natural to her spirit as royal command. She carried a cup of steaming tea to Samantha and sat at the side of her bed. "This concoction is more wild honey than herb, to mask its bitterness. Sip it slowly, dear one."

Brenna breathed in the mild fragrance of the tea, puzzled. "Echinacea?"

"Astragalus." Shann patted Samantha's leg sympathetically when she grimaced at the taste. "I had no idea we could find it this high in the hills."

"Astragalus?" Brenna blinked. "You're feeding your daughter, and my sister, a tea made of locoweed?"

Samantha pretended to choke, and Shann laughed.

"Luckily, my daughter, and your sister, is not livestock, Brenna. There's no harm in this root as an infusion." Shann brushed Samantha's auburn hair off her forehead. "And it might help clear this foggy young head."

Brenna leaned against the pine wall and studied her only living blood-kin. Jess claimed there was a familial resemblance between Brenna and Shann, but she had never been able to see it herself. There was no missing the likeness between Shann and her sister, though. Their profiles were similar, with high cheekbones tapering to strong chins. Brenna shared a lighter version of Shann's fawn-colored hair, but Samantha's curling tresses were the dark reddish-brown of their father, David.

Brenna had no conscious memory of him. He died when Sammy was still an infant. David and Shann had been fighting in an underground cell of the Resistance when the City Government launched a vicious campaign to crush the movement's leaders. David had been killed in an ambush of City soldiers and Shann had been imprisoned, and their two daughters placed in a spartan City Youth Home. Brenna and Samantha had only discovered their blood relation to Shann as adults, after fate reunited them in Tristaine.

Shann asked, "Will you feel abandoned, Samantha, if I take our wise seer away for a quick council?"

"Your seer, my sister, take her, take her." Sammy waved at them both vaguely. "But, Brenna, I have to meet your new horse, so don't let me die before you haul her up here to say hello."

"I'm not going to let you die." Brenna managed a smile. "I'll check you later."

❖

Jess stared at the beautiful oak carving of a winged woman in flight that graced an entire wall of the healing lodge's anteroom. The serene figure depicted was Gaia Herself to some of Tristaine's women, Artemis or gold-winged Isis to others. To Jess, She was simply one of the Mothers, and she had spoken to Her on a regular basis since she was a child. Jess reminded Her now that She promised centuries ago to protect Tristaine, Her last Amazon clan.

She listened to the low murmur of voices in the next room. Shann's soft laughter, a sound that had charmed and soothed Jess through her turbulent adolescence, helped calm her nerves now.

The curtain of bead-strings parted, and her queen and her adonai joined her.

Jess measured Brenna silently, reading a dozen subtle clues to her mood that only long seasons together taught her to interpret. Brenna's gaze was direct and warm, but there was a new stiffness in the usually flowing lines of her body. Jess touched her wrist, offering a brief comforting connection, and Brenna smiled her thanks.

"Have you eaten, Jesstin?" Shann tapped Jess's chin, then settled on a cushioned bench. "You're wearing your old rock-jawed glower again, my young friend. Stop it. We don't know what we're facing yet. Brenna, tell me your thoughts."

Brenna sat next to her mother. "I'm afraid we might be facing an epidemic, lady. Has Tristaine ever been through one?"

"Our journals tell us our clan has weathered many fevers over the centuries," Shann replied, "but we've read of no killing plagues."

Jess recognized Shann's intent focus on her elder daughter. Jess was awarded the same respectful attention whenever she spoke to the queen on important matters.

"Have you seen any signs other than the ravens?" Shann asked.

"No, but that was a pretty chilling sign." Brenna looked at Jess, who nodded grim agreement. She was acquainted with the forms death could take in Gaia's wild creatures, but the mortal throes of those dying birds had been eerie, gruesome in a way Jess couldn't explain.

"Jess and the others saw dying birds, lady." Brenna seemed to read Jess's mind. "I saw dying Amazons. I couldn't make out faces, just women weeping on their knees beside their dead sisters."

"Sweet Cybele." Shann swallowed visibly. "But can a pestilence of ravens truly threaten us, Blades? We've never known disease to jump from bird to human."

"They've known it." Brenna nodded toward the south. "Down in the City. It happened in one of the outer Burroughs about five years ago. Some form of influenza, fast and virulent."

"Fatal?"

"The mortality rate was almost sixty percent."

Jess drew in a sharp breath. "Lady. Should we call a clan council?"

"No, Jesstin." Shann regarded Brenna thoughtfully. "If this strain is infectious, it wouldn't be wise to call a full gathering of our sisters. Let's do this." She extended her hand to Jess, who stepped closer to take it. "In the morning, Jess, form a contingent of your most trusted warriors. Send them in pairs to each lodge and cabin to see if there's illness. Remind everyone, especially those with children and grandmothers, to take precautions."

"Would it be best to send them out tonight, Shann?" Brenna rubbed her neck, wincing. "If this is something really scary, time's going to be important."

"Hmm." Shann tapped her thighs. "I'll follow your counsel, Blades, if you feel strongly about this, but my own choice would be morning. Sounding an alarm at night can invite fear and rumor, and we don't have much true knowledge yet. I think we can allow ourselves these few hours."

Brenna hesitated, and Jess read uncertainty in her silence. Then her features cleared and she nodded. "In the morning, then. Jesstin, will you divorce me if I spend the night here? I'd like to keep an eye on Sam."

"I'll bed here too, lass, if you like." Jess moved behind Brenna and began a gentle massage of her neck. "Lady, get some rest. We can call you if our little sister in there stirs."

Shann smiled at them both, and when Shann smiled at the women she loved, they knew to their bones they were cherished. "Then with you two on watch, I'll retire to my humble cabin. Let me wish Samantha a good night." She parted the curtain of beads that separated the two rooms.

Jess grinned. Brenna was making cat-like sounds of pleasure as her strong fingers eased the tightness in her neck. "Why is my adonai so tense?"

"Your adonai spent most of the day watching your fine, unarmed self jump around with killer warhorses," Brenna reminded her. "And if that weren't relaxing enough, we had to stumble upon a possible plague that might wipe out half our clan."

"You think Shann is wrong to wait until morning." Jess's breath stirred the silky hair over Brenna's ear. She felt her uneasiness through the palms of her hands.

"Something's happening, Jess." Brenna leaned back into her, and Jess folded her arms around her waist. "I heard the queen's summons today."

Jess's embrace tightened slightly. "Just the summons?"

"'J'heika, rise,'" Brenna confirmed. "Nothing else. I didn't recognize the voice."

"Bren, did you tell Shann this?"

"Ah, Jess." Brenna sighed and rested her head on the smooth curve of Jess's shoulder. "Shann's right, a few hours won't matter either way. And everyone seems so intent on this queen...thing right now. I'll tell her if it seems important."

"I'll trust you with that." Jess rested her lips in Brenna's hair. "For now, I'll build us a nest by the window."

❖

Brenna dreamed of the veiled woman for the first time that night.

She was young—Brenna could tell that much by the easy grace of her carriage. She wore a simple white robe. The silver fabric that shrouded her head and shoulders shimmered in the scant illumination of troubled dreams.

Brenna couldn't see her features, but she knew with certainty that the veiled woman was watching her with an intensity that sent a shiver up her sleeping spine.

"Hello," Brenna said politely. "Have we met?"

The apparition didn't answer. To Brenna's astonishment, she lowered herself gracefully to one knee and inclined her head.

"I honor you, j'heika." The voice was rich and warm with respect, and Brenna had heard it before. After a moment of stillness, the woman stood.

"It was you." Brenna strained to see her features through her gleaming veil. "You called me earlier today."

"Yes, I sounded the queen's summons." The woman's tone was calm, but then it grew stern. "Hear me, Brenna. You have seen the face of our enemy. Now act."

And that was all. The veiled figure faded and Brenna awoke, unrefreshed, in Jess's arms.

❖

By dusk that day, three other women and two children had joined Samantha in quarantine in the healing lodge. Samantha and both children were running low-grade fevers.

Shann called an emergency summons of her Queen's Council.

❖

"We have to go back to the Clinic."

An appalled silence fell after Brenna's words faded.

Twilight found the grassy park in the center of the Amazons' village deserted. Tristaine's women had gathered early in their cabins, as if the protective walls of their lodges could hold out the pestilence. Shann and the six sisters who formed her Queen's Council sat in a loose circle around a small, snapping fire enclosed by stones.

"Brenna." Dana cleared her throat. "No disrespect, you know that. But have you flat out lost your flaming mind?"

"Dana," Kyla murmured.

"No, Ky. This is nuts." Dana got to her feet. "Have you forgotten everything you ever knew about the City, Bren?"

"Tell me again, lady." Sarah, the oldest of the queen's advisors, rubbed her bald head, scowling. "You insist on including this rude young weed on your Council because...?"

"Because our young bring us energy and insight far fresher than yours or mine, grandmother." Shann's gaze on her elder was affectionate. She nodded at Dana. "We're listening, sister."

"Good. Because we need to find another way, Shann." Dana's normally animated face was set and still. "Returning to the Clinic would be a suicide mission, you know that. The City has *guns*. They have technology and an entire Army with *guns*."

"An Amazon warrior can kill with her hands, little girl." Aria's sensual purr took the sting out of her words. She reclined in the thick grass and smiled up at Dana. "And Tristaine has always had her dealings with the City. Jesstin and Kyla survived their own exiles in that detestable sinkhole."

"Barely," Dana muttered.

"Tristaine has never needed the City," Sarah growled and spat delicately into the grass. "Lady, Amazons are hardy stock, or we'd have died out generations ago. And you're one of the greatest healers our tribe has ever had. Can't we use our own store of herbs and your knowledge of Gaia's healing lore to fight this illness?"

"We can and we will, grandmother." Shann lifted a kettle from a flat rock near their small fire and refilled Sarah's mug with a fragrant tea. "We'll call all the natural remedies we've harvested in these hills to our defense. But Brenna's vision was powerful, and it warns against easy cures. I've already begun our search for a new remedy, but that requires a great deal of testing, and time is precious to us now." Shann nodded at Jess. "I'd like to hear my second's thoughts."

Jess stared at the crackling flames in the center of their circle. "I've heard our sister's opposition to this plan, lady. I'm still waiting to hear what hope Dana has to offer in its stead."

"Jess, Brenna—" Dana sighed harshly. "Dang, please know I don't mean to doubt you. But this is the first I've heard about any outbreak of this weird flu in the City."

"Dana, if that surprises you, you've forgotten everything *you* ever knew about the City." Brenna rose and went to Dana. Her tone was warm, even loving, but absolutely firm. "It hit the South Borough—zoned for mixed races, Caucasians banned. The Clinic needed human subjects to make a vaccine. Where would you expect to learn about that, the *City Gazette*?"

"And they found a cure, Brenna?" Aria asked. "Those barbarians down in the City?"

"No resource was spared once the Government realized their own class could fall ill just as easily as people in the outer boroughs." Brenna smiled without humor. "Yes, they had a vaccine and a cocktail of drugs that beat this flu in record time."

"We need the Clinic's medicine to save our clan." Jess looked at Dana. "You're right to respect the danger of this quest, adanin. The City is a formidable enemy. But we don't shirk from danger when the prize is so dear and the cost of losing beyond bearing."

"We haven't heard from one of my wisest councilors." Shann drew their attention to Kyla, who sat quietly in the grass. Her expression was almost serene, but her features were pale.

"I might throw up," Kyla began politely. "Because I'm terrified. I hate the thought of any of us going back down to that slaughterhouse. But I can't think of any other way to help our sick, Shann, and we've got so little time." She looked at Dana with regret. "I think we have to go back."

Shann murmured agreement, and another silence fell as she met the gaze of each of her Amazons in turn. "All right. We're not in perfect accord, so I'll pray we follow our Mothers' lights. We'll send a party to the City."

A sigh moved through the Council, and Dana and Brenna sat down again in the hush that followed. Twilight had become full dark, and the stars were extraordinarily bright with no moon to rival their flickering. Overhead the Seven Sisters, the constellation that housed the spirits who guided Tristaine, glowed brilliantly.

Jess was the first to pull her gaze from the star-drenched heavens. "I'll need a team of six, lady. Four in the City, two as backup nearby."

"You'll need me to get into the Civilian Unit in the Clinic where the study was done." Brenna returned their grave regard. "I was assigned there as a medic before I was transferred to Military. I might still have contacts there."

"And a few enemies with grudges, I bet." Kyla frowned at Brenna and nudged her leg with her foot. "Caster had blood-kin, didn't she?"

"She was married, with two teenagers. Boys." Brenna's gaze grew distant. "But Caster was a scientist, Ky, not a Military leader. We haven't sighted any City patrols since we found this mesa. I don't think either Caster's sons or the Army have much invested in avenging her death."

"Caster's kin probably sacrifice virgins to Tristaine nightly in thanks." Sarah drew on the pipe that was perennially clenched between her strong teeth, lighting her withered cheeks with a robust glow. "Artemis herself owes us for freeing the world of that lunatic shrike harpy bitch, spit thrice on her grave."

"Sheer poetry, Sarah." Aria lifted one long arm and her many bracelets trickled down her wrist. "If we're to take on this dangerous quest, we must prepare. I can have food packed for our intrepid warriors by dawn, Shann."

"Thank you, sweet girl." Shann smiled at her old friend. "Jesstin, who will ride with you and Brenna?"

"I should go, lady." Kyla looked at Jess. "Camryn and I hid in the City before we broke into the Prison to find Jess. At least I know enough about how to act like a City dweller to get by."

"Well hell, if Kyla's going, I am too." Dana scratched her scalp fiercely, frowning. "And I'd have to anyway. I've been down there more recently than any of you guys."

"You train your warriors well, Jesstin." Shann looked at Dana with approval. "They speak their minds, but even if they don't agree, they'll fight for the good of their clan."

"I try," Jess sighed. "I'll take Hakan and Vicar too, lady."

"Time is of the essence." Shann stood in one graceful motion. "Aria will arrange provisions. Sarah, please alert Hakan and have her prepare our party's horses and weapons. The rest of you, to my lodge. We have maps to study and strategy to plan."

❖

Tristaine's cartographers were genuine artists. The parchments bearing their etchings were multi-colored, jeweled landscapes, richly detailed and accurate to the league. Jess spread out their largest map on the burnished surface of the oak table in Shann's private lodge. Finished only that spring, this map held their most up-to-date charting of the terrain between their mesa and the City.

Half an apple hovered beneath Jess's nose. Tristaine's apples were the size of the City's cantaloupes, and the fruit's fresh, tangy scent tickled her nostrils. She smiled and pushed the apple away gently with one finger.

"You should eat something." Brenna laid the fruit aside. "This is looking to be a long night."

"I will soon. Just don't want to drip juice on our maps." Jess lifted Brenna's hand and sucked a drop of juice from her thumb. She looked around the small cabin, illuminated with a mild gold glow by oil lamps and the fire in Shann's wide hearth. Shann was laying out a light spread of cold meats and cheeses on a low table along one log wall. Kyla and Dana were studying the entries in Brenna's journal that chronicled the clan's migration up to the mesa.

Jess wasn't hungry. Her body thrummed with a current of restless energy, a familiar sensation that came with shifting into crisis mode. She tried to ignore the uneasy churning in her gut, which was both unfamiliar and unwelcome. Jess had never wrestled this particular brand of gnawing dread before at the dawn of any mission. She stared down at the map and cracked her knuckles, and Brenna nudged her hip gently. She'd been trying to break Jess of the habit for years.

"Keep it up, ace," Brenna murmured. "See how much fun it'll be, pulling a bowstring with arthritic fingers before you're forty."

Jess heard the strain in her wry tone and knew it didn't concern the future of her knuckles. Brenna stood stiffly beside her, her gaze unfocused, worrying her lower lip with her teeth. Jess put a finger to Brenna's chin and turned her head. When their eyes met a low, reverberating pulse sounded in Jess's sex, followed by a rush of warmth. *Ah, battle lust,* she thought ruefully. *I'd take you on this table here and now, girl.* She brushed her thumb lightly across Brenna's full lower lip. "Second thoughts, lass?"

"Several dozen." Brenna looked up at Jess with naked uncertainty. "We're not really going to do this, right? We'll come to our senses soon?"

"Aye, querida, absolutely." Jess stepped behind Brenna and slid her arms around her waist. "This is a bad dream. We'll wake before you know it, and morning will find us both whole and well."

Brenna leaned back into Jess and sighed. "And damned if I don't believe that, coming from you. How do you do it, Jesstin?"

"What's that?" Jess nuzzled the lush softness of Brenna's hair, breathing in her clean scent.

"How do you make me feel so safe when I know good and well we're both about to pitch headlong off a cliff?"

Jess felt that unpleasant roiling in her stomach again. "I'll admit to wishing we had other cliffs to choose from, Bren. But this City drug offers us hope. It's worth the risk."

"You offer us hope." Brenna shook her head. "I swear, Jess, I don't think I've ever seen you rattled. The entire clan looks to you to lead our defense, and you're as calm and centered as a sage—even tonight."

Jess ached for Dyan's presence with a longing that was almost physical. It seemed many long years had passed since her mentor's death. She'd give much to feel that rough palm on her neck again and to hear Dyan's low brogue whispering guidance.

"Hey, Jesstin." Brenna turned in Jess's arms to face her. "Your hands are freezing." She reached up and touched Jess's forehead, concern darkening her eyes. "How are you feeling?"

"I'm not sick, Bren." Jess tried for a reassuring smile and found it. "Just eager to get started."

Brenna studied her and then nodded and laid her hand on Jess's chest. "I just want to promise you something, Jess, okay? I know this mission is dangerous as hell, and I won't let you down. I've got your back in this. You hear me?"

"I hear, adonai." Jess lowered her head and brushed her lips softly across Brenna's. "And I thank you for your promise. You know I trust you with my life."

"Brenna?" Dana was holding Brenna's journal, flipping through its last pages. "Where was that mountain pass you warned us not to take when the clan was trekking up here? The one you had the dream about, with the waterfall of blood?"

"Ah, yes, delightful memory." Brenna smiled weakly at Dana. "Yeah, the dream warned of a disaster if we tried to get the entire clan over that pass. I asked Shann to take another route. It added a good two weeks to our travels, but it was necessary."

"Well, I'm afraid we're not going to be able to avoid it this trip." Kyla took the journal from Dana and brought it to the table that held the unfurled parchment. "We'd lose way too much time going around."

"Six women travel more lightly than six hundred." Jess studied the break in the mountain range on the map. "We won't be hauling wagons of supplies. We can risk the pass."

"And Kyla's sharp eyes will find the safest path over it." Shann joined them at the table and slipped her arm around Kyla's waist. "Our young singer can best most of Tristaine's warriors when it comes to scouting a trail, Jesstin."

"Aye, lady, I plan to abide our little sister's guidance on this journey." Jess felt their gazes on her as she unsheathed the dagger in her belt. The women in the cabin fell silent, waiting for her to begin.

Jess touched the tip of the dagger lightly to the small swirl of color in the map's upper left corner. "Our mesa." She skated the tip across the map's surface. "And here, the site of our first village in these hills."

They all stared down at the vibrant patch of blue that marked the mountain lake that covered their first home. Then Jess traced an oblique, curving line from their mesa to the dark streaks at the base of the map that signified the City. "This looks to be the easiest grade down, lady. No sheer drops, once we're over the pass."

"The bloody waterfall pass," Dana said, and Kyla tapped her head smartly.

"Even the shortest route will still mean a very long ride." Brenna followed their planned path with her finger. "If this is the same strain of flu that appeared in the City, Shann, it could prove fatal within a week."

The tension in the cabin ratcheted a notch higher, but Shann answered Brenna calmly. "Our sisters have an advantage over the unfortunates who fell to this plague in the City, Brenna. Sarah was right; the women born to Tristaine are physically hardier than City-dwellers. Our life expectancy tops theirs by a decade. Our air is cleaner, our produce more nourishing, our immune systems are stronger. It will take this flu longer to kill Amazons."

"But we weren't all born to Tristaine, lady." Kyla touched the older woman and nodded at Dana and Brenna. "Many of our adanin came to us as adults. Will their few years under Tristaine's healthier sun be enough to protect them?"

"Those years will offer a welcome edge." Shann paused a

moment, then regarded all her women soberly. "But don't mistake me, sisters. Barring some miracle, we're going to lose precious lives before this is over. The very old and the very young among us are most at risk. All we can do is move heaven and earth to keep our losses few."

Jess reached for Brenna's hand and held it, their fingers twining.

"And we have good hope for that." Shann spoke with assurance again. "Tristaine has a rich, varied stock of natural remedies, and a talented guild of healers to help me find stronger ones. We may not be able to cure this pestilence, but we can slow its progress."

"We'll make all possible speed, Shann." Jess pointed to a spot on the map. "We should come out here, in the hills northeast of the City's downtown district. We can pasture the horses by this creek. How far from this position to the Clinic, Bren?"

"Far enough." Brenna bent over the table and tapped its wood surface, an inch from the edge of the parchment. "Somewhere here."

"That's a long way for six Amazons to walk City streets without rousing suspicion." Shann frowned thoughtfully. "You'll need help getting close to the Clinic, Jess."

"Aye, lady." Jess raised an eyebrow at Brenna. "We'll call on an old friend."

"Jodoch?" Kyla smiled with genuine pleasure. "Damn, Jess, I'd love to see our sweet bear of a brother again!"

Dana frowned. "We've got a brother bear in the City?"

"Remember the guy who helped Jess and me escape from the Clinic, Dana?" Brenna took Jess's hand. She frowned and chaffed her still-cold fingers. "That was Jode."

"Oh, yeah, Jode. He's an Amazon's son." Dana nodded. "His mother was Jocelyn?"

"My old friend raised a strong and loving man." Shann's tone was touched with sadness, and Jess shared her sense of loss.

Jocelyn had been like a grandmother to her. "Jode is Tristaine's true friend. Go to him, Jess, but protect him and Pamela from exposure to our enemies as best you can."

"We will, lady." Jess sheathed the dagger in her belt. "Vicar and Hakan can shelter with Jode and move on the Clinic if our first attempt fails. You're sure you can get us into this Civilian Unit, Bren?"

"I know how to find someone who can get us in. If she will." Brenna drew in a slow breath. "She's our best bet, Jess."

"As with all our missions, some spontaneous changes to our plan may be necessary." Shann put one arm around Kyla and the other around Dana. "Luckily, Amazons are nothing if not creative." She smiled at them, and Jess felt a warm tendril of reassurance ease the tension in her gut. "Trust in each other, adanin. The four of you have faced great danger together before and seen Tristaine safely through the night. The fate of our clan could not rest in more capable or courageous hands."

Jess met Shann's gaze and saw her queen's faith in her shining as tangibly as a nimbus of warm light. She swallowed.

"And now, you will all find your beds." Shann hugged Kyla and Dana, then released them. "Sleep and replenish your energies, sisters. The sun rises soon."

CHAPTER THREE

B renna stopped short, smiling in spite of her weariness. The thought of a praying queen conjured the image of an ethereal, devout woman appealing to the heavens with upraised eyes and clasped hands. Tristaine's queen was devout, but hardly ethereal, and her arms were waving in agitated circles as she paced in one of the clan's beautiful gardens.

It was how Shann prayed. Loudly, when she thought it necessary. She was having an earnest discussion with one or more of her Mothers, and Brenna waited respectfully until she had finished.

Shann's voice softened to a friendlier tone as she bid farewell to her guides, and then she turned and smiled at Brenna. She stepped out of the garden and through the dew-soaked grass, pulling her light shawl around her. The pre-dawn air held a mild chill.

"We're almost ready, lady." Brenna walked beside Shann toward the village square. The clan was beginning to stir. She saw women emerging from their lodges, preparing for the day's work. It was an oddly quiet dawn, though, bereft of the cheerful greetings and singing that usually hailed summer mornings in Tristaine. Even the sparse birdsong seemed faint and tentative.

"It will be a dangerous ride, little sister." Shann slipped her arm around Brenna's waist, and she was glad for its warmth. "You have treacherous ground to cover, and you must travel swiftly. Are you sure it's wise to ride your new horse?"

"I'm sure." Brenna nodded. "Hakan had her half-trained before we culled her, and Jess and Bracken will help keep her in line."

"Did you sleep at all?" Brenna felt Shann's appraising gaze.

"Even if your mount has a sure step, you'll bruise just as easily toppling off her asleep."

"Speaking of sleep." Brenna cleared her throat. "I've had a visitor."

She told Shann about the veiled apparition's first appearance, relaying all the detail and nuance she could remember. "And she came again last night."

"What did this woman say?" There was an element of awe in Shann's tone. She had no second sight, and Brenna knew she was fascinated by these glimpses into other realms. "Tell me everything, adanin."

Brenna waited until the drifting remnants of her vision swam clear again in her mind.

She found it unnerving, these sudden transitions from deep sleep to acute awareness. Brenna still didn't understand why other-worldly beings had to wake her up to talk to her, and she wasn't sure she would have signed on for the job had she known this. What was wrong with a simple prophetic dream—

"Greetings, j'heika."

The veiled woman faced Brenna again in a timeless circle of light that seemed suspended between reality and illusion.

"Hello again." Brenna surveyed her mysterious emissary. She still wore a plain white robe, and the silver fabric draping her features shimmered with a soft glow. The girl's body was supple and strong, and her stance held an almost regal confidence. "Did you ever tell me your name?"

"My name is unimportant, Brenna." Light sparkled around the woman's shrouded head. "You begin your quest today. You and your adonai ride with Tristaine's finest, and our home will be left vulnerable. I will be your lifeline to our clan. Tell your queen I will clear her path."

"What—wait!" Brenna reached toward her as the light around them began to fade. "Hey! Don't you dare shimmer out on me again, ma'am, come back here!"

The woman shifted, as if startled, and the illumination rose again.

"Want to clarify all that, please?" Brenna asked. "Start with the lifeline reference."

"Forgive me, j'heika." The specter spoke with genuine respect. "But you'll understand soon. You must focus on reaching the City with all speed."

"All right. I can live with that." Brenna relented. This apparition was obviously on Tristaine's side, and she appreciated her help, whoever she was. And while the energy coursing from her aura was urgent, it held a certain benevolence that Brenna trusted. "I do need to know what to call you, though. Withholding your name for no reason is a little rude."

The veil dipped as the woman inclined her head. "I'm called Elise."

"And that was all?" Shann asked.

"That's all she said." Brenna looked at Shann curiously. "What is it, lady?

"My grandmother's name was Elise." Shann studied the awakening sky. "Your great-grandmother. I never knew her. She lived and died fairly young, in the City. But she was of our line, Brenna. If this is our Elise, she might well be able to clear a path between our worlds."

"But why would she want to?" Brenna wasn't sure she wanted to know the answer. "What are you supposed to do with this cleared path, if you get one?"

"I have no idea, dear one."

Brenna shivered, and Shann stroked her back comfortingly.

It was fully light now, and Brenna stood beside Shann on a small rise and drank in the beauty of their village below. She would travel far and face great danger before seeing her home again.

"I'm afraid I have to burden you further, Blades," Shann said quietly.

"No, you don't have to. That's okay." Brenna turned to meet Shann's knowing smile and sighed. "All right, I guess you have to. What burden?"

"I want you to find out if your niece is alive."

Brenna stared at Shann and her throat went dry.

Samantha was told her infant daughter died at birth in the City Prison. But the woman bearing that news had been Caster, the Clinic scientist who hated Tristaine beyond all imagining. Caster had tortured Jess in the City Clinic. The Amazons had had to destroy their first village to keep it out of her grasp. She had been killed in the flood that drowned their former home.

Shann had long believed Caster might have lied about Sammy's baby.

Brenna had seen what losing her husband and child had done to Samantha. The younger sister Brenna had grown up protecting had been an exuberant spirit who, even motherless, found delight in the simplest of life's pleasures. The Sammy they knew today was a wan shadow of that girl. Still loving, still warm, Sammy had remained quiet and withdrawn in her two years with the Amazons. Brenna could only imagine the joy of returning a living daughter to her arms.

"But, lady," Brenna whispered. "I wouldn't know where to start."

"Just find out what you can. When you can." Shann folded Brenna's arm in hers. "If Samantha's child lived, what would have happened to her?"

Brenna had to swallow hard past the angry knot in her throat. "She would have been placed in a City Youth Home."

"As you and Sammy were, when you were taken from me." Shann looked out over their village, the shadow of an old pain drifting across her features. "Start there, Blades."

They continued, arm in arm toward the village square as the sun inched over the eastern ridge. Brenna could see several horses assembled in the square, and Jess among the Amazons preparing them for travel.

"This quest for my granddaughter," Shann said. "You know I ask it as queen as well as the child's blood-kin."

"I guess I'm not seeing the difference, right now."

Shann stopped and faced her. "What did Artemis promise Tristaine, Brenna?"

"Which time?" Brenna rubbed her temples. "She promised Tristaine a lot of things. Her protection, for one."

"Yes. And what form will Her protection take?"

Brenna tried to concentrate. She wanted to see Sammy. She wanted to be with Jess. She wanted to get going before her nerve failed. She remembered the passage in their ancient scrolls. "'In the time of Tristaine's deepest travail, she will be led by three generations of blood-bonded queens.' That's the first part of Her prophecy, at least."

"If Samantha's daughter lives," Shann said calmly, "She might be fated to rule this clan after you and I are dust."

"You mean after your reign." Brenna drew in a long breath. "And mine?"

"So I believe, yes."

"Still?" Brenna couldn't speak for a moment. "Are we back to this? Lady, you've heard me deny Tristaine's crown, time and again."

Shann said nothing. Brenna grit her teeth, refusing to soften at the compassion in her mother's gaze. "What about the second part of Artemis's prophesy, Shann? Why didn't you ask me to quote that?"

Shann nodded. "'Of these three blood-bonded queens," she recited, "One will be blessed with great powers. The final destiny of Amazon Nation lies in her hands. She will prove Tristaine's salvation, or her destruction, for all time.'"

"And what if these so-called 'great powers' refer to my second sight?" Brenna felt tears threaten, and she blinked them away angrily. She knew she sounded like a petulant child, but she couldn't seem to help herself. "You realize that means a time might come when the lives of all our sisters will rely on *me*. The fate of our entire clan. And it's just as likely that I would destroy Tristaine as save it!"

Shann studied her for a moment. "I see how this prophecy has haunted you, daughter. You fear failing Tristaine when she needs you most. But tell me, what queen who has ever ruled Amazons escaped such a fear?" Shann's smile was rueful. "I've shared it myself, Brenna, more times than I care to recount. May Gaia save Tristaine from ever crowning a queen too arrogant to imagine failure."

"But lady, Shann..." Brenna was desperate to make her understand. "You're a real queen. Okay? You're the most amazing leader I've ever seen. You brought six hundred women and children through a mountain range and founded a new village. You outwitted a deranged scientist and destroyed a shrieking demon. And that's just since I came to Tristaine! I'm a *medic*, Shann."

"Yes, Blades, you're a fine healer, and much more." Shann appraised her keenly. "I've seen her in you, this young queen you won't recognize. At times you've seemed filled with the power to lead and inspire. All of us have seen this gift, and so have our Mothers. Haven't you wondered at the wording of the queen's summons, Brenna? *J'heika, rise.* You're called to awaken. These voices you hear *know* that this queen is already within you—"

"Didn't those voices see me drop a full haunch of venison into the cooking fire?" Brenna broke in. "And last winter, I might have poisoned Adik with a remedy she was allergic to if you hadn't stopped me. I'm the one who tripped Oisin in the training drill when she broke her wrist. Shann, I've got all I can do just trying to make myself a half-decent Amazon, much less lead a whole tribe of them!"

"Brenna, one of a queen's most important tasks is to accept her humanity." Shann looked stern now. She cupped Brenna's chin. "Yes, you might stumble, and badly. You might make the wrong choice at a crucial time. But the same is true for every woman who walks beneath the Goddess' sun. You can't allow the fear of failure to absolve you of your obligation to your clan."

Brenna's head was pounding. She couldn't think about this anymore. "You're asking too much, lady."

"I'm not asking anything, dear one. I'm not one of the Mothers you need to convince. You must argue your future with your spirit guides." Shann took Brenna's shoulders. "But for now and always, Brenna, you are an Amazon of Tristaine. Whether or not you ever serve as her queen, you owe your sisters the very best of your powers. The best of your courage. In every way you can offer them."

They stared at each other, mother and daughter, queen and seer, City-born both and Amazons to their last breath. Strength seeped back into Brenna's legs, and she straightened.

"Besides." Shann's eyes warmed again. "Why assume *you* are the most powerful queen?" She kissed Brenna's forehead fondly. "Go see Sammy. She wants to say goodbye."

❖

Brenna opened the outer window that stood above Sammy's bed in the healing lodge. Her horse's twitching nose pushed its way through the bead curtain, questing for the apple Brenna had placed on the sill. There were a few muted chuckles from the other women in the room who shared Samantha's exile.

"She's beautiful!" Samantha was slightly hoarse, but her delight was obvious. She slid up against the furs folded behind her to stroke the mustang's cheek. "What's her name?"

"Hippo."

Sammy looked at Brenna. She was pale except for the pinpoints of color the fever brought to her cheeks, but a smile dawned on her lips. "You're naming your first horse after my beloved Hippo?"

"I am." Brenna grinned as the horse chomped on the apple contentedly, her long ears twitching. "That name carries good juju in our family."

Hippo had been a small stuffed toy, the only one allowed Samantha in their early years in the Youth Home. As a toddler, Sammy rarely let it out of her sight.

"And hippo is an old Amazon word for horse," Brenna added. "So our clan approves as well."

The mare had had enough of beads tickling her neck, and she shook her massive head with a snort and backed delicately out of the window.

"I've got her, Bren." Jess's rich alto sounded outside, and Brenna waved her thanks.

"Our clan," Sammy repeated.

"Hmm?"

Samantha's glassy eyes focused on the colorful glyph at the base of Brenna's throat, and she touched it with one finger. "Your clan's been very good to me, Bree."

"Hey, it can be your clan too, kid." Brenna registered the chill in her sister's fingers, and she folded them gently into her hand. "You know you can choose a glyph of your own, whenever you feel ready."

Samantha just smiled at her with a look of such sad sweetness Brenna felt tears threaten again. They both knew Samantha wouldn't be choosing a glyph. She wasn't an Amazon.

Blood relation had nothing to do with it. Either the long, harrowing history of Amazon Nation resonated in your bones, or it didn't. In Sammy, it never had. She loved many of the women she met in Tristaine and was loved by them in return. She took to riding horses as naturally as Brenna breathed. As the daughter of their queen, the clan had welcomed Samantha with affection and respect. But by her own choice—out of grief for the loved ones she'd lost, or through the simple lack of some vital bond more spiritual than genetic, Samantha remained a visitor among them.

"We're ready, lass." Jess swept aside the curtain of beads and rested her elbows on the windowsill. She smiled down at Samantha and brushed the backs of her fingers against her cheek. "How's my ornery little sister?"

"Full of phlegm," Sammy sighed. She clasped Jess's hand and kissed it. "You be careful on this trip now, Jesstin." She nodded at Brenna. "And bring her back unscratched, please."

"Aye, adanin. I'll do my very best." Jess looked at Brenna with concern. Brenna nodded slightly, acknowledging the fever that worried them both. "Be well, my Sammy." Jess ducked back out the window, and the bead curtain clicked closed.

Brenna knew she had to say goodbye now, neatly and quickly, or she'd be reduced to a slobbering mess. She bent over Sammy and rested her cheek against her warm forehead. "Be good. Do what Shann says. I'll see you in a few days."

"Okay," Samantha murmured. Brenna sat up. Sammy's eyes were drifting closed, but she smiled again. "Shann said...you have to give me the keys to Hippo...and let me ride her when you come back."

"That's a promise," Brenna whispered. She kissed Samantha's cheek and then got up.

❖

Jess finished tying her last pack to the sling across Bracken's back. She stroked her horse's neck, and he lifted one hoof and clocked it impatiently against a stone. Bracken's sentiment was clear—enough mush, time to hit the trail.

"Work on your patience, old friend." Jess grinned and gave her mustang's neck a last pat. "And keep your little sister over there under close watch on this journey. She carries precious cargo."

She turned and watched Hakan help Brenna climb aboard her bay mare. Hakan's arms were layered with muscle, but her big hands on Brenna's waist were gentleness itself. She served expertly and well as the clan's master of horse, but Jess valued Hakan equally as a warrior and a friend. The ebony sheen of her skin was marked with several scars earned fighting in Tristaine's defense. Jess couldn't ask for a more able sister to ride with her on this mission.

Dana and Kyla were just mounting their horses. The last of their party, Vicar, Jess's blood-cousin, frowned as she straightened the blanket that would cushion Kyla's legs from her gelding's coarse hide. As fair as Jess was dark and just as tall, Vicar's frown could strike terror into more than one stout Amazon heart. She shared Jess's reputation as a fierce fighter, as well as her protective adoration of Kyla. Kyla grinned down at Vicar and gave her nose a playful tweak.

It was a good cadre, Jess thought, a balanced collection of skills and brave spirits.

More women were trickling into the square now to wish them safe travel. Jess closed her eyes and inhaled, long and deep. She smelled horses, the faint smoke from cooking fires, bacon sizzling in a nearby lodge. And as always, the light, green scent of pine and spruce.

"What we smell lingers in our minds more clearly than what we see."

Eyes still closed, Jess smiled. Shann's quiet voice at her side was deeply familiar and welcome.

"Aye." Jess blew out a long breath. "It's what I yearned for most in my time in the City. The Clinic reeked of chemicals and fear." She suppressed a shiver. "I conjured the aromas of home to pass the nights."

"And now you lead the sisters you love most back to the source of your nightmares." Shann touched Jess's corded forearm. "Jesstin, does Brenna understand how much you fear returning to the City?"

Jess blinked. "We're all scared, lady. And we know what we need to do, in spite of our fear."

"It's different for you." Shann looked at Jess searchingly. "Captivity was an unimaginable horror for you, dear one. Not just the physical hardships you suffered—dreadful as those were. You were locked away from the stars and the sky, night after night, for seven months. I feared such a thing would kill you. It was a full season before that haunted look began to leave your eyes."

"Shann—"

Shann nodded encouragement, but Jess found nothing to say. She wiped a small bead of sweat from her upper lip.

"It doesn't matter, lady," Jess said finally. "We both know I have to do this."

"Yes." Shann lowered her head and sighed. "All right, but hear this, Jesstin. Let your sisters take care of you, when you have need. Don't be so strong that you shut out their comfort. You are not alone this time."

"Aye, Shann. I hear you."

Shann cradled Jess's cheek for a moment, then stepped back so she could swing aboard her horse.

Bracken turned with gentle pressure from Jess's knee. Jess looked at the column of five mounted Amazons who waited with gathered reins for her signal. She looked at Brenna and tried to convey all her love and pride in her brief smile. Jess turned and nodded at Shann. "Your blessing, lady?"

Shann stepped back until all six riders could see her, and then lifted one hand in benediction. "Amazons, may our Mothers guide your path," she called, her words ringing clarion clear in the crisp morning air. "Your sisters will hold you safe in their prayers until we see you again. You carry with you all our hope. Ride for Tristaine!"

Jess let out a short, sharp whistle and was answered with immediate discipline by five others. The women standing in the square unleashed a lusty war cry of farewell, and Jess nudged Bracken into an easy canter. She heard the other horses fall in behind her in ordered cadence, and she led them toward the tree-lined path that would take them down off the mesa.

Jess knew she was not the only one whose vision blurred with tears at this parting. Shann was right. This time she wasn't alone.

CHAPTER FOUR

Jess set a brutal pace, and they held it for days.

Brenna trusted Jess to prioritize safety. They couldn't risk a horse stumbling from exhaustion, or a rider so weary she couldn't sit erect. Care had to be taken when they traveled steeper trails. But keeping those practicalities in mind, they rode steady, hard, relentless hours, and breaks were kept to an absolute minimum.

I'm sore in places I would have sworn under oath I didn't have, Brenna thought. She stared down between her horse's silky ears, envying Hippo's ability to shake off the clouds of small black gnats they kept riding through.

Hippo was proving an able mount. The little mustang was what Jess called a natural ride, suited by personality, temperament and build to carrying a human passenger. Jess's Bracken had literally leaned into Hippo every time she decided to outpace Brenna's command, and horse and rider soon reached a friendly accord, but the long miles of rugged terrain were telling on them both.

The path Kyla found that morning was wide enough to allow riding two abreast. A sheer rock wall rose on the left side of their trail. Brenna knew Jess could tell her if the wall was composed of limestone or granite or basalt, but all she truly cared about was it was solid rock. She found that reassuring, as the right side of their path was bordered by an equally sheer drop into empty space.

Jess always rode the outside of any precipitous trail, and Brenna's ever-present discomfort with heights was somewhat eased by her protective presence. If Brenna wanted to peer over the edge, first she'd have to see past the rock-jawed Amazon warrior who rode beside her, and she much preferred to dwell on Jess's profile.

It was late afternoon, and the jagged cliffs were casting dark, slanted shadows across the rocky plains far below them. Brenna was almost too weary to appreciate the majestic beauty of their surroundings anymore, but the glory of the summer day still managed to register now and then. Having spent the first twenty-two years of her life in the City's urban sprawl, Brenna had never lost her sense of wonder and pleasure in the rugged loveliness of the high hills.

The forests had grown thicker as the Amazons descended from their stronghold, though the section of rocky ground they rode now was almost bare of vegetation. They had galloped through fields of dazzling wildflowers under blue skies rich with birdsong. They had forded cold, glittering streams, fast and deep with summer snowmelt, their passage carefully chosen at the rivers' shallowest points. Their party was covering ground more quickly than they could have hoped, but Brenna knew their pace would slow soon. They were nearing the pass of her dream.

"So how do we know one of us still won't come down with this devil-flu?" Dana called back. She clung grimly to the neck of her horse, having achieved an efficient, if not graceful, style of riding. "We still could, right?"

"We still might," Brenna confirmed. She and Jess rode directly behind Dana and Kyla, and Vicar and Hakan brought up their rear. "One of us, or all of us, could still get sick. Everyone in the clan was exposed, but some will fall ill later than others."

"That's why Jesstin brought backup, adanin, to improve our odds." Hakan sat her large stallion with ease, the silver glyph on her cheek glittering in the light of the afternoon sun. "Vicar and I will stay with our brother Jodoch. If the four of you aren't back by our deadline, we'll make our own sojourn to the Clinic."

"We'll be needed to break Jesstin's skinny butt out of the lock house," Vicar predicted. She winked at Brenna. "And bribe the rest of you out of whatever bordello she's sold you into."

"You could never begin to afford me, warrior." Kyla turned on her horse to see virtually everyone staring at her, and grinned. "I know, I sounded just like Aria, didn't I?"

"Just." Dana snickered.

Brenna was relieved to hear this gentle teasing. Despite their fierce reputation, laughter played a surprisingly large role in Amazon life. Thus far their journey had been a tense and silent one, and it was good to see her adanin smile again.

They were reaching a wide break in the rock wall that ran along the side of their trail. Brenna felt a cool breeze lift her hair as the wall gave way to a rolling vista of hills stretching toward the east. The pure mountain air provided miles of visibility, and Brenna was struck by the checkerboard of forested fields reaching to the far horizon.

Ahead of them, Kyla pulled her horse to a stop. "Jesstin? Is that—" She pointed out over the wide expanse of valley, and Brenna shaded her eyes and tried to follow her gaze.

"Aye, lass. I see it."

Brenna glanced at Jess, surprised by her flat, somber tone. She looked out over the valley again.

For several moments Brenna searched in vain for whatever had caught her sisters' notice. Then she found it. The mountain lake was an impossibly distant glint of color, made miniscule by the many long leagues that lay between it and their present course. It was probably the largest body of water in these hills, but when Brenna finally sighted it, it seemed a tiny, far away spark of diamond-blue light.

A sigh moved through all of them, a brief, mournful breeze.

"*Sigmen sulla nostra sede*," Hakan murmured.

Kyla leaned closer to Dana. "Blessings on our home," she translated softly.

They were seeing, for the first time, the final resting place of two dozen of their Amazon sisters. Those distant, pure waters covered the graves of women lost to Tristaine in the final battle with Caster, including Kyla's beloved Camryn. The village that had housed their clan for generations was destroyed by the flood the Amazons unleashed to wash Caster's rotting soul from the world at last.

Brenna saw Jess and Vicar make identical hand signs, a subtle and silent weaving of fingers to end their prayers. Jess patted Bracken's neck and regarded them quietly.

"Let's ride on, adanin. The pass waits."

❖

"Sheesh, Brenna." Dana threw her an incredulous look. "Do your dreams have to be so dang literal?"

The pass through the last high portion of the hills was not marked by any dramatic dip in the trail they had followed since dawn. The cliff wall bordered them solidly again on the left. From what Brenna could see, the path narrowed significantly just ahead, and that was worrisome, but the series of bloody waterfalls was worse.

All right, that's an exaggeration, Brenna scolded herself. There were no great gushing gory spigots of blood cascading over the rocky trail ahead. But there was a good quarter mile of smaller falls dotting the cliff's sides, wide streams of reddish, mud-colored water that splashed down on the path and over its side, like fitful squalls of rain.

"That trail aims to be wicked slick," Vicar drawled behind Brenna.

"Aye, it'll be tricky footing." Jess leaned out to see around a bend in the pass far ahead, and Brenna automatically hooked a finger in her belt, as if to anchor her on Bracken's back.

"The track looks wide and solid enough for single passage, Jesstin." The calm assurance in Hakan's tone soothed Brenna.

Somewhat. "The waters might have eroded the stone, but from here I see no crumbling edges."

"Bren." Jess spoke softly as she brushed Brenna's thigh. "This is probably the stretch where Samantha's friends fell."

"Yeah. Yes, I think it is," Brenna said faintly.

Some sad and certain insight told her the two women who had helped Sammy leave the City both died here. Her sister's recounting of those final brutal moments was still vivid in Brenna's mind. A fist-sized rock had bounced off the cliff and struck Lee Ann in the head. Her wife Karen lunged to catch her. They both slid off the trail, clutching each other and screaming, and were gone in a heartbeat. Samantha had been left alone in the wilderness, grieving yet more loss, and forced to find Tristaine on her own. Karen and Lee Ann were remembered around the clan's storyfires, whenever the names of loved Amazons lost to this world were evoked.

"Are you steady, lass?" Jess's gaze was patient and measuring.

"I am, Jess." Brenna drew herself up on Hippo's back, mentally inserting steel in her spine. Jess had enough on her mind without worrying about her. "Let's trot."

Jess smiled and cupped the back of Brenna's neck. "All right, sisters, move with care. We'll cross in roped pairs. Dana and I will lead."

Kyla sighed. "Are you going to butch me out again, Jesstin? I've ridden lead all day."

"And you're well capable of heading our line now, Ky." Jess shook out the hemp rope looped on her sidebelt. "But I'd rather have my Bracken's wee frame test any weakness in the rock. You'll walk behind Dana. Hakan? Keep a close watch on Brenna's beast. Adanin, string out and dismount."

They shifted cautiously, positioning their horses. Brenna bit her lip on a groan as she swung her leg stiffly over Hippo's back and dropped to the ground. She brushed her wrist across her forehead and realized she was sweating. The shrill cry of a hawk reached her, and she caught a glimpse of it, descending to the rock floor far below in lazy spirals.

"Hey, Bren." Kyla was beside her, twirling one end of the rope already secured to her waist. "Want to try out some of those neat trick knots Sarah showed us last season?"

"Let's just stick with the basics, shall we?" Brenna smiled weakly and tied the loop of hemp around her waist with surgical precision. She started when Hippo suddenly shook her massive head, the coarse hair of her mane slapping across her face.

"Easy, little sister."

Brenna clawed her matted bangs out of her eyes and saw Hakan's encouraging smile. "You're with your adanin, and Artemis smiles on Tristaine. All will be well."

"Thanks," Brenna said softly, and meant it. Like Jess, Hakan was a warrior strong enough to allow connections of tender honesty, and her reassurance meant something.

Vicar's melodic whistle cut the air, signaling the readiness of their line. Brenna took in a deep breath and then coughed out the rock dust stirred by their movements. Kyla stood just ahead of her, roped to Brenna and holding the reins of her sturdy dun gelding. If she stood on her toes, she could see flashes of Jess's head beyond Kyla and Dana. Brenna tried to quell the fluttering in her stomach.

"Leave maneuvering space between our teams," Jess called. "If there's a misstep, find a brace fast and go flat. Mind the woman in front of you."

"Aye, Jesstin," Vicar acknowledged from the rear of the line.

"Aye, Jesstin," Dana echoed, in a much higher voice, and Kyla giggled nervously.

Brenna watched Jess and Dana start out, the slow clocking of their horses' hooves on the craggy stone the only sound in the clear afternoon light. The trail narrowed almost immediately, and Jess led Bracken at a slow and careful pace. Dana clicked at her sorrel, following Jess closely, but leaving slack in the line connecting them.

When they were several yards ahead, Kyla glanced back at her, and Brenna nodded. She stepped closer to Hippo and stroked her soft nose. "You stay cool, shaggy sister," she murmured, then turned to follow Kyla out to the first slope of the pass. Hippo responded readily to her tug on the reins.

Jess and her horse had reached the first of the mini-waterfalls, and Brenna watched her tensely. Jess moved with athletic ease, keeping her back close to the wall, her slow side-step sure on the slick rock. She and Bracken were both drenched in that brief deluge, but they shook off the cold, muddy water without missing a stride.

Relieved, Brenna fastened her gaze on the rump of Kyla's horse in front of her. They had reached the narrowing of the trail, and there was a more distinct descent than she'd anticipated. Behind her, she heard Hakan whistle softly to her towering stallion as she and Vicar set out.

The going was precarious, but not overtly harrowing. Brenna had advised Shann wisely when she warned her to avoid this pass—trying to move hundreds of women and wagons across its narrow length would have proved sure calamity. But Hakan's assessment held true—the solid shelf beneath Brenna's feet offered ample space for the breadth of a horse, and her heart began to slow to a more bearable rhythm.

"Yee...shikes!" Dana's shrill cry rocketed Brenna's pulse back to full speed, and her head snapped up. Dana was passing beneath the first wide splatter of muddy water, and she shook herself vigorously. "Damn—frigging—freezing—"

"Girl, if you yell like that again, I'll kick you off this mountain myself!" Kyla snapped, her voice echoing off the cliffs around them. "You scared the holy pink bile out of me."

"Dana, there's a widish ridge to step across," Jess called. "All of you, mind your step here."

Brenna figured it was just as well that she couldn't see Jess at that moment.

Kyla was entering the spray of water now, leading her dun mustang with small, efficient steps. Brenna swallowed hard when her turn came to pass through the wide spatter, and she gasped as the chilly drops hit her. Cold, yes, but no worse than Tristaine's streams in winter. She blew out explosively to spit muddy water from her lips and tugged Hippo safely through after her.

Even with her heightened blood pressure, Brenna felt a small thrill of pride as she looked up into her horse's mild brown eyes. Tristaine's herds were no strangers to rocky peaks, and Hippo was taking this treacherous trail like the mountain-born mustang she was.

Brenna stepped on a flat slate of wet shale and her heel shot out from under her. She dropped hard and landed on her butt with an impact that snapped her jaws shut. Hippo snorted at the abrupt pull on her reins and pranced uneasily.

"Brenna!" Jess's shout whip-cracked against the rock wall.

I'm not near the edge. Brenna's left foot indeed dangled over the abrupt drop, but she was in no danger of falling. The first pain was so sharp she thought for an awful moment that she'd broken her coccyx, but then the spasm subsided to an almost bearable ache. "Don't try to get to me," she called breathlessly. "I'm fine."

She heard Hakan behind her, chanting soothingly to Hippo, who quieted readily. Brenna brushed her dripping hair out of her eyes and put a shaking hand to the wall.

"Get up slowly, Bren." Kyla was crouched against the cliff ahead of her, watching her anxiously. "I should have warned you about that patch of shale, honey, I'm so sorry."

"N-no harm done." Brenna gathered her feet under her and pushed up gingerly, wincing at the flare of pain in her hip. She couldn't see Jess, but she could feel her anxiety coming at her in palpable waves. "I'm all right, Jesstin," she called.

Jess whistled in response, and they moved on.

The rocky path was descending more noticeably now. Enough so that Jess risked a controlled slide of a few paces, banking her speed with the soles of her feet. She led Bracken through another brief downpour of reddish water. Dana was following her a little too closely, and she signaled her to lay back.

Jess half-regretted insisting on taking the lead. Like Tristaine's horses, Jess had been born to the high hills, and this precarious part of their trek held no great fear for her. But Brenna's fall had jarred her. She hated having women and horses blocking her way to her wife.

They were better than halfway across the pass. Jess's mind began to move on to the next challenge, to making up the time they'd lost creeping along this damned ridge. At first she thought the low buzzing noise must have been coming from some winged insect, until it registered more clearly in her ears as a growl.

Jess turned slowly, the pores of her skin opening, her senses narrowing to an intense focus. She recognized the source of the sound before she saw the tawny cat.

She and Dyan had encountered cougars at a distance twice on their night hikes, both small females. This was a large male, better than eighty pounds. It stood on a wide ledge approximately twenty feet above Kyla's head. The big cat was crouching, its long tail twitching in small arcs. Jess stepped closer to Bracken and unlaced her bow from his side pack.

"Hey! Easy, boy!" Dana tried to curb her horse, who was back-stepping skittishly. Jess's sisters hadn't seen the cougar yet, but their horses were more than aware of its presence. Vicar's roan unleashed a nervous whinny at the rear of the line.

Jess sent out a low, reverberating whistle to warn her adanin. For a heartbeat, she held out hope that the cat would retreat. It wasn't starving—well fed by summer game, its silver-gold cloak was sleek and layered with healthy muscle. But they had obviously passed very close to its holdings. The cougar dropped deftly to a lower ledge, closer to Kyla, and Jess knew they had no time.

And she had no space. The bulk of Dana's horse blocked her view of Kyla and Brenna, and she had no clear line to the cat. Jess whispered a prayer to her Mothers, measured the width of the path, and took two long running steps. She vaulted off the rock trail and over Bracken's head, her feet landing solidly on the mustang's broad back. Her horse started beneath her but quickly stilled, and Jess was able to stand erect.

She took in everything in the scant seconds needed to notch the arrow and raise her bow. Dana looking up at her, her mouth agape. Brenna, lying flat on the rock, staring up at the cougar in fearful fascination. Vicar, stringing her own arrow. Hakan, calming her stallion as well as Brenna's mount. And Kyla, trying to soothe her horse, her back to the cougar that crouched above and behind her.

"Kyla, down!" Jess clenched her teeth and let fly. The obsidian-tipped arrow sizzled from her bow, split the air in a sharp arc, and punched solidly into the big cat's chest. It convulsed on the ledge and emitted a high-pitched snarl. A moment later, Vicar's arrow pierced its side. The cat staggered and fell from the ledge, narrowly missing Kyla's head. It struck the edge of their trail and then dropped into empty space.

It was too much for Kyla's horse. It neighed shrilly and reared, its hooves flashing dangerously close to Kyla's raised hands.

"Kyla, get clear of her!" Hakan was struggling to get past Hippo to reach them.

Jess saw one hoof clip Kyla's shoulder. Brenna cried out, and Kyla teetered on the edge of the path, her arms pinwheeling wildly.

She fell over the side.

"No!" Dana screamed, giving voice to Jess's horror.

Even knowing Kyla was roped, that Brenna was flat on the ground and braced, Jess's breath iced in her chest until she was able to convince herself that Kyla hadn't just plummeted to the stone floor far below. The hemp cord arrested her fall, though her weight dragged Brenna a good two feet toward the edge before Hakan reached her and braced her. Jess saw Kyla clutch the rope and knock against the stone wall as her abrupt descent stopped short some fifteen feet below their trail.

Jess set her foot on Bracken's rump and jumped off his back, landing close to the cliff wall. Dana was fighting her way past her horse to get to Brenna, so recklessly Jess feared she might go over too. She followed her, moving carefully but fast, minding the rope between them didn't snag.

"We're well set, Jesstin!" Hakan was half-draped over Brenna, her big hands gripping the rope. Brenna's smaller ones were white-knuckled around the cord, but she looked up at Jess and nodded wordlessly, her eyes enormous.

"Vicar!" Jess saw her cousin stilling their horses on the narrow stone shelf.

"They're steady, Jess," Vicar called. "I'm on my way."

"Kyla, hang on!" Dana was lying on the rock, her head dangling over the edge of the trail. "Don't move!"

"Okay." Kyla's voice sounded high and faint.

"Dana, you're off rope." Jess untied the knot around Dana's waist with quick efficiency, her blood pounding in her ears. "Find an anchor and hold on."

Vicar reached them, muttering a low litany of curses. She stretched out on the ledge beside Dana. "Kyla, you hear me! Don't you dare let go!"

"Gee, thanks, Vic, okay," Kyla snapped.

Jess crouched at the edge of the drop and saw her, her red hair a splash of color against the tans and grays of the canyon wall. Kyla's face was upturned, but her eyes were squeezed shut against the grit and small bits of gravel dislodged by her fall. She had managed to find a protruding stone wide enough to brace one foot. Her other boot dangled over empty air. The rope tethering her to the world had slid up under her armpits. If Jess didn't get to her soon, Kyla risked hanging herself or dropping through the loop entirely.

"You have me?" Jess barked.

"Aye, Jess!" Vicar and Dana both held sections of Jess's rope, ready to lower her over the ledge.

Jess wound the cord around her wrist, pivoted, and stepped over the edge of the cliff. She risked one glance at Brenna, who still lay beneath Hakan, clenching Kyla's rope. Brenna's plea for her safety, and Jess's answering reassurance, passed silently between them in that quick look.

"Heads up, Ky." Jess stepped down the wall carefully, letting Vicar and Dana ration out her line in even intervals. The cord bit into her back, and she heard small pebbles bouncing off the rock in her wake. A light gust of wind rocked her slightly.

"Careful, Jess!" Kyla was trying for calm, but fear strained her voice. "You're almost here."

Jess checked her line and covered the last few feet, coming down on Kyla's left side. "Hold," she called to Dana and Vicar, then squinted at Kyla and smiled. "Hello, little sister."

Kyla smiled back tremulously, but she had reached the end of her bravado. Her face was ashen, and she was gripping the rope bloodlessly. Her right leg was trembling, holding all of her weight.

"We'll do this." Jess balanced carefully, and then slid her right arm beneath Kyla's hips. "I'm going to lift you a bit."

"I'm s-scared to take my foot off."

"It's all right, lass." Jess was close beside her now. "I've got a good hold on you. Hakan and Brenna have your line, Dana and Vicar have me. We'll go easy."

"Okay," Kyla whispered.

Jess winked at her, then tightened her left hand on the rope and slowly raised Kyla a few precious inches. Kyla gasped as her foot left the rock, but she managed not to flail and kept her upper body straight.

"I've carried you on my shoulders a hundred times, adanin."

Jess let Kyla feel the solid brace of her arm beneath her. "You steady?"

"Yeah. Better." Kyla's teeth were chattering.

"Good. Keep your eyes on the rock in front of us. Take one hand off the rope, and pull the loop down around your waist."

Kyla made a whimpering sound, but she complied. The slack in the coil allowed her to arrange it more securely around her body.

"They'll pull us up in stages, Ky. Nice and slow." Jess checked their stance, and then looked up to see Vicar peering grimly over the ledge. She whistled.

"On three," Vicar barked.

Jess heard her count down, and then felt a strong tug on her rope, raising her several inches. She kept her right arm firmly under Kyla's hips, and they moved smoothly upward together.

"Let your feet touch the wall," Jess coached quietly. "Look straight ahead. You're doing well, lass."

"Thanks." Kyla gasped as they rose another two feet, and she flicked Jess a glance. "Jesstin?"

"Aye."

"You can butch me out any time. Okay?"

"Okay."

It wasn't a long climb, but every inch of it was torturous. Jess whispered assurance to Dyan, promising her she wouldn't fail, she wouldn't let her blood-sister die.

"We're right here, Ky!" Dana leaned over the ledge and extended her hand, still a good three feet from Kyla's head.

"You're not roped, you bloody fool!" Vicar snarled. "Keep well back! Again now, don't jerk—one, two, three!"

Kyla crested the edge first. Vicar reached down and snagged the cloth of her tunic, and she and Dana hauled her bodily over the lip of the ledge. A deep wave of relief swept Jess as Kyla's weight left her shoulder, and she saw Hakan's broad hand above her head. She grasped it, and felt herself hoisted as if she were light as a child. She scrambled up onto the trail, panting.

Kyla lay back against Vicar, ghostly white, her eyes closed. She still gripped the slack hemp rope. Dana knelt next to her.

"Dana, rope on." Jess shook out her stiff fingers and tossed the end of her line to Dana, then felt Brenna's cold touch on her forearm.

"Well done, hotshot," Brenna whispered and kissed Jess's cheek. She was as pale as Kyla, but she stepped nimbly past Jess and knelt on the ledge beside her. She laid her hand gently on Kyla's head. "Honey? Can you open your eyes?"

"No," Kyla muttered, opening them. She released a shaking sigh. "Sheesh."

"I know." Brenna felt the back of Kyla's head, and then her neck and shoulders. "Are you hurt, Ky?"

"I don't think so, I'm just shook." Kyla shrugged, wincing. "My shoulder smarts a little."

Dana snatched her hand from Kyla's shoulder as if she'd touched a hot iron. Jess noted that both Kyla and Brenna were regaining their color, but Dana's features were still the shade of old linen.

Brenna examined Kyla's shoulder. "I can't see it well here. Can you move your arm?"

"Sure." Kyla demonstrated feebly, then gaped at Dana. "Dana, did you see the size of that cat?"

"Yeah." Dana smiled sickly. "So, you're okay?"

"That was a fine shot, Jesstin." Vicar was still seated on the stone, supporting Kyla. "You're still a bloody second faster than me, damn your eyes."

"Your arrow hit true as well, Vic." Hakan brushed rock dust off her palms, leaning against the cliff wall. "Dyan would smile on us all today."

Her old friend's smile chased the last of the chill from Jess's blood.

"Hey, Jess? Come here, please." Kyla sat up, looking calmer.

Brenna rose, and Jess took her elbow as they exchanged places on the narrow shelf. Jess knelt beside Kyla, who looked at her silently for a moment.

"Well, you saved my life again," Kyla said. "Thank you, Jesstin. I'm going to bake you a big pie."

"You're welcome, little sister. Blackberry apple."

Kyla kissed her soundly on the lips, and Jess grinned. "Think we're ready to put the last of this pass behind us?"

"Yeah, I'm game." Kyla let Jess pull her carefully to her feet. Kyla craned past Jess to see Brenna. "Aren't you amazed that neither of us threw up, Bren?"

"I was just thinking that!" Brenna was taking in her line carefully. "Shann's going to be so—"

She was interrupted by the sound of Dana, still on her hands and knees, vomiting copiously into the canyon.

CHAPTER FIVE

B renna found the ghostly hooting of a horned owl fitting music to mark the end of this nightmare-inducing day. In their urgency to reach the City, sleep was snatched in judiciously rationed hours, and she intended to wring every drop of peace she could from this brief respite.

Kyla was already fading, curled on her side not far from Brenna. They hadn't laid a fire yet, but the full moon cast enough light to reveal Vicar laying out a meal of dried meat and berries. Hakan was setting their horses to graze in a small grassy field this side of the trees.

Brenna winced as her bruised hip protested, and she stretched out gingerly on the folded blanket Jess had spread on the sparse grass of their campsite. She could still see the moon, embodied as Selene in Amazon lore, kissing the tops of the trees before beginning her long, slow glide across the night sky. Brenna silently petitioned her to take her sweet time.

Brenna examined the rope burn across her palm, longing for her journal the way she used to long for a drink, with the same fretful nostalgia. Carrying any written account of life in Tristaine would be pure folly if they were captured, but Brenna missed her nightly ritual, the scratch of her quill across the page in the peaceful cabin she shared with Jess.

As if summoned by her thoughts, Jess emerged from the trees, her tall figure silvered in moonlight, carrying an armload of dry kindling. Brenna sat up, deciding she craved her adonai's touch more than food, sleep, her journal, or air in her lungs.

"Grub's about ready, Stumpy." Vicar sucked two fingers noisily as Jess layered the wood in the firepit dug in the center of their circle. "We'll have enough left over for a tasty stew."

"Your recipe, Bigfoot?" Jess gripped the small of her back and stretched, wincing, then smiled at Brenna. "Hope my lovely lady has packed strong colonics."

"Ah, this is just your runt of a horse, he'll go down fine." Vicar sprinkled an herb over the dried meat. "I'll get our fire started. At least I'm still faster with a flint than you, cousin."

"Spark away, mate." Jess lowered herself on one knee next to Brenna and kissed her lightly. "I'll bring us water, Bren, then join you soon."

"Dana's already gone to the spring." Brenna patted the blanket beside her. "Sit down, Jesstin, rest your bones. This is me butching you out."

Jess offered another tired smile and settled stiffly onto the blanket beside her. They sat quietly for a moment, leaning into each other. It was possibly the first time in days neither of them had some urgent task to perform, and Brenna relished their shared stillness.

Jess nodded at Kyla. "Ky's shoulder?"

"It'll be tender for awhile, but she's all right." Brenna breathed in Jess's familiar scent, marveling at the quiver of arousal that managed to sneak through her weariness. "She's out like a light. Let's let her sleep. We'll feed her a Bracken sandwich before we mount up."

"What's this?" Frowning, Jess took Brenna's hand and turned her palm toward the light beginning to flicker from the campfire.

"It took me a second to get the right grip up there." Brenna shuddered, remembering the ghastly sight of Kyla teetering on the edge of the abyss. "It's not bad, love."

"Bet it hurts, though." Jess examined the thin burn the rope had left across the base of her palm, then turned and rummaged in Brenna's pack. She drew out a serrated leaf of aloe and snapped it smartly in half, then squeezed a drop of its thick juice onto her callused finger.

Brenna watched Jess smooth the cool unguent across the burn, her touch as tender and healing as Shann's. "Speaking of the pass," she said, "was it strictly necessary, Jesstin?"

"What's that?"

"Shooting a raging cougar…while standing on top of a horse…on a mountain ledge less than four feet wide?"

"I thought I looked great." Jess's mild brogue twirled the word. She blew softly on Brenna's palm. "Keep this clean, now."

"Well, Kyla better bake me a pie too." Brenna brushed woodchips off Jess's lap. "Spiked with enough cannabis to make me forget watching you shimmy over the edge of a cliff."

"Ah, even better than blackberry apple! We'll take two." Jess raised Brenna's fingers to her lips and kissed them. "You did stunning well on the pass today, lass. There was a time coming anywhere near a drop like that would have frozen your bones."

"Yeah, and that time was about six hours ago." But Brenna smiled, hearing her praise and warmed by it. Jess was right. She had conquered a lot of her fear.

She remembered another horrific day, years ago, when she had clung to the side of a cliff next to Kyla. Jess's description nailed it. Her bones had frozen so solid she couldn't move. Vicar had to all but pry her fingers off the rock to get her going again. That rescue had been Brenna's introduction to Jess's wild cousin, and it had taken some time to overcome that withering first impression. She remembered Vicar's gruff pat on her back today as they left the pass.

Brenna smiled a welcome at Hakan as she stepped into their camp, marveling again at the big warrior's ability to move through brush in absolute silence. "How's Valkyrie's foot?"

"Hoof," Vicar snorted, feeding kindling to the fire.

"Val's foot is fleet again, thank you, little sister." Hakan peered down at Kyla fondly, and spoke softly. "It was a small stone, Jesstin, it won't lame him."

"Good, adanin. Get something to eat and tie a feedbag on

Vicar." Jess rolled her head slowly, and Brenna heard her neck crackle. "The night's passing fast. I'd best go see what's keeping our water-bearer."

Brenna touched Jess's arm. "Let me go, Jess. I'd like to splash some of this trail grit off my teeth before I eat anyway." She got up, stifling an unladylike grunt, and planted a kiss on the top of Jess's head.

"I miss ye already," Jess murmured. Her tired blue eyes looked almost vulnerable. "Be safe."

Brenna bent and kissed her again, this time on the mouth, slow and deep. Rich tendrils of pleasure swirled through her. She made herself straighten, feeling color fill her cheeks and hoping a cold splash of water would cool her ardor a bit. Jess's plaintive look made it harder to leave her, but she wanted a moment alone with Dana.

She stepped carefully around Kyla and made her way through the brush toward the faint sound of the rippling stream that ran just north of their camp. Brenna found she had energy left to appreciate the beauty of the night. The ebony, star-drenched bowl of sky above her would be a bank of smog-choked clouds in the City. She drank in the flickering glory of Tristaine's constellation while she could.

The pine-scented air had cooled Brenna's cheeks when she found the stream, wide but shallow, running swift and glittering beneath Selene's gold light. Dana stood in its center, the dark water swirling around her knees. She was gazing back toward the high cliffs they had struggled through that day. It was too dark for Brenna to see her clearly, but every line of Dana's body was slumped and pensive.

"Hey." Brenna didn't want to startle her, and she didn't. Dana turned toward her with a kind of calm resignation, as if she'd known her solitude wouldn't last. "You need any help?"

"Nah, I'm good." Dana nodded at the dripping canteens stacked neatly at the river's edge. "Just wanted to catch us some fresh trout before heading back."

"Good idea." Brenna bit her lip. She had seen Jess plunge her hands into fast-running streams and pull out flapping salmon. She'd seen Dana fall butt-first in the water trying to do the same. No need to draw on her psychic sense to know the young warrior wasn't up for fishing tonight. Brenna sat down on the mossy bank and watched Dana wade slowly to shore.

"We're making good time, huh?" Dana settled cross-legged beside Brenna, shifting to keep from getting her wet. "Even with the pass."

"Yeah, we're doing well." Brenna waved a mosquito away from her ear. "Better than Jess hoped."

"We've still got that long stretch from the foothills to the City." Dana picked a smooth pebble from the earth and skipped it across the stream. "Dang, Brenna, I hate us having to sleep. We need to get this drug back to Sammy."

"Samantha's young and strong." Brenna rubbed Dana's forearm. "I worry more about our elders. Shann and our healers will do all they can to keep them with us."

She let the quiet spin out between them. Dana would talk to her, usually, if she didn't push. She probably confided in Brenna more than anyone, other than Kyla, and she couldn't talk to Kyla about this. Brenna tried to see her face without appearing to stare. Dana's jaw was clenched, and her eyes were muddy and unhappy.

"I think I would have followed her over." Dana kept her gaze on the swift-moving river. "If that rope hadn't caught."

"No, honey, you wouldn't have."

Dana scowled. "Why do you say that?"

"Because four Amazon sisters who love you very much would have stopped you." Brenna imagined Jess knocked off the edge of the cliff, and she shuddered. "It must have been terrible for you back there, Dana."

"I died inside." Dana spoke without inflection. "I don't know what I'd do if I lost Kyla, Bren."

"I know how that feels." Brenna hesitated. She couldn't

promise that Kyla, or any of them, would survive this quest, and the thought of losing any of their adanin chilled her heart too. "Maybe we can take today as a reminder, though, that we should tell our friends the truth about important things, while they're still around."

"Yeah, like that's gonna happen." Dana skipped another stone across the stream. "Hey, Kyla, I'm crazy in love with—*blat!*" She pretended to throw up. Brenna laughed, and Dana smiled at her ruefully. "And your stupid girlfriend is still showing me up, I hope you noticed."

"Yes, I spoke to her about that." Brenna turned her head and spat delicately to fend off another whining mosquito. "I'm getting feasted on out here. Care to escort me back to our posh holdings?"

"I can do that." Dana sighed and climbed to her feet and gave Brenna a hand up. "Don't tell Ky I went all mushy on you."

"Nope, your mushiness is yours to reveal." Brenna snagged the straps of three of the canteens and wound her arm through Dana's. "Come on, or there won't be any horse cutlets left."

"Oh, dang. Vicar's cooking?"

❖

Curled in Jess's arms, Brenna slept hard and deep.
"We must talk, j'heika."
Brenna groaned. Not again. Surely whatever this was, it could wait until morning.
"Brenna, wake up."
The voice, while still respectful, carried a certain command this time.
Brenna lifted her head, and stood facing Elise. She discovered a new element had been added to this spectral plane—a marble basin stood on a waist-high pedestal between them, full to its oval surface with clear water.

"If you're going to sleep this rarely," the younger woman said politely, "You must find a way to reach me while awake."

"Good evening, Elise." Brenna greeted her just as politely. "Do you have news of home?"

"Some." The sparkling veil moved, as if Elise had inclined her head. "The plague progresses, j'heika. More of our sisters fall ill."

Brenna discovered her hands could still prickle with anxiety in the spirit world. "How many, Elise? Do you know how my sister is? Her name is Samantha."

"I'll bring you to one who can tell you." Elise hesitated for a moment, and something in her uncertainty made her seem fully human to Brenna for the first time. Her hands rose slowly, slipped the silver veil off her brown curls, and settled it around her shoulders.

Human or divine, Elise's beauty was ethereal. She gazed at Brenna through dark-lashed jade eyes, and her skin held the pale perfection of porcelain. Brenna took in the girl's exquisite features in one glance and felt her heart constrict with sorrow.

Tears moved soundlessly down Elise's face. Her expression was sweetly composed, but there was a depth of grief in her lovely eyes that punched Brenna in the chest. An immediate need to offer comfort filled her, and she stepped closer and touched Elise's hand. The graceful fingers resting on the edge of the marble basin felt warm and real.

"Little sister," Brenna said softly. "Tell me why you're weeping."

"I have always wept." As Elise spoke, a tear fell from her calm face and dropped into the basin of water between them. Ripples spread in gentle circles, joining tears shed for unknown years. "I will always weep, if the path of Amazon Nation continues on its present course."

Brenna was at a loss. "Can you tell me any more?"

"You are our best hope, j'heika." Elise smiled, a heart-

breaking contrast to the falling of the next tear. She gestured to the circular pool between them. "Look closer. Seek counsel from Tristaine's wisest queen."

Brenna peered into the basin's clear marble depths. The surface of the water shimmered, reflecting both Elise's visage and her own. As she watched, more ripples spread across the small pool, blending their images and dispersing them. Brenna drew a long breath, feeling her body relax.

A new face began taking shape in the water, and Brenna strained to see its features. Just as they seemed ready to form, the image drifted apart, and Brenna cursed silently.

"Breathe deeply and evenly, adanin," Elise coached her quietly. "She wants to appear. Give her time. Be patient."

"You don't know me very well," Brenna muttered. But then the face dawned clearly in the water, and it was dear to her. Brenna drank in the kind wisdom in those gray eyes, relief and pleasure sluicing through her.

"Sweet demon's bile!" Shann cried and pressed a hand to her breast. "Brenna?"

They were standing together on either side of the marble basin, Shann in Elise's place. Brenna took her mother's hands across the small pool.

"It's all right, lady. It's really me."

"How did you do this?" Shann looked down at herself, fascinated. She wore the spun silk robes of her high office.

"I didn't. I think Elise did. This must be what she meant by clearing your path."

"I bless this Elise for bringing me to you." Shann's gaze warmed. "Tell me, how are Jesstin and our adanin?"

"We're all safe, Shann. We draw close to the City." Brenna tried to quell the anxiety gripping her throat. "How is Sammy?"

"Our Samantha holds her own. I'm with her every moment I can be."

"And Tristaine?"

"Two-score of us have taken ill since you and Jess left, Brenna. We've mixed remedies that seem to slow the fury of the fever, but we haven't stopped it. And we've lost two, dear one."

"Oh, Shann," Brenna whispered. "Who?"

"Aracina, Aria's blood-grandmother. She was over a hundred years old and her heart was weak, and she slipped away quickly. And this morning, Elsbeth's baby daughter, Lynne, left us without a cry."

"Ah, lady." Tears filled Brenna's eyes. "I'm so sorry. I promise you, we'll return as quickly as we possibly can."

"Other winds blow through Tristaine that concern me deeply, daughter."

"Tell me."

"There is unrest. Only this morning..." Shann paused, and gazed down into the full basin. She lifted her hand, and looked at Brenna questioningly. "Someone is telling me—"

"Go ahead," Brenna encouraged her.

Shann dipped her hand into the water and stirred it gently. As Brenna watched, Shann's glyph, worn on her wrist, began to pulse with a gold light. Her signets of royalty and healing emerged clearly through the shimmering water.

Colors and shapes began to flicker again on the turning surface of the pool. Brenna began to recognize forms—the stand of aspens that marked the trail leading to Tristaine's mesa, and then their village square. She saw their lodges, and a gathering of their sisters, and then—

Then Brenna was there, standing next to Shann, witnessing the scene as if she had been present at the time. She could smell fresh pine and heard a roiling of angry voices.

"With all respect, Shanendra." A wiry Amazon with long gray hair stood with her fists on her hips, scowling at Shann. She was surrounded by half a dozen other women, and most of

them looked just as angry—or afraid. "You're showing signs yourself of this vile plague. How can we be sure you still rule us with a clear head? How can you be sure?"

"What?" Alarmed, Brenna touched Shann's arm and watched her hand pass right through it. Shann didn't turn or respond to her. Brenna might be witnessing this scene, but it was in the past, and she was seeing it as a phantom. Shann was flesh and blood here, and she couldn't see or hear Brenna. And her cheeks were lightly flushed with fever.

"I can trace your line back six generations, Bethany." The queen's tone was rather dry. "I'll recite them for you, if you wish. My mind is my own, and I'll trust my Council to tell me if my judgment falters."

"I'm not sure we can share your trust in the Queen's Council," Bethany retorted. "Not with the lives of our children at stake."

"Shann. Lady." Another Amazon stepped forward, her hands lifted in appeal. "Forgive Bethany's passion. As leader of our mothers' guild, she carries the safety of our little ones close to her heart."

"No closer than mine, Ethne." Shann gestured gently. "Go on, tell me your fears."

"Elsbeth's sweet baby breathed her last at dawn, lady. The youngest of our clan are at greatest peril from this terrible sickness." Ethne clasped her hands, pleading. "We must get the children out of the village!"

There was a grim stirring of agreement among the women.

· "And take them where, adanin?" Shann went to Ethne. "What safe haven do you hope to find out there?"

"Anywhere but here," another voice called. Brenna saw Martine, another of the mother's guild, push past Ethne to face Shann.

"To the City?" Shann met the woman's glare evenly. "That's where the only cure for this illness lies, sister."

"Of course not the City, lady," Martine snapped. Brenna had always found her unpleasant, and her fervor was a little frightening now. *"There are a dozen small settlements on the other side of the range. One of them will take us in."*

"And in thanks, you'll bring them the plague." Shann shook her head. *"The harm is already done here, Martine. All of Tristaine has been exposed. If you enter another village, its people will have even less defense against this sickness than we do. More will die."*

Brenna was drawn by the effortless leadership that was part of Shann's natural aura. She wore royal command as comfortably as her own skin. She walked among her Amazons, looking into each face. Several were from the mothers' guild, Brenna noted, but not all. Strong, loving sisters for the most part, but carried away now with fear for their young.

"Have courage, adanin. At least here, our children can be strengthened by the remedies we've managed to find. And our sisters will return soon, with medicine that can save most of us. Amazons will not sacrifice the lives of innocents in a futile bid for safety."

"Shann—" Martine began.

"No, Martine." Shann turned and faced her. *"You've heard my decision. No Amazon leaves this mesa."*

"And if we feel we must?" Bethany had regained her composure, but her respect was tempered by anger.

"If you try to leave Tristaine, you will be stopped." Shann held Bethany's hard stare until the older woman dropped her eyes.

The mountain village and all its Amazons vanished, dwindling from reality to darkness in a heartbeat.

❖

Brenna started awake, her back chilled by a lonely draft. She sat up quickly, wincing, hoping against hope that Shann's comforting presence had somehow followed her onto the physical plane.

It wasn't yet dawn, and birdsong rang clear and sweet. Vicar sat cross-legged across the fire, feeding it twigs and keeping watch over their camp. She grunted a morning greeting at Brenna, her expression sour.

Brenna turned and confirmed what she'd known in deepest sleep—Jess had left their shared blankets. She raised an eyebrow questioningly at Vicar, who pointed vaguely over her left shoulder. Brenna nodded and got to her feet in slow, stiff stages. Fit or not, between clinging to Hippo's back and cuddling up on the ground night after night, she felt she'd aged decades.

She stepped quietly around the still forms still huddled around the fire. Every head but Dana's was covered with blankets or arms or packs, or anything that might block out her trumpeting snore. The snoring explained Vicar's morose glare and made Brenna smile.

Wrapping a shawl around her shoulders, she went in the direction Vic pointed to, remembering the small meadow near this grove of trees. She walked through the high grass, vestiges of her vision still drifting through her mind. The pre-dawn light made tracking Jess's steps in the fresh dew easy enough, but Brenna would have been able to find her now even in full darkness. At times she was simply drawn toward Jess, wherever she was, following some silent beacon that ended in her lover's arms.

She saw Jess now. She was dressed in her lightest breastwrap and leggings, performing a complex series of dance-like drills in the center of the meadow. Brenna rested against a young aspen and enjoyed the sight, knowing Jess needed privacy for this meditation.

Her limbs gleamed with a light sweat—she must be nearing the end of a long session. One leg whipped in a fast, deadly arc, cutting through the pasture grass, and then Jess balanced and slowed, her movements becoming sinuous, coiled power in the muscle of her back.

Brenna knew Jess prayed to her Mothers in words, but this controlled, lethal dance was her best means of seeking the wisdom of her spirit guides. Her arms wove in a sudden flashing series of blows, and then her body straightened again and grew still. Brenna watched Jess's shoulders lift in a deep, cleansing breath, and then they settled into a more relaxed posture than she'd seen in days.

Doubtless aware of Brenna's presence since she entered the meadow, Jess turned and sauntered to her, smiling. She slipped her arms around Brenna's waist.

"Looks like that did you more good than an extra hour's sleep." Brenna patted Jess's damp chest with the edge of her shawl.

"It did. Good morning, lass." She dipped her head and brushed Brenna's lips with her own. "Are you well?"

"I'm well. But Shann isn't, Jesstin." She met Jess's stunned look, feeling slightly guilty at finding relief unburdening her fears while adding them to Jess's load. "Elise was able to bring us together through my dreams. Shann's caught it. So far she's still on her feet, but Bethany and others are pushing hard to take our children off the mesa."

Jess's brow furrowed. "That's idiocy. Don't they see—"

"No, that's the problem, they're not thinking." Brenna ran the soft cloth of her shawl down Jess's muscled arms, drying them. "Shann's in control, but I wish she had either Vicar or Hakan with her. What if this panic spreads?"

"Our lady has Aria and Sarah," Jess reminded her. "They're both formidable allies. Sarah will bellow sense into our sisters, and if that doesn't work, Aria will scratch out their eyes."

"But what about muscle?" Brenna grimaced at the thought. "May every goddess alive save us from raising arms against our own, but if it comes to that—"

"Oisin and Jackson are young, but they're both able warriors.

Better, they're honorable, cool-headed, and smart. They'll back Shann's every breath and hold any force to an absolute minimum." Jess stroked Brenna's hair. "Shann has coped countless times with dissent in our clan, adonai. Have faith in her. Just as our lady trusts us to bring swift help."

"I will." Brenna sighed and leaned against Jess. She knew they both still feared for their clan, but as always Jess's strength offered welcome reassurance.

She closed her eyes as a rough hand moved down her back, probing gently, easing her stiffness. Brenna cupped the gleaming swells of Jess's shoulders in her palms. Jess touched her chin, and tipped her face to receive her kiss.

It began as a warm, languid exploration of soft lips, reminiscent of their usual greeting on peaceful Tristaine mornings. Then Brenna felt a creeping thrill of arousal work through her as Jess's mouth roughened against hers and became more demanding. She ran her fingers through Jess's wild hair and pulled her head closer against her.

"I've offered my prayers," Jess growled into Brenna's neck. She lipped her way wetly to the top of her shoulder. "I'm sure my Mothers will grant me a moment of worship."

Jess lifted her head, and Brenna saw the heat building in her, the silvering in her lover's blue eyes that signaled her growing need. A similar sensual chord resonated in the depths of Brenna's belly.

Jess's arms went suddenly still around her, a courtly restraint that allowed Brenna time to make her choice. Once given, her permission would not be requested again, but it wasn't a difficult decision. Brenna signaled assent by softening her body and allowing her breasts to brush Jess's taut ones.

Jess's eyes turned feral and she buried her lips against Brenna's neck again, her long fingers deft and quick on the laces of Brenna's light topshirt. She clenched the cloth in her hands and yanked it open, baring Brenna to the waist with shocking abruptness. The first rays of the rising sun dappled across her exposed breasts, her pink nipples quivering to life in the cool morning air.

"Ssssucculent..." Jess's sibilant brogue was impossibly enticing. Her rough palms swarmed over Brenna's full globes, cupping them, squeezing. A jagged bolt of desire surged through Brenna, and she threw her arms around Jess's neck too eagerly, knocking them both off-balance.

"Ooof!"

Jess landed hard on her back in the high grass, Brenna sprawled on top of her, and for a moment they enjoyed that lovely combustion of laughter and arousal that often flavored their lovemaking. But Jess was too heated to tolerate much distraction. She turned Brenna on her back and moved over her with urgent efficiency, stripping her leggings and lowering her own, then pinning Brenna's arms and legs to the ground beneath her.

Their kiss ran deep this time, the joining and melding of their mouths a lush banquet of sensation that was at once both tender and crudely demanding. Jess's lips moved lower and coasted over Brenna's cool breasts, pausing to suck at one turgid nipple, then the other, biting it gently, and she arched hard against her. Gasping, Jess stared down at her, and Brenna drank in the image, not of her friend and lifemate, but a crazed Amazon warrior pinning her to the earth, her muscular legs forcing her knees widely apart.

"You're mine to pleasure, querida." Jess's predatory smile sparked a rush of carnal heat through Brenna's groin. Jess lowered her hips, and the coarse hair of her mound brushed across Brenna's open sex. "And you'll not escape my touch."

Brenna's breath grew ragged, and she ground the back of her head into the grass as Jess thrust her hips, continuing the lewd scrubbing between her helplessly splayed legs. The intensity of the pleasure growing in her center almost frightened Brenna, and she knew Jess could see it in her face and in the hectic color rising in the smooth paleness of her exposed breasts.

Climax hit Brenna almost silently, propelled by the breath

that hissed explosively between her clenched teeth. Jess timed her ecstasy with expert care, slowing her movements as the waves of release washed through Brenna. Then she collapsed beside her in the grass, panting.

"Amen," Brenna gasped.

"Aye." There was a definite note of cocky satisfaction in Jess's tone, so well deserved Brenna couldn't even tease her for it. She was still coming down from the shivering heights of this shared prayer, and Jess stroked her arm with gentle patience.

Brenna hadn't realized how dearly they had both missed this most tangible expression of their love. Since the first ravens fell on Tristaine's mesa, she and Jess had had little time or privacy for intimate communion. Relatively modest, even demure in public, Brenna tended toward rather embarrassingly loud declarations of appreciation when pleasure took her. This morning, though, the immensity of her climax had been contained in that one long, drawn-out hiss, and tendrils of that liquid delight still swirled through her.

Vicar's faint, surly whistle reached them through the trees. The signal was a general summons, not an alarm, but it needed to be answered promptly.

"Ears," Jess whispered, and Brenna covered hers gratefully before Jess's sharp whistle split the morning air. They helped each other up and adjusted their clothing, snickering as they slapped grass off each other.

Brenna wound her arm through Jess's and they started back toward the camp. Their spirits were replenished now in every way possible, and they couldn't linger.

The City waited below.

CHAPTER SIX

Jess let out a low whistle. To most ears it would be indistinguishable from the birdsong filtering from the surrounding trees, but the five women riding with her were instantly alert. They reined their horses to a halt.

Jess listened, her head tilted slightly to catch the smallest nuance of sound. She glanced at Vicar, who pointed to two sections of heavily forested terrain on either side of the path ahead. Jess nodded. She turned on Bracken's back and signaled Dana and Hakan with a complex flourish of hand signs. Dana squinted, then flashed Jess a silent thumbs-up.

Both Brenna and Kyla were fit and well-schooled in the basic tenets of close fighting, and Jess knew they could hold their own in any fair match. But Kyla was pledged to the guild of artists, and Brenna to Tristaine's seers, and they lacked the intensive training of Jess's warriors. She wanted them both placed with more experienced fighters.

Dana and Hakan paired with Kyla, and Brenna nudged her mount closer to ride with Jess and Vicar. The two parties peeled quietly off both sides of the trail and moved into the shadows of the trees on either side.

Jess felt a polite tap on her shoulder.

"I still don't know what we're doing," Brenna whispered. "Not that I have to. Just letting you know."

Jess checked the breeze to see how sound might travel before she answered. "I heard a man's voice, Bren, just over the rise ahead. Sounded like a command. We need to assume we've found hostile natives, until they prove us wrong. Shh, now."

She raised a hand, and their horses stopped. Jess lifted her leg over Bracken's neck and dropped soundlessly to the ground, then turned and helped Brenna slide down Hippo's side. Jess took her coiled rope from her belt, and Vicar unlaced the sleek bow and quiver from her horse's back.

The summer earth was blanketed in soft grass and moss, which helped silence their approach. Jess dropped to the ground and crawled to the top of the curved ridge. She scanned the grove of trees below and the six uniformed figures filtering through them.

She heard Dana's brief whistle and acknowledged it, but the signal was unnecessary. She'd fought enough City soldiers to recognize the breed on sight. Jess shivered as a coldness worked through her, a familiar chill that ran through her blood and prepared her to fight. She looked to her left and returned Vicar's steely smile.

They weren't outnumbered, but they were certainly out-gunned. The City patrol was armed with bolt-action rifles. The Amazons carried daggers, slings, bows, and escrima sticks, short, thin clubs favored for close fighting. Strategies clicked through Jess's mind in fast, methodical order. There was no going around this patrol or out-waiting them. If they weren't stopped now, her adanin risked encountering them again between here and the City.

And the Amazons would have to draw lifeblood. If any of these soldiers escaped and lived to warn their commanders, the protective cloak of secrecy guarding this mission would be lost. Shann bade Tristaine's warriors to fight without harm whenever they could, but lives must be taken today. Jess just needed to ensure soldiers died, not Amazons.

She reached for Brenna's cold hand and covered it with her own. Brenna's eyes were worried, but they crinkled with her smile, and she offered Jess a simple nod of confidence. Jess drew a deep breath and whistled a clear, mild series of notes. Their deceptive beauty signaled the necessity of killing, and the attack fell fast.

War cries burst from six throats and echoed crazily through the trees, sounding twice their number. Jess darted over the edge of the rise, feeling Vicar and Brenna surge with her on either side. They ran hard, kicking through the high grass, and then Jess dodged right, pushing Brenna with her, as one of their startled prey finally managed to squeeze off a shot in their direction. The bullet sang harmlessly wide.

"Base," Jess barked at Brenna, slapping the trunk of a large oak as she raced past it.

"Base," Brenna acknowledged behind her, sliding to a stop near the tree. It would provide her adequate cover while she sighted her targets.

There were roars and shouts from the City patrol, and more shots punctured the air. Jess and Vicar, running side by side, lengthened their stride and left the ground at almost the same second. Vic vaulted high into the branches of a tall oak, Jess into those of a red cedar.

Jess darted through the lush inner limbs of the tree, the rope coiled high on her shoulder. She balanced easily on a thick branch, then crouched and knotted the rope to it with a few deft twirls.

"This way, Sergeant!" Two soldiers were jogging closer, a man and a woman, clenching their rifles and stretching to see through the trees ahead.

Jess checked Brenna's position, and then dropped into thin air. The rope caught her and she swung in a vicious arc, using her momentum to kick powerfully into the first soldier's chest. He sailed backward and crashed into the woman behind him, his arms spinning helplessly, his rifle flying when he hit the ground.

Jess shrugged off the rope and snatched the rifle from the grass, and her fingers flew over the bolt release. Unfamiliar with firearms but understanding the general principle, she snapped the rifle's stock to her shoulder and fired twice.

Half expecting the twang of her bowstring, the two sharp cracks in her ear were painfully loud—but arrow or bullet, Jess's aim was true. The reclining soldier was struck in the chest, and the woman behind him in the head as she started to rise.

Jess didn't wait to see her fall. She whirled and took in their small battleground. Vicar, still crouching on the limb of the oak, had felled two soldiers with arrows—clean shots and swift deaths. Hakan was finishing off the man she knelt over now, thrusting a dagger through his heart with a trilling cry. Jess searched for Brenna and saw her checking the two soldiers who fell from her bullets.

Then Jess heard Dana's full-throated roar and saw her grappling hand-to-hand with a soldier as tall and solid as a stone block. Kyla had jumped onto the man's back and wrapped her arm around his throat to cut off his air.

Even as Jess broke into a run, Dana executed the escape she had performed perfectly in drills a hundred times. She pivoted and twisted, using the man's superior strength against him, and broke his hold. Dana's dagger flashed, and the soldier bent double, bellowing in pain. Kyla slid quickly off his back, and he crashed to the ground on his side.

Jess reached them, and released a sharp whistle. Her adanin answered at once, and Jess closed her eyes in relief. All her sisters were still standing. Dana was next to her, panting, staring down at the soldier curled at their feet. Blood was trickling from her nose, but she looked otherwise unhurt. Jess gripped Dana's shoulder and then knelt beside the fallen man.

Boy, she corrected. The pale face that was revealed when she turned the soldier onto his back still held traces of acne. He clenched the gory shirt over his stomach, his teeth gritted in pain, and stared up at Jess through wide, shocked eyes. She studied the wound dispassionately. Dana's thrust would prove fatal, but only after long hours of suffering.

Jess put a hand on his chest. "What's your name, son?"

"Private Curtis Voakes, *bitch*!" the soldier spat, and a drop of blood flew from his lips and struck Jess's breast.

Jess felt Dana stiffen, but she didn't hold the boy's rage against him. He had just watched Amazons wipe out all of his brothers. She glanced up at Kyla, who understood at once and turned away. Jess wrapped her hands around the soldier's head and felt his convulsive trembling. A quick snap and this bloody fight would be over.

"Jess, wait." Brenna knelt beside her, breathing hard. She showed her the flask she held. "It's painless and very fast."

Jess looked into Brenna's beautiful eyes, soft and pleading, and slid her hands from beneath the boy's head. Brenna pressed her arm in thanks, then moved closer to the soldier and lifted his head with effort. She held the flask to his gaping lips.

"You're dying, Curtis." Jess sat back on her heels and studied him. "This drink will ease your pain and take you quickly. We can't force you to swallow, but you are dying today. I'd choose the easier path."

The boy let out a few explosive breaths, his heavy brows furrowed, looking from Jess's face to Brenna's. When his gaze fastened on Brenna's compassionate gaze, she tipped the flask. His sharp Adam's apple bobbed as he swallowed, and he coughed, hard. Jess looked up as Hakan joined their circle, then Vicar, shouldering her bow. Their expressions were impenetrable, but Kyla looked down at the dying soldier with tears in her eyes.

"You gonna throw us into a ravine?" The boy still struggled for defiance, but the pain and his fear were weakening him.

"Your remains will be treated with respect," Jess told him. "Your kin will find you."

"That's more kindness than you'd have shown us, boy." Vicar only spoke the truth, and no one contested her.

Jess watched the drug take hold. The soldier's big body relaxed slowly as the pain left him, and he let out a hitching sigh of relief. His eyelids began to flutter.

"Annie," he whispered. His eyes closed, and Brenna lowered his head gently to the grass.

Jess waited until the boy's chest rose and fell one last time. Then she rose and helped Brenna stand. "Have we any injured?"

"No." Dana stood with her fists braced on her hips as Kyla examined her bleeding nose. "We're just *fine*."

"All's well, Jesstin." Hakan snapped her dagger into the sheath on her belt. "We took no mortal hits."

"And perhaps we've gained some time." Jess looked thoughtfully at the dead soldier at her feet. "We're long leagues from the City limits. These soldiers didn't walk up here, they had some kind of transport."

Dana lit up. "You're right, Jess! Let's go find us some jeeps!"

"Just as soon as we honor the dead, youngster." Hakan studied the small clearing, frowning. "Or at least find them some shelter from the wolves."

Jess raised her aching arm, and Brenna sighed and nestled against her side. She rested her lips in her adonai's soft hair and sent silent thanks to her Mothers that Brenna hadn't had to draw lifeblood in this skirmish. Her breathing was even now, and she seemed to be recovering fast from the sick adrenaline surge of the fight.

Violence had been alien to Brenna when she first came to Tristaine. Jess had known that within minutes of meeting her. Caster's vicious attacks on Jess and the rest of their sisters had ignited a protective passion in their gentle healer. Brenna had fought fiercely in Tristaine's battles, but so far she had been spared dealing out any killing strikes. Jess prayed she always would be.

She kissed Brenna's forehead. Then she went to Dana, and peered at her nose.

"It's not broken, Jess." Dana winced. "Don't you *dare* do that cracking thing with your thumbs."

"No cracking needed, adanin." Jess tapped Dana's cheek. "But you could have ducked. We were hoping not to draw notice in the City. This honker of yours will be swollen and bruised."

Dana sighed. "I guess I should have yelled 'not the face.'"

"It's still a very pretty face." Brenna checked Dana's injury. "I doubt we can find much ice around here, Dana, but at this altitude, river water is cold enough to help with swell—"

Jess heard the click and spun, and saw the soldier she had shot in the chest weaving on his knees, raising his rifle. Her hand rocketed to her belt, pulled her dagger, and threw it in one blinding motion.

The split-second before Jess's blade thudded home in his neck, the soldier fired, and Vicar staggered and fell.

❖

"This is my fault." Tears threatened to blind Brenna, and she dashed them away impatiently. She needed to be able to see to lay out her instruments. "I should have checked that soldier more carefully, Jess."

"Bren, it was a battle." Jess was washing her cousin's upper back, and Brenna could see the faint tremor in her hands. "If anyone's to blame, I'm the one who botched that kill."

"I'll take hush-money from ye both," Vicar grumbled. She was stretched out between them on a folded blanket, naked to the waist, her hands loose on either side of her head. She hadn't lost consciousness when the bullet smacked into the back of her shoulder, but the strong herbal sedative Brenna had given her was finally taking effect. Vicar's words were slurred. "Just dig it out, healer."

"Brenna, can you tell us anything?" Kyla stood nearby, watching their preparations anxiously. "There isn't much blood."

"No, we're lucky there. It missed the subclavian artery." Brenna summoned her will and silenced the sick guilt in her gut. "Vicar? I'm going to ask Jess to hold you. I don't want you twitching at the wrong moment. Can you hear me?"

"Aye," Vic mumbled. "Cooties..."

Jess draped herself carefully across Vicar's back, and Hakan settled into the grass near her head and clasped her wrists, more for comfort than restraint. Brenna had seen it many times, the gentleness and love in the touch of Tristaine's warriors when they helped tend one of their own, and it still moved her.

"Here we go." Dana spoke quietly, as if entering a church. She set their two brightest lamps near Brenna and Vicar, adding their light to the wan glow of the setting sun. "Is there anything else I can do, Bren?"

"Watch our periphery, Dana." Jess was watching Brenna closely as she measured Vicar's pulse at the throat. "We don't need more cougars or soldiers tonight."

"Will do, Jess."

Vicar's pulse was slow and even, and her long body was relaxed. Brenna knew she was hurting by her deliberate, rhythmic breathing, but there were no signs of shock. Brenna was calming herself, now, as she lifted a slender probe from her instrument case. Healing was her home territory. She knew what to do here, how to help. She rested her hand on the blond hair curling around Vicar's neck.

"Vic, I'm going to take a look. Try not to move. It's going to hurt a little, but nothing unbearable. Okay?"

"I'm set." Vicar closed her eyes.

And so was Brenna, once she had positioned the probe in the wound and vision couldn't guide her further. She advanced its slender length gradually, with meticulous care, her inner senses following its passage. The bullet had hit the trapezius on Vicar's left side—on an Amazon warrior, a thick and powerful muscle. Judging by the trajectory, it had missed both the scapula and humerus. Brenna blew out a breath in relief.

A soft grunt escaped Vicar.

"Good, adanin, we've found it." Brenna withdrew the probe smoothly, and selected a thin pair of forceps. These instruments had been a gift from Sammy when she became a medic, and they fit her grip like old friends. "I think the bullet's intact, Vicar, it's embedded in muscle. Keep breathing slow and deep. This is going to smart a bit."

"Just lie easy, adanin," Hakan murmured at Vicar's head. "We've got you."

Brenna found the bullet. Her forceps gripped it, and Vicar moaned. "I'm sorry, Vic, I'll be as gentle as I can. We're almost there."

Jess held on to her cousin more tightly as she stiffened, and then Brenna drew the small bloody bullet out into the light of the lamps. She heard the collective sighs of her sisters, and Vicar echoed them with a long, trembling exhalation.

"Well done, lass." Jess cradled the back of Brenna's neck. Brenna returned her weary smile.

"We're far from home free." Brenna patted the sluggishly bleeding hole with a dry cloth. "We have goldenseal to guard against infection, but this wound will take careful watching. How are you, Vicar?"

"Just keen," Vicar muttered. "Jesstin, give me an hour. I can ride."

"Aye, then you ride," Jess answered easily. "The rest of us will catch up later. We camp here tonight."

They laid their holdings near the field of their battle. Dana and Hakan had stripped the dead soldiers of their weapons and arranged them respectfully side by side. The branches laid over their bodies would help protect them from small predators until they were recovered.

"This surgical wizardry is how you got your nickname, Bren." Kyla knelt beside Vicar and helped her drink from her canteen, smiling at Brenna. "Shann started calling you 'Blades' after you cut a bullet out of Camryn's leg."

"Ah, poor Cam." Brenna smiled sadly at the memory. "She must have thought Shann had lost her mind, letting a Clinic medic waving a scalpel anywhere near an Amazon."

"Our lady was showing her trust in you, adonai." Jess patted her cousin's bare back and climbed to her feet. "That helped Cam trust you, too."

Brenna saw Jess grow still and turn slowly toward the thick grove of trees that bordered their camp.

"Jesstin?" Dana called from her post across the clearing.

"I hear it, adanin." Jess turned and looked at Hakan, who nodded.

"Do we have company, Jess?" Kyla asked. Her stance over Vicar was suddenly protective.

"Aye," Jess replied, checking the dagger sheathed in her belt. "Not many—two or three."

Vicar started to lift herself on one arm, and Brenna stilled her quickly. "Absolutely not, Vicar, you lie still. Let us handle this." Vicar grumbled and lowered herself again.

Brenna got to her feet and went to Jess. "What exactly are your freakishly sharp ears hearing, dearest?"

"Our guests' blundering passage." Jess smiled apologetically at her. "Sorry, lass, but whoever they are, they're crashing through the far brush like mules. These aren't trained troops." She went to the soldiers' rifles they had stacked near their packs and took one, then tossed a second to Dana. "Hakan, stay with Vic. The rest of you, fast and quiet. Stay behind me."

Jess broke into a sprint through the trees and the others ran with her, shadow-close. Strident cricket-song helped cover the sound of their steps. Brenna kept up pretty well, she thought, given the fact that her knees were jelly again. This long, harrowing day just refused to end.

Jess sailed over a bush everyone else had to veer around, and in spite of her fear, Brenna was swept by a moment of breathless appreciation for Jess's sheer physicality. She shook herself mentally as they neared the base of a large oak that split their path, its branches heavy and thick with leaves.

Brenna, balancing lightly on her feet and ready to launch toward any threat, looked hard into the shadowy depths of the oak. She spotted two separate patches of oddly shivering twigs about halfway up the gnarled trunk.

"How many, Bren?" Jess's voice was a low burr from a nearby shadow.

Brenna gulped. She was sure. "Two, Jesstin."

"Kyla, are they armed?"

"Not with anything that threatens us at this distance." Kyla stood close behind Jess, panting lightly. "They would have taken potshots by now."

Jess lowered her rifle and rested her hand on her hip, looking thoughtful. "*Come down!*" she bellowed.

Brenna actually ducked, as did Dana. When Jess wanted to roar, she could flatten the grass for a mile in any direction. Complete silence followed the command. Even the crickets had the sense to shut up.

Then there was a sudden, frantic rustling of branches and leaves, a breathless yell, and a body plummeted from the tree and thumped to the ground at their feet.

"Oh shit!"

Brenna heard a feminine cry from the figure above them, still clinging to the oak's trunk.

"Don't you hurt her!" There was an immense crashing of boughs as she descended.

Brenna knelt beside Jess and helped her steady the woman lying on the ground. She looked to be in her forties, reasonably fit. The breath had been knocked out of her, but she seemed basically unhurt. She lay gasping with her hands raised protectively, a pair of dark-framed glasses askew on her face.

Moving carefully, Brenna adjusted the frames so the woman could see them clearly. She rested her palm gently at the base of her throat and measured her thrumming pulse. "I think you're all right," she told her. "Just lie still a moment and catch your breath."

The crashing finally ended as the second woman leapt from the tree. She darted toward them, long brown hair whipping around her face, but Dana caught her around the waist and hauled her back. She performed a quick search, then nodded at Jess and released her.

The woman skidded to a halt on her knees beside her friend. "Hey! You're okay, right?"

"Right," the second woman gasped. She lifted her hand, and it was taken with a tenderness that didn't escape Brenna. "Get me up."

They struggled to their feet, and Brenna rose with them. The women clung to each other, still a bit wild-eyed. They were dressed for travel, but their clothing was torn and muddy.

"I'm Brenna." She smiled in a way she hoped was reassuring. "Who are you?"

The first woman opened her mouth to answer, but then Jess rose from her crouch to stand beside Brenna, and her voice faded. It was obviously not unlike watching a tree sprout slowly before her eyes.

"I'm Je-Je-Jen—" she stammered, and Brenna bit her lip in sympathy and nodded encouragement. "I'm *Jennifer*," she finished at last, still ogling Jess. She squeezed her friend's arm. "This is Evelyn."

"I'm Eva," the second woman corrected, pushing wisps of her abundant silver hair off her forehead. "This is Jenny."

"We're Jenny and Eva," Jenny confirmed. "You're very tall," she said to Jess.

"This colossus is Jesstin. Our sisters there are Kyla and Dana." Brenna wound her arm through Jess's to humanize her. Her adanin seemed willing to let her develop this first contact. "Tell us what brought you here."

"We escaped from the City, and we're going to find Tristaine." Now that Jenny knew her partner—the women were obviously adonai—was unhurt, she spoke with calm precision. Her lively green eyes studied them curiously. "We didn't get very far. That Army unit you guys tackled was looking for us."

"We heard you take them out." Eva had almost caught her breath. She swallowed, eyeing Jess's rifle. "We wanted to try to get closer to you, to be sure. You're Amazons, right?"

"Aye, we're Amazons." Jess extended her hand to shake Eva's, but Brenna stopped her quickly, and she stepped back at once.

"Listen, this is important." Brenna half-lifted one hand to hold their attention, and realized she was mirroring Shann. "We've all been exposed to a sickness. If you stay around us, you might catch it, and it's serious. Have you had all the City inoculations?"

"Oh." Jenny looked at Eva, and an unspoken communication passed between them. "Well, our boosters are up to date. And even if they weren't, we decided a long time ago we would throw in our lot with Tristaine, if we could find it."

"We decided your lot would be our lot," Eva agreed. She stuck out her hand, smiling, and Jess grinned and shook it firmly. "Tell us how we can help."

CHAPTER SEVEN

B renna turned her head on Jess's thigh and peered sleepily at the four women clustered on the other side of their small campfire. Dana and Kyla had drawn second winds with the knowledge Eva and Jenny carried of the ways in which the City had changed since they had last seen it. They were revising their map of City streets, whispering and pointing out new routes.

Vicar was resting well. Jess's cousin had one of the highest pain thresholds Brenna had ever seen. She just wished she'd stop having opportunities to marvel at it. Hakan was stretched out on a blanket beside her, deeply asleep. Like most of Tristaine's warriors, she had mastered the art of finding sleep fast in the few hours of rest allowed them. Brenna noted one stubborn holdout had refused to submit.

She gazed pensively at Jess's still profile above her. The heavy muscle of the thigh beneath her head still thrummed with energy. She could see the outline of Jess's clenched jaw in the firelight. Brenna reached up and popped her lightly on the chin.

"Yesssss?" Jess turned half-shuttered eyes on her.

"I was looking for your off-button." Brenna caressed Jess's thigh with her knuckles. "Why so tense, Jesstin?"

"I'll be ready for sleep soon." Jess stroked Brenna's hair gently, and she struggled to keep her eyes open. "I like our new friends."

"I like them too." Brenna turned her head, enjoying the mild scratch of denim against her cheek. She saw Jenny's and Eva's heads huddled next to Dana's and Kyla's, looking as if they had joined their clan's planning sessions for years. "They love each other; they survived meeting you. My Amazon flags are flying."

"Aye, Eva and Jenny are both Tristaine." Jess spoke with a certainty rare for her on first meeting, but Brenna agreed with her. Some women were born Amazon, destined for Tristaine from their first breath. Others were not.

"No, the entire downtown district has changed." Eva polished her glasses with her shirttail, then slipped them back on and pointed at the map Dana held. "There's construction going on here, so none of these streets will get you through."

"Right," Jenny said and pointed to another section. "And both of these rural roads are guarded by Army details now, twenty-four-seven. There's usually only two guards posted here, though, at the City Line."

"Damn, Tristaine's lucky we ran into you, sisters." Kyla scratched her head. They all desperately needed baths. "Our map of City streets is at least two years old."

"Yeah, so much has changed since I was stationed down there." Dana frowned down at the map. "Your good intel is going to come in real handy, ladies, thank you."

"Well, we researched it enough." Eva looked at Jenny with rueful affection. "We planned this field trip to Tristaine so carefully for months!"

"Yes, and we still managed to attract the attention of an Army patrol three days out." Jenny leaned into Eva briefly, the laugh lines around her eyes deepening. "Scared the holy screaming hell out of us both."

"Were they looking for you in particular?" Brenna turned on her side and rested her head again on Jess's leg. "Are there warrants out for you in the City?"

"Not any we know of. These are excellent, by the way." Jenny peered at the nuts cradled in her palm. "Much better than those mealy peanuts the City dares to call trail mix. Anyway, we don't think the patrol was sent specifically after us, Brenna. I teach Public School, Eva's a psychiatric nurse. We're not really on the Government's radar. There's no reason the Army would be tipped off if we went missing for a few days."

"Jenny's theory is we got sloppy covering our tracks at our first two campsites." Eva accepted a nut Jenny held to her lips and chomped it thoughtfully for a moment. "Those guys were probably on a routine patrol of the outskirts, and they picked up our trail. We moved as fast as we could." Eva's friendly face sobered. "We heard the gunshots behind us, and those yells. It was pretty terrifying."

"Yeah. They were unlucky." Dana folded the roadmap of the City, her jaw set. Brenna realized the clash with the soldiers must have hit close to home for Dana. She had been one of their kind before coming to Tristaine. And no matter how many of their clan's enemies Dana killed, her inherent decency would always quail at the visceral horror of punching a knife into a human being. "They were all pretty young. Brave enough, but not well trained. And they weren't a clan. They didn't fight together like one."

"I'm sorry they had to die." Kyla looked at Jess with a compassion that told Brenna she understood the necessity of the command to draw lifeblood. "Amazons don't kill unless we must, Jenny. We just couldn't avoid it this time."

"We've heard that—that Amazon warriors honor all life. We've heard so many stories about you." Jenny patted Kyla's knee. "Rumors about Amazons still swamp all the women's bars in the Boroughs. Tristaine is very real to a lot of our friends down there."

I never heard those rumors, Brenna thought. *And I spent more nights in those bars than I can count.* A shiver of sadness worked through her, and she hunched closer to Jess. She had been single-minded in her City years. She went to bars to get drunk, as efficiently and quickly as possible, not to listen to gossip.

Dana snorted in disgust and gave up folding the roadmap, handing the snarled parchment to Kyla. "Well, at least we know the army's training is still no match for Tristaine's. There's not a single soldier in my old outfit I'd lay money on against any of Jess's warriors."

"Don't underrate the City's Army, Dana." Jess's low brogue was a pleasant burr against Brenna's cheek. "Some of the best Amazon warriors I've known have come to Tristaine from their ranks."

Dana looked startled. Then she smiled and began feeding twigs to their fire. Kyla bopped Dana gently on the head with her neatly rolled roadmap and then kissed her cheek.

Brenna closed her burning eyes, Jess's soothing touch in her hair lulling her toward sleep. She tried to listen to what Jenny was saying, but her voice kept changing, growing younger.

❖

This transition to the spirit plane felt disjointed, almost chaotic, and Elise's first words told Brenna why.

"Our queen grows weaker, j'heika." A tear wended its way down Elise's high cheek and dropped into the basin between them. *"See our home."*

The clear water swirled, and suddenly Brenna stood in the center of Tristaine's village square.

It seemed to be a full clan gathering, and somehow Brenna knew it was happening now, as she slept in Jess's arms. Perhaps not a full meeting—Brenna saw about two-thirds of Tristaine's number sitting on the log benches lining the square. Her stomach gave a nasty lurch, and then she realized the missing Amazons couldn't all be sick—those who were ill needed caretakers.

Brenna's sleeping senses were overwhelmed. Here, in this corridor between spiritual planes, she could feel every emotion coursing through the four hundred hearts around her. There was ragged tension in the women's silence, and Brenna saw armed warriors standing at intervals throughout the benches. That sight shriveled her soul more than the coming of the plague. Amazons prepared to lift arms against their sisters.

She sought out Shann with something like desperation and found her, seated on an elevated, high-backed chair at one end of their circle. The fact that Shann didn't stand before her Amazons told Brenna all she needed to know about her mother's health. Oisin and Jackson, the warriors Jess had praised, stood protectively on either side of her throne.

"The force used last night was unforgivable, lady!" Bethany was not addressing the queen, but the clan. Outrage sparked her eyes as she turned in a slow circle to include all present. "When did Tristaine become an accursed police state?"

"We suffered one broken ankle, Bethany, when Martine wouldn't stop running and Jackson had to sling her legs." Shann's complexion looked gray to Brenna, but she sat with graceful posture and apparent ease, her hands folded in her lap. There was a slight threadiness to her voice, and she had to work hard to produce the volume needed to reach all ears. "Don't portray last night's foolish skirmish as a bloodbath, sister. You and your guild had clear warning not to try to leave the mesa."

"You're lucky you weren't all skewered on Dyan's labrys, Bethany!" Sara's cracked snarl sounded behind Brenna, and she slumped in relief. Shann's eldest Councilor was still hearty and hale. "And I'll gouge out your liver myself if you pull such a mutton-brained stunt again!"

"Your warriors can't be everywhere, Shann, not with so many of them down with this fever." Bethany was treading dangerous ground now, Brenna could see it in the stiffness of the women watching her. "We'll get our children out. By one's and two's, if we have to. You can't stop—"

"All right, I've heard enough of this codswallop." Shasa stood on the other side of the circle, one of Kyla's close friends in the artists' guild. "You can't just defy the word of the Queen of Tristaine, Bethany, Shann guides us all. And you definitely bloody hell *can't address our lady with such blatant disrespect, not in my hearing!"*

Shouts of agreement rose, many of them. But Brenna heard other voices too, some pleading, some angry. She saw three women arguing with Aria, whose smiling, crossed-arm charm budged not an inch. Thank Gaia their lady had these strong sisters to back her.

Shann waited until the noise subsided, biding her time. Brenna realized she needed it to gather her strength.

"Amazons have walked the earth for centuries, adanin." Shann rose smoothly, showing no sign of infirmity, her voice strong and clear. "Tristaine is the last of Artemis's daughters, Her last Amazon clan. We will not implode from within after defeating generations of powerful enemies!"

The gathering was quiet, watching Shann avidly, and Brenna saw Oisin and Jackson exchange looks of relief.

"Sisters, believe me when I tell you the medicine from the City offers our children, and all of us, our greatest hope. We must give Jess and our sisters time." Shann's expression darkened again. "And they will bring the cure home to a family of Amazons, strong and united, not a gaggle of frightened, vicious alley cats. Do you hear me, adanin?"

"We hear, Shann!" A hundred women roared in answer—not all or nearly all, but enough for now, Brenna hoped.

"While we prattle here, our orchards go untended." Shann wisely turned them to practicalities. "We still have animals to feed and crops to tend and ill to nurse. Our council here is finished. Let's be about Tristaine's business."

Shann made her way back to her throne as her clan began to rise and filter from the square. She lowered herself to the chair's cushioned seat, her eyes closing. The usual small crowd of Amazons gathered around her, hoping for a moment of private council.

"Can you hear me, Brenna?" Shann whispered.

Startled, knowing she was invisible, Brenna leaned closer to Shann's lowered head. "Come back to us soon, Blades. Your sisters are frightened, and this rebellion is far from over."

Brenna wanted desperately to touch her mother's hand, but knew she could not. She murmured reassurance she knew Shann couldn't hear. "We're coming, lady. Please hang on."

❖

Selene was just beginning her fading descent into sunrise when Jess shook Brenna gently awake. The twittering music of morning larks reached her as she fought off sleep and sat up, wincing at the painful bruise on her hip.

"Bren? Have a look at Vicar."

Jess sounded calm, but Brenna's eyes flew fully open. Vicar was sitting up, braced by Hakan's arm. Brenna could see her shaking from ten feet away. She went quickly to Vicar and knelt beside her.

"How are you, Vic?" Brenna felt Vicar's forehead, which was clammy and cool.

"She woke a moment ago, cold as Hera's tit." Hakan's usually courtly language had deserted her. She shifted to keep from brushing Vicar's bandaged shoulder.

"Vicar?" Brenna said softly, measuring her rapid pulse.

"It's just the shakes." Vicar successfully quelled any trembling in her voice.

Brenna looked up at Jess, her hands prickling with dread. Fever would follow, if the pattern in Tristaine held true. Vicar's eyes were already hollow and glassy. "This might be more serious than chills, Vic."

Vicar cursed, but didn't try to refute her. "Jesstin, I have to be able to ride. Brenna can dose me with what remedies we have to keep me upright."

"No, cousin." Jess knelt and touched Vicar's leg. "You can't ride with us. Between the bullet and the flu, you'll lose strength fast."

"Jesstin—" But Vicar broke off, and she and Jess locked eyes. Brenna sensed an intense communication pass between them, the same kind of silent exchange she often shared with Jess. She watched Vicar absorb the knowledge that she had to stay back. It must be killing her to accept it.

"She can't stay up here alone, Jesstin," Hakan said.

Jess turned, and Brenna followed her gaze to Jenny and Eva, who sat quietly talking with Kyla near their packs. "Eva is a nurse. She and Jenny can tend Vic here."

Kyla nodded, and she and Jenny and Eva got up and joined them. None of them looked as if they'd slept much.

"Vicar, I'm so sorry you're ill." Eva crouched and patted Vicar's foot. "I'll do everything I can to help Brenna make you comfortable. But Jenny and I think we should go with the rest of you down to the City."

"What?" Brenna was sure she hadn't heard correctly.

"We can help." Jenny folded her arms against the dawn's chill. "We know the City's layout, and where guard stations are posted much better than any of you, Jess. Really, your map's almost useless. We can help you reach your friend's trailer safely." Jenny looked a little pale, but when she smiled her eyes lit up. "To put it plainly, we want to be Amazons. This is our chance to earn our stripes."

"Jenny, you guys just escaped from that madhouse!" Dana draped her jacket around Kyla's shoulders. "Honest, you don't have to pass an entrance exam to join Tristaine. They didn't make me."

"Your sister, Jen," Kyla urged quietly.

"Oh, right," Jenny said. "Brenna, Kyla told us you need to try to find your niece, who might have been placed in a Youth Home. My sister is a social worker in the City. Maybe she can help find this little girl."

"But…" Brenna trailed off as she felt Jess's touch on her arm.

Jess was studying their faces, and then she nodded. "Hakan, you'll stay here with Vicar. Jenny and Eva will come with us."

Hakan's mouth fell open. "Jesstin!"

"You know enough about tending to watch over Vic, adanin. And a much better chance of fighting off any attack than Jenny and Eva would have. We're close enough to the City that we risk another patrol. You can defend her if one comes this way."

Vicar made a withering spitting noise, which Hakan ignored. When she spoke, her tone was respectful. "But you'll need backup, Jess."

"That's still you." Jess checked the position of the sun. "If we find that transport, we should be back by tomorrow's dawn. If two days pass, consider us captured or lost, Hakan. That would mean leaving Vicar, and going down alone. You'd be our last hope of getting that cure to Tristaine."

Hakan swallowed visibly. "I hear, Jesstin."

Brenna tried to reel in her chaotic thoughts, still fogged with her sleeping vision of Shann and the village. As always when she needed to center herself, she reached for Jess's hand. *We look to her with such trust,* Brenna thought. *We all count on this one brave warrior to lead us safely through this nightmare. It's just the salvation of her clan. And I wonder why she can't sleep.*

Jess smiled down at her, then went to Eva and Jenny. "In our queen's name, we thank you both for your help. You show great courage in taking on this quest."

"Now, please don't let us fuck up." Jenny sighed, and Eva chuckled nervous agreement.

"Let's break camp." Jess bent and tossed a folded blanket to Dana. "Leave two rifles and our food stock here with our sisters."

Brenna went to her satchel and took out several packets, then sat beside Hakan and Vicar. "Here, Hakan. Make a tea of this, using about this much. Vicar, I want you to drink a cup every six hours." Vic was still shaking, and Brenna helped Hakan adjust a blanket around her. "We'll bring you your own personal dose of that remedy very soon, Vic."

"Aye, Bigfoot." Jess knelt at Vicar's other side. "We'll test the cure out on you, to ensure it's not poison."

"Jesstin." There was no humor in Vicar's voice, and her brogue was low and grating. She clasped Jess's wrist, and in that moment, Brenna thought the two warriors were alone together in these high wilds.

"They raped our mothers, Jess." Vicar jutted her chin toward the City. "Them, down there. For generations, they've hunted us. They murdered our sisters, and they murder them still. They took Dyan from us. And young Camryn."

Brenna shivered. Jess's features were growing as stony and feral as Vicar's.

"Strike without mercy, Jesstin, if they try to stop you." Vic grasped Jess's collar. "With a righteous heart and a vengeful arm that seeks only the Goddess's justice. Bring down the rage of Artemis on the enemies of Tristaine if they bar your path."

Jess's hand covered Vicar's, still clenching her collar, and Brenna saw the words run deep in her. Then Jess looked at Hakan.

"Our Mothers grant your safety, adanin. You'll see us again soon."

❖

"What *is* that?" Dana sniffed the air, then held her injured nose. "What's that bloody stench?"

"The City," Jess replied tersely. She'd been smelling it since they emerged from the forest. Shann was right. Memories were revived more vividly by smells than by sight, and she was not enjoying hers.

"Man, you really can smell it all the way from here." Jenny's nose crinkled. "I didn't realize the City air had gotten that bad."

Dana took another cautious whiff, then spat on the ground. "What'd they do down there, bomb all the smelters?"

"The City stank just like this the whole time you lived there, Dana m'dear." Kyla slipped the green army jacket over Dana's shoulders and buttoned it shut. "You've just had a few years of pure mountain air to blow the poison out of your lungs. I remember it smelling this bad the first time Cam and I got close."

"It's auto exhaust and pollution and chemical waste. And fear." Brenna was lacing her boot closed with quick, tense snaps.

"You don't notice it if you're breathing it in every day. I'd forgotten too, Dana."

Jess saw that the sun had cleared the eastern ridge behind them. "Let's finish this, adanin. We need to get on the road."

They had found the Army transport easily enough. The boot tracks of the soldiers were clearly marked on the dusty trail. Rather than jeeps, the patrol had ridden into the hills in a large, canopied Army truck, a dark muddy green, with white stars painted on each door. The set of keys they had taken from a dead officer cranked its engine to life.

They had taken the soldiers' light jackets, too—the ones not too visibly darkened with blood—and Jess's broad shoulders strained against the scratchy fabric. She helped Brenna button her own jacket, knowing she shared her discomfort wearing clothing so recently owned by the dead.

"Eva, Jenny, one of you should ride in front to guide us." Jess went to the back of the truck, figured out the latch, and lowered the rear gate. The bed was lined with two short metal benches. "The rest of us will stow away here."

She whistled to Dana and lofted the keys to her. Dana snatched them out of the air with one hand, grinning. "You might be able to outrun me on a mustang, Jesstin, but I'm a maniac behind a wheel!"

"We're counting on it." Jess helped Brenna take the high step up into the truck's bed, then assisted Kyla and Jenny before jumping in herself. Immediately it felt like the canopy-shrouded interior was closing in on her. It took more effort than it should have to pull up the gate, latch it, and tie the canvas covering over its bolts. Jess settled on a hard bench next to Brenna, facing Jenny and Kyla, and started the breathing exercises Dyan had taught her to ground herself.

Dana slid open the panel that separated the front seats from the bed of the truck. "Listen, there are no seatbelts back there, and we'll be going over rough terrain. Hold on to what you can."

The truck's engine sputtered to life, and Jess braced herself for a lurch. But Dana backed the transport around smoothly and then accelerated down a small hill. In spite of their driver's skill, the women in the back had to brace themselves as they gained speed, and Jess slid her arm around Brenna's waist to anchor her.

Dana drove all out. The greenery of the foothills gave way quickly to the sandy, gently sloping terrain that lay between the mountains and the City. They covered ground in minutes that had taken Jenny and Eva long, laborious hours to cross on foot. Jess closed her eyes and thanked the Goddess for smiling on Tristaine at last. This truck would save them entire days of travel.

Brenna's fingers curled around hers, her touch as welcome as warm water on her hands after a cold night's hunt. Her adonai's lovely smile was tired, but soft with affection. "Good morning, Jesstin. We never got around to saying that." Brenna had to raise her voice to be heard over the clattering of the transport. "I'd kiss you, but I'm afraid we'd hit a ravine and I'd knock out your teeth."

"I might want to risk it." Jess blew a tuft of hair gently out of Brenna's eyes. "Good morning, querida."

"So, we're hoping a bunch of rabid Amazons can pass for City soldiers for ten seconds?" Brenna asked. "Long enough to get past that guard post?"

"That's what we're hoping." Jess braced Brenna as the truck took a jarring bounce. Jenny and Kyla steadied each other quickly. "Dana has a fair shot at it. She knows the Army's lingo. With Gaia's luck, we'll be taken for yesterday's patrol, checking back in."

"And if there's trouble," Jenny said gravely, looking at the rifle tucked behind Jess's feet, "we'll shoot it out, if we have to."

"We'll be fine, Jen." Kyla slipped a companionable arm around her. "If anything happens, just do whatever Jess says. Like, right away."

The landscape flew past the small, plastic-shielded windows

near the bed's roof. They had a good hour of this rocky ride ahead, and Jess shifted to ease her lower back. Brenna sat with her eyes closed, and Jess figured she was still so spent after last night's scant rest, she might doze off in spite of the rattling truck.

A quiet urgency rose suddenly in Jess. She frowned a moment, puzzled. She wasn't usually prone to phantom impulses, but she decided to abide this one. "Brenna."

"Hmm?" Brenna opened her eyes at once.

"You own my whole heart, Bren." Jess turned on the bench, needing to see her face. "I love you more than my life."

"Jesstin." Brenna smiled and drew her head back a bit, as if to see Jess more clearly. "Thank you, adonai. But where did that—"

"Just needed to be said, I guess."

Jenny was looking politely away, but Kyla smiled at them openly.

"You guys are so great." There was a sweet poignancy in Kyla's tone that Jess heard even over the rumbling of the engine. Her little sister's features were soft and sad. "You two have the love every Amazon ever born dreams about, you know that?"

"You've felt that kind of love, Ky." Brenna touched Kyla's knee. "You know if you find a woman worthy of it, she'll change your life forever."

"Jesstin?" Dana knocked on the front panel, and Jess saw Kyla start. "Eva has us headed toward the entrance by the north access road, the one with the smallest guard post. We should pick it up pretty soon."

"Aye, Dana." Jess swallowed past a rawness in her throat, missing the canteen she'd left at their base camp. "Signal when we're close."

❖

Army units patrolled the outer perimeter of the City limits constantly. The vast bureaucracy of Homeland Security had achieved what its shortsighted Citizens thought they wanted—all possible protection against foreign terrorists. But even their willingness to sacrifice basic human rights in the name of safety hadn't rendered the City immune to penetration.

The small guard post Jenny and Eva identified was manned by only two soldiers on an isolated stretch of rural road. Craning her neck between Dana and Eva in the front seats, Brenna caught a glimpse of the long, red-striped gate in the distance that barred the path past the station.

Jess and Jenny and Eva had finished tying up their hair. Through the scratched plastic windows, the women in the back of the truck should just be shadowy forms to anyone standing outside, but Jess wanted their silhouettes to resemble the genders of the soldiers in the lost patrol.

"Here we go, adanin." Dana was wearing the pair of mirrored sunglasses she'd found in a dead soldier's pocket. "Jess, like we agreed, I'll say 'kilo' if this starts to turn funky."

Jess whistled acknowledgement, and Brenna was grateful she still had hold of her hand. After an hour in this dank, enclosed space, Jess seemed as calm as if they were trundling up to a Tristainian picnic, but Brenna saw the faint line of sweat beading her brow. Jess looked down at her and winked, and suddenly they were there. Dana slowed the truck and cranked down her side window. They came to a creaking halt.

"Unit Red Fourteen, end of watch."

Brenna closed her eyes. Dana sounded bored and tired. She knew she was extending the female officer's plastic ID through the window, and Brenna whispered a swift prayer that this inspection would prove as brief and cursory as Dana predicted. A few unbearable seconds ticked by. Kyla and Jenny kept their gazes on the corrugated tin floor of the bed.

A khaki-colored form appeared near the front of the truck. Brenna could see it through the first window. It was impossible to tell whether the sentry was male or female. Jess's gaze was keen and still as they waited.

"End of watch," a man droned.

Brenna let out an explosive breath and then stifled it instinctively. Their tense silence held as the striped gates swung slowly open, and Dana pulled past the station with a laconic wave. They continued down the dirt road for a full minute before anyone spoke.

"Hoo," Dana said softly.

"Oh my, damn straight, hoo," Eva agreed fervently. She twisted in her seat to see Jenny through the panel window. "You okay back there?"

"We're just fine." Jenny fanned herself briskly. "Beautiful job, Dana!"

"Thanky, ma'am." Dana cranked the truck around a bend in the road, and Brenna saw Jess's face go still as she stared through the dusty front windshield.

A dense mass of buildings loomed ahead of them, high rises and squat factories of every shape and size, surrounded by a yellow cloud of low-lying smog. The City was opening its maw to swallow her and Jess whole again.

Brenna gripped Jess's hand tightly and held on.

CHAPTER EIGHT

There was only so far they could drive an Army truck into the City in broad daylight without drawing attention. Smaller Military vehicles were a common sight on paranoid urban streets, but one of them was bound to question the presence of a troop transport in the City's core.

"Keep a sharp eye, adanin." Jess shucked off the dead soldier's jacket gratefully. "We need a large space, untended."

The untended part should be easy enough, Jess thought. *Eva and Jenny chose this neighborhood wisely.* While well within the City Lines, this shabby street seemed all but deserted at high noon on a Friday. Dana trundled the truck slowly past a series of shabby, shuttered retail stores, most of them closed for good.

"There, Jess." Kyla was pressed against one of the small plastic windows.

"Aye, Kyla, good catch. Dana?"

"Yep, I see it." Dana cranked the wheel, and the truck lumbered into the wide entrance of a large, abandoned storage shed. Its concrete floor and walls were coated with dust and cobwebs, and it was deep enough that the truck was parked in shadows. It wouldn't go undetected here forever, but they only needed a day.

Jess slid off the metal bench, crouched stiffly, and unlatched the truck's tailgate. They clambered out quickly, and Dana and Eva joined them. Under the army jackets, the Amazons had donned several items of clothing Jenny and Eva had packed, to lessen the strangeness of their hand-sewn Tristaine attire.

"What do you say, Jenny?" Jess asked. "Do we look ready?"

"Hmm." Jenny went to Jess and straightened the collar of her long chambray shirt. "You still look a little über-Amazon in this, Jess, but then you would look butch in a bikini. I think you guys are disguised well enough as City dwellers to pass, yes."

"Now, the streets that lead to your friend's place outside the East Borough are just north of here." Eva slid the strap of her backpack over her shoulder. "It's a pretty rough part of town, folks, so be careful."

"We will, sister." Jess cast a longing look at the truck, sorry they had to abandon the rifles. At least their hand weapons could be concealed in their clothing. "Jenny, Eva, tell us your plan again."

"We'll walk east of this neighborhood until we find a land line." Jenny recited their strategy with confidence. Jess had heard her whispering it a dozen times while they traveled. "We'll call my sister, who will come and pick us up. Then Gina will help us find out everything we can about Brenna's niece."

"We'll find a way to refuel this hulking jeep." Eva adjusted her glasses and frowned at the truck. "Then tonight, at 3:00 a.m., we'll be parked on the frontage road that runs behind the City Clinic."

"You think you've got the gears of this rig down, Eva?" Dana looked worried. "It's not like driving a compact."

"Yeah, I watched you pretty carefully." Eva smiled and extended a trembling thumbs-up. "It might not be pretty, but I'll get us there."

"Thank you, Jen." Brenna clasped Jenny's arms. "For helping me look for Sammy's baby. We'll try to check the Clinic's database, but your sister has a much better chance of finding Foster Care records."

"We'll look hard, Brenna." Jenny patted Brenna's cheek. "I hope we find something that helps."

Jess knew it was time to move. The sun was high in the sky now, and they had to find Jode. "We'll see you tonight, adanin. Walk by our Mother's light."

"You two watch out for each other." Kyla hugged Eva tightly, then Jenny.

Jenny went up on her toes and kissed Jess's cheek, and then she and Eva were gone.

❖

Brenna remembered the East Borough as a sparsely populated ghetto on the outskirts of the City's Downtown District. The people who lived there were lucky to get basic services—water, electricity, heat—and were reminded of that fact forcefully when any unrest threatened.

The few schools were as ramshackle and antiquated as the policies that ran them. Housing consisted of dilapidated apartment complexes, Government-run developments, and the occasional isolated trailer.

In one of those trailers lived the son of an Amazon and his wife, driven into poverty because of their loyalty to Tristaine. It was still a stone in Brenna's heart that after helping her and Jess escape, Jodoch and Pamela had to leave their jobs and their home and go into hiding to escape Caster's wrath.

The cramped streets of the Borough baked in the high sun, and they encountered only a few other pedestrians on the cracked sidewalks. Brenna was relieved to see that none of the people passing by took any particular notice of their small cadre. In fact, none of them met their eyes, a defense mechanism among Citizens that was all but unheard of in Tristaine.

"Should we cut through, Jess?" Dana eyed the shoddy storefronts on either side uneasily. "This seems like the right neighborhood."

"Eva wanted us a bit farther north." Jess paused, and Brenna saw her frown darkly at two shabbily dressed men who stood looking at them from the curb. The men exchanged glances, then moved quickly on.

"Adanin, I give you Jesstin's killer stare of death." Brenna smiled and nudged Jess. "Works every time."

Jess led them several more blocks, then checked an alley darkened by the buildings on either side. "Through here."

The alley was wide enough that they could walk side by side down its stinking length, avoiding the overflowing trash bins on either side. They were halfway through the dingy passage when Brenna heard the sound of approaching footsteps. Jess snapped her fingers, and Dana and Kyla moved smoothly behind them.

A loose clump of five people lurched around the corner into the alley. Four men and one woman, and judging by their gait and raucous voices, they had hit happy hour early and hard.

"Wonderful choice, Jesstin," Jess grumbled aloud.

"We could try your killer stare of death, Jess," Dana suggested.

Any hope that they could simply slip past this group faded as the men bunched across their path, falling silent as they drew closer.

"*Good* afternoon to you lovely ladies!" The largest of the men kept walking, his bleary eyes fixed on Brenna, until he almost touched her. Jess put out a calm hand and laid it on his T-shirted chest, and he backed off, his arms raised in exaggerated surrender. His friends clustered behind him.

"Man, it's so cool you girls came along!" A second man grinned, blowing beer breath through his beard into Jess's expressionless face. "Me and my family, we all got stranded when our van broke down over on Yesler."

The woman with them giggled, holding onto the vest of the man who had his arm around her, almost too intoxicated to stand. They were all drunk, but there was an ominous sheen in the eyes of the two men closest to them. Brenna was all too familiar with the toxic street drugs that were the constant plague of the outer Boroughs, and these two looked ripped on them. It seemed unlikely that they could talk their way out of this.

"Maybe you guys could stake us a few bucks, just enough

for bus fare back home?" The bearded man grinned at Jess, scratching a small sore on his nose.

"We have no money." Jess checked their positions. The fourth man, more a skinny kid, had rested his butt against the brick wall, and was yawning widely. "We're just passing through."

"Well, what say you come party with us for a while?" The second man stepped closer to Jess, still smiling. "Then maybe we can pool all our resources, see what we got, and make everybody happy."

Jess felt Dana shift behind her, and she reached back and touched her wrist. "We have plans we can't change, and no time for this. Either let us pass, or draw arms."

The bearded man let out an explosive hoot. *"Draw arms?* We're just having a friendly conversa—"

But apparently his partner welcomed Jess's invitation, and he lunged at Brenna with a lusty roar. Jess shot sideways and rocketed her fist into his chin, cutting off his bellow abruptly and spinning him off his feet. She whirled and saw Dana and Kyla tackle the bearded oaf, taking him down against a trash bin. The woman's shrill scream echoed crazily off the brick walls around them. The kid bolted back down the alley, obviously wanting none of this.

Jess advanced on the man holding the hysterical woman, and he backed away quickly, dragging her with him, one hand raised in panic.

Jess heard the meaty impact of Brenna's boot in the midriff of the big brute, who was still scrabbling over the concrete to get to her. He grabbed her ankle and she fell. Cursing, he grappled in his shirt and yanked out a blue steel revolver.

Time condensed into seconds. The small black bore of the gun's muzzle weaved toward Brenna, who was crouching only inches away. Jess heard Dana's warning cry even as her dagger filled her hand, and then it was flying, all the strength in her arm launching the blade in a sizzling trajectory toward the center of the man's chest. Its wicked edge passed so closely to Brenna's head that it sheared off a strand of her blond hair before slamming to the hilt in his heart.

"Jesus!" screamed the woman, careening in her boyfriend's arms, her hands plastered over her face. *"Jesus, stop!"* He yanked her away, and they staggered into a run back down the alley. Jess gestured to the others to let them go.

The bearded man lay slumped and insensible in piles of wet garbage. Jess went to Brenna and helped her to her feet. She was shaking and pale, but unhurt, and Jess kissed the top of her head. She walked to the man sprawled on his back and knelt beside him.

The last spark of life was leaving his eyes. Jess watched dispassionately as it faded, waiting until the last guttural breath left his spit-flecked lips. Then she grasped the hilt of her dagger and drew out the obsidian blade. She wiped the blood off on the man's shirt methodically.

"It was a necessary kill." Jess heard Dana behind her. "Well done, Jess."

Jess stared at the ebony sheen of the blade, a gift from Dyan. She rose and sheathed it in her belt. "Are we injured?"

"We're whole, Jesstin." Kyla put her arm around Brenna and squeezed her shoulders, and Brenna was able to offer her a tremulous smile. It had been very close.

"This kind's not likely to run to the police for help." Dana nudged the leg of the bearded man with her foot. "I don't think we need to worry about pursuit."

"Then let's find our brother." Jess stepped over the dead man, and they left the alley and its silent denizens behind.

❖

Their shadows slid across the cracked plaster wall of a utility substation. Brenna crouched in the high weeds beside Jess. "Do you think that's it?"

"Aye, seems likely." Jess tossed a dead bush aside so she could see the tinny length of the trailer that stood a stone's throw away. The land it stood on looked barren and parched, but splashes of color from a carefully tended flower garden pleased the eye.

"Can you see any security system?"

"Guard dog." Dana nodded toward a small white puppy high-pawing across the fenced yard, sniffing the air industriously. "I can take him."

Jess touched Brenna's knee. A screen door on the trailer was creaking open, and a large man backed carefully down the two rickety steps. She twirled her fingers sharply, and the others rose with her.

The area was fairly deserted, but Brenna knew Jess wanted them inside as quickly as possible. They ran as one body, and Jess vaulted the low fence in one easy leap, sending the puppy into a frenzy of alarmed yaps. "Jodoch."

The man had been bending over something, and now he spun into a defensive stance. Jess skidded to a halt, obviously startled by the wild light in her gentle brother's eyes. "Jode, it's me."

Jode gaped at the four women who had magically appeared in his backyard, and his body relaxed. A smile wreathed his acne-scarred face. "Jesstin!" He took two steps and clapped his burly arms around Jess.

"Jodoch!" Jess grinned, returning the embrace. "Get us inside."

"Jeeze. Yeah, sure." Jode released her, looking around the empty lots adjoining his. "Come on in."

"Hello, Jodey!" Kyla, holding the squirming puppy, rose on her toes to kiss Jode's cheek.

"Hey, my sweet little sister!" Jode ushered them quickly up the wooden steps into the trailer. "Uh, Pam? Company for dinner!"

Light splashed through the small windows, but it took a second for Brenna's eyes to adjust to the relatively darkened interior. Jode's home was tiny but clean, cluttered only by the pleasant disorder of daily life.

"Kee-rist, is that *Jess*?" A short, stout woman with a beautiful sway to her hips tossed a dishcloth over her shoulder, smiling. She bounced on her toes and peered past her. "What, did you bring the entire tribe? We're having Jell-O."

"Pamela." Jess bent down and kissed her cheek. "Forgive us our ambush."

"Something big must be up. You guys look like roadkill."

"Aye, there's trouble." Jess made quick introductions. Adding four women to the cramped living room made for much shifting of positions.

"Is Shanendra all right?" Jode ducked back in through the screen door, carrying the reason he had reacted with such swift protection when Jess startled him.

"Jode, you're a father!" Brenna brushed the backs of her fingers across the baby's downy cheek. It ogled up at her comically, wearing an infant's classic pleased to meet you, freaked out to be here look. "And yes, Shann's still with us."

"Hey, Brenna." Jode smiled down at her with a sudden shyness, jiggling the baby gently in his big arms. "You look fantastic."

"Yes, right," Pam called from the kitchen. "Now, if we could get all Amazons and all hulking carpenters to please sit the merry hell down, even short people might be able to see what's going on."

❖

Pamela claimed she could concoct a feast from two cans of pea soup and a chicken leg, and she proceeded to do so. Fresh spices and vegetables from a second garden supplemented an excellent meal that filled Jess with nostalgia for Aria's home cooking. Though artfully prepared, the vegetables were puny and stunted specimens compared to Tristaine's lush produce.

"It's been hardest on Pam." Still chewing, Jode brushed his

callused, scarred hands together, his elbows balanced carefully on a TV tray. "She grew up in a pretty well-off family in the City, with nice things. She's got nothing out here."

"Precious, feel free to throw yourself off the nearest cliff." Pam smiled at her husband with undisguised affection. She glanced down at the baby nursing at her breast. "I can name a few wee compensations for the loss of my stupid rice cooker."

"Are you finding work?" Jess measured the care-lines etched at the corner of Jode's eyes, but he nodded with enthusiasm.

"Yeah, plenty, actually. There's steady work on construction crews, at least in the summer. Pay's not much, but we won't starve. I've got a good hand with a band-saw."

And a good mind for mechanical engineering, Jess thought. Dreams of a more prosperous life were probably forever beyond this small family now.

"And this little guy will be handy too." Dana tickled the soft black hair on the baby's head with uncharacteristic tenderness. "Jodey Elijah Junior."

"Named for my mom, really, not for me. Jodoch is the male form of Jocelyn." Jode smiled at Jess sadly. "I sure miss her, Jess."

Kyla stopped stroking the puppy sleeping in her lap and laid her hand on Jode's leg. "All of Tristaine misses her, sweetheart." Though Jode was Jocelyn's only child, she had been spiritual mother to dozens in their clan, and one of Shann's most trusted advisers.

Jess checked the lowering of the sun through the window. "We have a few hours until we move, adanin. We'll spend them resting."

"Pam's great grub brought me back to life, Jess." Dana rubbed her belly. "I could stand to head out now."

Jess shook her head. "We're on schedule, Dana, let's stay with it. We won't find rest again until we leave the City. We need to replenish our energies while we can."

"I'll get the pickup ready," Jode said. "Jess, I don't like the idea of just dropping you guys off downtown. You won't have any way of signaling for help if things go sour. What if your friends don't meet you? If I went in with you, at least you'd have one more pair of—"

"You'll get no closer to the City than the edge of the Borough, Jodoch." Jess swallowed and rubbed her throat. "You've risked enough for Tristaine, and your little one needs you home safe tonight."

Pam threw Jess a grateful look and rose from the sofa, balancing her gurgling infant easily. "All right, we have a baby to burp, and beds and a couch to make up. You," she said to Dana, "will sleep on the floor. Grub, she calls my dinner."

"You never learn," Kyla told Dana and knuckled her hair affectionately.

❖

"Shanendra, he is my son."

There was no transition this time, and no sign of Elise. Brenna just suddenly found herself standing in a corner of Shann's private cabin.

She could see her mother seated in the wide padded chair near the dark fireplace. Shann's head was resting against its high back, and her complexion was gray. But she gazed compassionately at the large warrior standing before her. Oisin and Jackson flanked Shann's throne, and they looked much less sympathetic.

"Perry, I know you cherish your son." Shann lifted a small cup of steaming tea and sipped it before she continued. "Tristaine cherishes all her children. But you cannot take your family off the mesa."

"Lady, I'm Tristaine's true daughter. I asked for this private council out of respect for your reign." Perry's large fists bunched at her sides. Brenna didn't know this warrior well, except as a quiet woman who was intensely devoted to her adonai and their five-year-old child. "But I'm telling you that we're leaving.

Alex has blood kin in the settlement south of the gorge. We'll go there."

"I'm not hearing much respect for our lady's reign, warrior." Jackson eyed Perry warily, her thumbs hooked in her belt. *"You serve under Jesstin's command, and we follow our queen's will."*

"Jesstin isn't here." There was a dangerous tension in Perry's low voice. *"And she took her top commanders with her. I don't follow your orders, Jackson."*

"Then you'll abide mine, Amazon." Oisin unsnapped the sheath on her belt, her threat unmistakable.

Shann reached out weakly and touched Oisin's arm, and she stepped back reluctantly. *"Perry, all you will accomplish by leaving our village is bringing death to Alex's kin. I'm sorry, adanin. But I will use all the force necessary to stop anyone who tries to leave Tristaine's mesa."*

Brenna saw the muscles in Perry's jaw stand out, and for a moment she thought Oisin would have to draw her knife. *"I'm not alone, Shanendra. It's not just the women of the Mothers' guild who chafe at your rule now. Many of our warriors are sick, but some of us still standing have young to protect. I pray you remember that."* The big Amazon straightened, nodded respectfully to Shann, and strode to the cabin's door.

Shann waited until it had closed and latched behind Perry. Then she rested her head on the chair's back again and closed her eyes. *"Jackson. Double the sentries around our periphery tonight. We must guard our boundaries closely until Brenna and Jess return."*

"It'll be done, lady."

"Thank you." Shann smiled up at the young warriors. *"You've both been a wonderful support these last frightening days. I'm going to check in on Samantha before I lie down."*

Brenna saw Jackson and Oisin exchange concerned glances.

"Carelle told us this morning your daughter is resting more

comfortably, lady," Oisin said. "Don't you think you should sleep now?"

"I'll sleep better if I see my girl myself, adanin." Shann grasped the arms of her chair and rose slowly. "Oisin, please go to our healers and ask if we should harvest more—"

Brenna saw the color fall out of her mother's face, and she tried to cry a warning she knew they couldn't hear. Luckily Jackson's reflexes were swift and sure, and she caught Shann as she fell.

"Cripes!" Oisin gasped. She helped Jackson lower the queen gently to the white pine floor. "Jackson, find Aria and Sarah. Bring them here. And a healer. Go!"

❖

"Brenna, Jesstin, it's time to go."

Brenna felt Jode shake her awake gingerly, and Jess stirred against her on the narrow bed. Shivering, she turned into Jess's arms and clung to her as Jode moved on to wake Kyla and Dana.

"Bren?" Jess sounded alarmed. "Are you sick, lass?"

"No. I'm okay." Brenna didn't want to move, but she had to. "Shann's running out of time, Jesstin. Please, we have to move fast."

CHAPTER NINE

Conversation was impossible while Jode's flatbed pickup rattled over the poorly kept roads, the worst of the jarring potholes cushioned by the sleeping bags they lay on. Brenna sweltered in the close confines of the truck's bed. The green tarp covering them was just inches above her nose, braced over plastic cartons at each corner. Jode had strewn small tools and sawdust over the tarp, effectively concealing the presence of the four women below.

Brenna felt Kyla's warm side on her left and Jess's on her right and drew reassurance from the contact, hot or not. When the road began to smooth beneath them, she groped until she found Jess's hand. "Darling. It's like our first date."

She heard Jess's rumble of grim amusement. Jode had helped them escape from the City in much this same way, and she was having flashbacks of green tarps and sick fear. Jess had to be affected by this claustrophobia more than any of them. The bed of the Army truck had been expansive compared to this close space.

"Bren, are you sure she'll be at this bar?" Kyla was invisible in the murk and barely audible over the thrumming of pavement beneath them. "Your friend?"

"It's Friday night," Brenna said sadly. "She'll be there. Are you sure you can find the utility doors at the back of the Civilian Unit?"

"You drew out a good map of the Clinic's compound." Dana squirmed, grunting in the darkness.

"You're on my hair," Kyla said.

"Sorry."

"There's plenty of cover behind the Clinic. You won't lack for hiding places." Brenna knew she was reassuring herself as well as her adanin. "No expense is spared when it comes to landscaping Government facilities."

"Brenna." Jess sounded a bit hoarse. "Everyone down here has had this vaccine the Clinic brewed? Even those in the outer Boroughs?"

"Yes, I'm sure. Inoculations are mandatory." Brenna squeezed Jess's hand. "I know. I worried about exposing Jode and his family too, but they're protected." A sudden chill worked through her as she remembered the faint rasp in Jess's voice. "Jesstin. How are you feeling?"

"I'm fit enough for the night."

Brenna shuddered, fresh anxiety sinking into her gut. Then she slammed on her mental brakes, hard. Her imagination could not dwell on Jess in the grip of this lethal flu, not if she wanted to function.

"We're starting to hear traffic." Jess shifted against her. "Brenna, you're certain you can make safe passage from this tavern to the Clinic?"

"Yes. It's close, and I'll start out well before curfew. We left plenty of time." Brenna fingered the sheathed knife in her belt. "I'll be fine."

"Just be sure we don't have our butts wagging out there when curfew hits," Dana grumbled. "Perimeter checks are done ten minutes after the siren at every base I've ever known."

The speed of the truck abruptly lessened, and Brenna's throat went dry as Jode pulled off the pavement to park. The bed tipped slightly as he stepped out of the cab. The tarp rippled above them, and she felt a welcome gust of fresh air as Jode threw it back.

"Downtown and points north," Jode announced, cloaking his tension in joviality. "Everybody out."

Brenna sat up and searched the night sky, yearning for Tristaine's starfield, and as expected, saw only a shroud of City smog. The polluted clouds were lit a dull gray from the murky illumination of streetlights. She pressed Jess's hand one more time, then followed Kyla stiffly off the tailgate of the truck, steadied by Jode's supporting arm. Her heart was beating a queasy tattoo in her breast.

Jode had chosen their drop-off point well, deep in the shadows behind a large retail outlet. He closed the tailgate with a firm click, then joined them. They stood quietly for a moment, hands joined in the center of their circle.

"Our thanks, Jodoch." Jess cleared her throat. "You served Tristaine well. Now our trails part again. We'll send you word when we can."

"See that you do, treetop." Jode swallowed audibly. "Don't get killed, please. And give my love to my Amazons."

Jess nodded and returned the gazes of her women. "We hold the life of our clan in our hands, adanin. May the Seven Sisters guide our path."

"Amen," Kyla whispered. She hugged Jode in farewell, and Jess took Brenna in her arms.

"Please, Gaia," Brenna whispered into Jess's shoulder. "Please don't let me fuck up."

"You have all my faith, lass." Jess kissed her, her lips lingering gently for a moment, and then she released her quickly.

"Don't you dare take any chances, Brenna." Kyla held her. "No falling off cliffs, no jumping into rivers. Don't you make me tell Sammy you got squashed by a City bus. I hate to let you out of my sight."

"I hate it, too." Brenna sighed.

Dana leaned over Kyla and kissed Brenna's cheek. "You be safe, little sister."

"You too. I'll see you in three hours." Brenna threw Jess another look and made herself move.

When she looked back moments later the shadows were empty, and gravel spun beneath the tires of a flatbed truck turning back toward home.

❖

Brenna had convinced Jess and the others that she should approach Nell alone. The shock of seeing her again would be enough of a jolt to her friend's fragile psyche without adding strange Amazons to the mix. She kept reminding herself of the wisdom of this strategy as she neared the entrance to Bruner's, her craving for Jess's protective presence as keen as thirst. She stared at her image reflected in the bar's glass door, then pulled it open.

The smell of alcohol was chemically pungent in the dim, high-ceilinged tavern, sparking in Brenna an almost atavistic revulsion. She used to inhale those stinging fumes as naturally as she now breathed Tristaine's pure mountain air.

Music from a jukebox jangled loudly from one corner. Whistles and sharp yells broke out as a new song started, evidence that the night's liquid intake was well underway. The single large room was crowded and dank.

Brenna found Nell where she thought she would, where Nell had been almost every Friday night for the last nine years. Many other nights too. She commanded a full booth without apology, her heavy backpack, filled with books, slung across the opposite seat.

Brenna stood beside her table. She knew Nell realized someone was there, she just wasn't looking up from her book in hopes that the intruder would go away. Brenna announced her presence the same way she had every time she'd joined Nell for a beer during medical school. She lifted her backpack, laid it gently on the seat next to Nell, and sat down opposite her.

Nell's eyes were owlish behind thick glasses as she glanced at the backpack beside her, then at Brenna. She jerked in her seat, her book clapping shut like gunshot, and hit the bottom of the table with her knee. The half-full pint near the edge of the table almost toppled, but Brenna righted it quickly.

Nell seemed frozen for a moment, staring at her with a lack of comprehension that was almost bovine. Her friend had one of the finest clinical minds Brenna had ever known. Gaia grant it was still working under that alcoholic fog.

"Sorry. Heightened startle reflex. It's the meds." Nell spoke in a monotone. She blinked at Brenna in incredulous silence.

"Will you talk to me?" Brenna tried to keep her dismay out of her voice. She had prepared herself for the ravages four years might have wreaked on Nell's appearance, but she was Brenna's age and looked two decades older. "If you're going to freak out or yell for help, Nell, let me walk away now."

Nell didn't answer at once. She downed a few swallows of the dark ale Brenna had salvaged. "If I were in my right mind, I'd make you go. You're taking a hell of a chance, Brenna, showing your face around here again. And you're not only risking your own hide, but mine as well. What do you want?"

"I need your help." Brenna swallowed. "Nell, I want you to give me your keys to the Civilian Unit."

"Sure. Here you go." A hint of Nell's glittering intelligence appeared. "Why do you need them?"

Brenna expelled a low breath. When Nell was calm and not too drunk, she could be reasoned with. "Because my family is at stake, and everyone I love. You'd be saving hundreds of lives, Nell. You don't need to know more, and the less you know the better."

"So I can't give away too much when the Fed's goons interrogate me? Brenna, how can I even consider helping you?" Nell's chewed fingertips gripped the edge of the table. "I've been through this once before. I was called in for *three* interviews after you disappeared. Because we worked together in Civilian, before you were transferred to Caster's Military unit. They thought I knew something about—"

"I'm sorry, Nell." Brenna reached for Nell's hand, and after a moment, she let her take it. "More sorry than I can say, for the trouble I brought you. And I can't promise I'm not bringing you more now. But we're desperate. Will you listen?"

Nell looked down at Brenna's hand covering her own and rubbed her forehead. "Yeah. Talk."

Brenna checked their surroundings, grateful for the general clamor of the bar, and leaned closer over the table. "You give your keys to me and go straight home. I'll leave them under the pagoda, in the park across from the Clinic's main entrance. Then show up to work Monday as usual. You never saw me."

"And what will I find out on Monday?" Nell slid her hand from beneath Brenna's and lifted her glass again, draining it. "That political radicals have stolen a chemical weapon to wipe out the Army?"

"All they'll find missing is enough kestadine to save six hundred women and children. With luck, the Clinic will never learn who took it."

Brenna sat back, trying to calm her pounding heart. If Nell refused, they could get into the Clinic through the ventilation ducts. It could be done—probably—without triggering an alarm. But breaking into the pharmacy would sound sirens they had no way of disarming. *Please,* Brenna pleaded silently.

"You said, 'with luck.'" Nell smiled without humor. "Luck has not been my life's forte, Brenna. What if you're caught and they find my keys on you?"

"At the first sign of trouble, your keys go into a medical waste drop shaft. You know Clinic orderlies aren't paid enough to go through that slimy mess to find them."

She studied Nell's closed face. She was alone in the world and bitterly unhappy since adolescence. But she was a good woman, and she became a medic for the same reasons Brenna had. Nursing political prisoners involved monitoring their physical interrogations, even in the Civilian unit. Seeing her patients tortured was shriveling Nell's soul as surely as it had Brenna's.

"Six hundred lives," Nell mumbled.

A passing server plunked down a full pint of ale in front of Nell and collected her empty glass, an automatic refill born of long practice. Brenna shook her head when he raised an eyebrow at her, and he went on without comment.

Nell reached for her backpack, and Brenna held her breath. She unzipped a side pocket, and drew out five silver and brass keys on a simple ring. She put them on the table in front of Brenna.

Air gushed quietly out of Brenna's lungs, and she curled the keys in her palm. She stared at Nell, a small spark of hope igniting inside her. "Nell, come with us."

"What?" Nell sat up, alarmed.

"Not to the Clinic," Brenna said quickly. "Join us later tonight. Come with us to the mountains, to our village. It's a different life there. You could have a different life, honey."

"As a political criminal?"

"As a free woman." Brenna gripped Nell's hand again. "Nell, there's peace and beauty in Tristaine you will never know here. Please, think about it. What would you be leaving behind that you could possibly miss?"

Nell said nothing, staring into her beer.

"You could heal there," Brenna whispered. "I have."

The chaos and noise in the bar faded, and the murky light dwindled down to illuminate this one booth and Nell's worn face. They had never been the kind of friends who had heart to heart talks, she and Nell. They'd rarely spoken of their childhoods, and less of their dreams. They hadn't even talked about work. They drank together to forget what happened there. But Nell was her friend, and Brenna hadn't had many in the City.

"You'd have to sneak out after curfew." Brenna hoped she was hearing her. "Wait for us in the pagoda. We'll come for you, Nell. We'll bring you with us."

Nell patted Brenna's wrist, and her smile was wistful. "I've missed you, Bren. I can see you've changed. I wouldn't have known you."

Brenna tried to read her expression. "Nell. Please. You have so much to gain and so little to lose. You have three hours to decide."

"I'll think about it. I will." Nell patted her hand again, then lifted the strap of the backpack over her shoulder. "It's late for me, I'm going home. Be careful tonight, Brenna. And remember, if this goes wrong, I've never heard of you."

"Thank you, Nell," Brenna whispered. She watched her climb out of the booth and make her way toward the exit doors. She didn't look back, and Brenna didn't need her psychic sense to know she would never see Nell again. She lowered her head.

The harsh clank of a glass on the table jerked Brenna erect, her nerve-endings firing like pistons. A full snifter of whiskey sat before her. A dead man, holding a second glass, slid into the booth across from her.

He was dirty and emaciated, and his bare forearms were etched with needle tracks. He still would have been handsome, though, were it not for his missing eye, a dark, lid-covered dent beneath his brow. His one eye was whole but blood-shot with drink, and Brenna remembered that he used to have beautiful eyes, a crystalline blue, shining down at Samantha on their wedding day.

"Matthew." It was all she could say, the only sound she could make.

"Brenna." Matthew slurred her name, his teeth clenched so tightly his jaw trembled. "I couldn't believe it was you. I couldn't believe it. I had to buy you a drink." He pushed the other snifter toward her, sloshing cheap whiskey over its rim.

"We heard you were dead." Brenna pressed her hand to her mouth and tried to steady her voice. "Matthew, sweet Gaia—"

"You heard right." He took a healthy slug of his drink and studied her in sullen silence. "We were going to name our child after you, Sammy and me, if it was a girl. Did you know that? We were going to name our baby Brenna, after you."

"Matt, Sammy is—"

"She loved you that much. She thought you hung the stars in the sky." He leaned his elbows heavily on the table. "Hell, I loved you too, Brenna, like you were my own sister. Why did you kill us? Why did you blow my family apart?"

"Please, Matthew, listen." Still trying to draw even breath, Brenna clenched her hands in mute pleading. "Sammy is alive—"

"I don't want to hear about Samantha." Matthew slammed the snifter down on the table hard enough to crack its base, and a pocket of quiet formed around them. He stared at her with a muddy hatred, and soon the curious lost interest and the noise swelled again.

"I gave her up." The fury faded from Matthew's eye, and he looked at her dully. "I told them where to find her. It didn't even take them very long to convince me. Just one prick." He pointed vaguely at his empty eye socket. "My wife, with my baby inside her, and if the tip of that scalpel came any closer to my other eye, I would have led them to her hiding place myself. I don't think about Samantha anymore."

Brenna tried for words and failed, gripped by waves of desolation.

"I hope it was worth it," Matthew said softly. "Whatever you killed my family for. That woman you escaped with, are you happy together? Do you have a daughter? Did you name her Samantha?"

"Stop," Brenna gasped, and that freed her tongue. "She's alive, Matt! She escaped. Sammy is safe, she's—"

Fire filled Brenna's eyes as Matthew threw the contents of his glass in her face. The burning liquid splashed over her throat and drenched her breasts.

"I...don't...think...about...your sister...anymore."

She couldn't see him get up, but she heard his parting words.

"Rot in hell, Brenna."

Darkness clouded Brenna's vision as she sat there, trembling, whiskey dripping from her chin. She was inundated by its noxious, familiar smell.

Finally she lifted her head and saw the full snifter Matthew had set before her. Almost without her bidding, Brenna's shaking fingers reached out and grasped it. She emptied it in three long swallows, then coughed spasmodically as it burned its way down her core.

Nell's second beer still stood untouched on the table. Brenna drank that too.

CHAPTER TEN

Jess was shivering with cold, wracked with it in defiance of the mild summer night. So far, this malaise creeping through her was limited to a dry ache in her throat and these bloody chills. Jess's mind was clear and her legs were still strong. All she could do was pray to her Mothers they stayed that way.

"Hey. Jesstin." Kyla's touch on her arm was gentle. "You're shaking like an aspen treetop. Come here."

Jess hesitated but then shifted closer to Kyla and allowed her to slip her arm around her. Kyla rubbed Jess's arm briskly, and then moved the flat of her palm across her back in warming circles.

"Thanks, lass," Jess whispered.

"You don't have to thank me for this, Jess."

Jess tried to relax into Kyla's ministrations, but Brenna was due to join them soon, and she couldn't turn off the invisible beacon that searched the air constantly for her adonai. She frowned as a mild crunching sound came from Kyla's other side.

"These candy bars are great." Dana smacked her lips. "Chocolate candy bars are one of the few things the City has over Tristaine. Want one?" She extended a wrapped bar to Kyla and Jess. "Pam gave me two."

"I can't believe you're eating candy at a time like this." Kyla frowned, still rubbing Jess's back. She snatched the bar from Dana. "I didn't say I didn't want it."

A bricked circle of lush, high vegetation on the Clinic's outer grounds provided them secure shelter while they waited. It was hours sitting in wet grass with leafy boughs in their faces, but only Jess seemed chilled by their damp vigil. She reached out cautiously and moved a thin branch an inch.

The Clinic awaited them like a malign sentinel, bathed in the harsh arc lamps posted at even intervals around the grounds. Beyond it, partially visible over the Clinic's north roof, were the looming walls of the Prison.

Jess had served hard labor there for six months. She'd been beaten there, and starved, and locked into a dank hole a thousand leagues from the sky. She was forced to leave Kyla and Camryn behind those gray walls when they took her to the Clinic, forced to imagine them beaten and starved.

"Jess? You want some of this? Dana's right, it's great."

Jess stared at the white sheen of the Clinic, and her shaking grew worse. The beatings had become torture there. Caster had made Brenna hurt her, Brenna with her gentle, healing hands, forced to apply a stunning electric shock to Jess's shoulder.

And Caster had stripped her. Her Brenna. Stripped her, tied her with ropes, and ordered Jess to whip her. That was her choice, scourge Brenna or betray Tristaine.

"Jesstin."

Kyla sounded so firm Jess started, thinking for a disoriented moment that Shann sat beside her.

Kyla's hand slid beneath Jess's dark hair and cupped her neck, then pulled her head down on her shoulder. Jess's muscles tightened, every fiber in her being resisting such intimate surrender.

"Stop it," Kyla said quietly. "Let me hold you."

"Jess? What's wrong?" Dana touched Jess's leg. "Is she all right, Ky?"

"No, but that's okay." Kyla stroked Jess's hair, rocking her gently. "Jess doesn't need to be strong right now. Don't worry; she will be when we need her. She always is."

Jess let out a hitching breath. A soft melody issued from Kyla's lips, not a lullaby, but a cheerful, lilting song Amazons sang at their harvest festival. Her rigid back began to relax, and her shivering lessened. Dana's hand still rested on her leg. Jess felt its warmth.

Kyla's sweet song ended, and Jess sat up slowly, feeling as if she'd had ten hours of solid sleep. Kyla rested two fingers against Jess's lips.

"Again, you don't have to thank your adanin for simple comfort, Jesstin," she murmured. "Our love for you is your birthright, and it runs very deep."

Jess's sore throat tightened, and she kissed the tips of Kyla's fingers.

"Are you okay now?" Dana still sounded worried.

"Aye, I'm fine now." Jess tried to see through the smog to check the position of the moon. "How's our time, Dana?"

"That's the thing." Dana rose up on her knees cautiously and peered through the foliage. "It's got to be close to curfew, Jesstin. And I don't see any sign of—"

The raucous curfew siren blasted through the night, shattering the silence into quivering shards.

"Jess," Kyla gasped.

Jess steadied her, searching the skies as if the Goddess might drop salvation into their laps.

Brenna, Jess's mind screamed. *Where are you?*

❖

Brenna lurched out of the booth, her thighs knocking the heavy table painfully, barely registering the jangle of keys as they fell to the wooden floor. She bent to snatch them up, and nearly fell headlong as dizziness coursed through her.

Dear Gaia, she thought, *what have I done. How much time has passed?*

Surely, surely she had sat there only a few minutes with Matthew's whiskey drying on her face and boiling in her stomach.

Time enough had sped by to allow a dismaying number of

people to leave the bar. It was almost empty. Brenna focused on moving, the sheer physical mechanics of putting one foot in front of the other and following the few remaining patrons outside. After four years of sobriety, the alcohol hit her broadside like a horned ram, and she gave her head a fierce shake.

Brenna stepped out onto the sidewalk and looked around wildly. The streets were almost deserted, just a few pedestrians and vehicles heading directly home before curfew sounded. She leaned against a light pole and commanded her mind to stop reeling, then pushed off it and ran.

She was fast when she had to be, and she hit a dead sprint within seconds. The Clinic lay just adjacent to a park six blocks over. She could make it in good time if she wasn't stopped. Then Brenna realized that racing through City streets like a frenzied banshee increased the possibility of drawing unwelcome interest, and she made herself slow to a trot.

She rounded the corner of a bank and plowed directly into a police officer.

The young woman gave a bark of surprise and steadied Brenna, gripping her arms. "Hey, slow down!"

"I'm s-sorry—"

"Phew." The officer's nose wrinkled beneath her visor. "Smells like you've been hitting it pretty heavy tonight, ma'am. You know it's almost curfew?"

"I know." Brenna stared at the hand still clenching her upper arm. "I live close. I can make it."

"Better show me some ID." The policewoman released her and slipped a small notebook out of her breast pocket. "Public drunkenness may go down in the Boroughs, but not on my beat."

Just do it. You have no choice.

For years, the silent voices that instructed Brenna came from spectral sources. Tonight she heard her own voice. She didn't need otherworldly advice. She understood what she had to do for the clan she loved.

Brenna reached into her belt and drew out the small dagger. Calling on a move Jess had taught her years ago, she swept her right leg in a sharp circle and kicked the woman's feet out from under her. She went down with a shocked gasp and Brenna was all over her, the dagger clenched in her fist.

At the last moment she twisted, turning her blade from the exposed throat and cutting the leg, slicing the cop's Achilles tendon with surgical precision. The officer bellowed in pain and threw herself backward, smacking her head into the heavy cornerstone of the bank building. Brenna froze, her teeth bared, and she watched her sag into unconsciousness.

Brenna clenched the collar of the woman's uniform shirt and heaved with all her might, pulling her dead weight around the corner of the building and into the alley behind it. Panting, she knelt and tried to check the woman's pupils, a futile effort in the darkness, then she tore a strip from the officer's shirt and bound her badly bleeding leg. She was no older than Dana, her slack features youthful and fresh.

Brenna hovered over the senseless woman, her eyes squeezed shut, and tried desperately to make the surreal decision as to whether to take the life of a defenseless human being. The liquor made her brain sluggish and slow. If the head wound wasn't fatal, she would awake within hours. In hours, Brenna expected to either be locked in a Clinic cell or well outside the City limits, headed for the foothills. Any alarm this cop raised would be centered downtown.

Brenna snatched the police radio and gun from the woman's belt. She had crippled her. She would need time to crawl for help. She whispered a fleeting prayer over the motionless form and lunged to her feet.

She raced to the end of the alley and dropped the gun and radio into a deep tin trash bin, flinching at the hollow clang of their impact. Cramps hit her belly and she bent double and vomited copiously. She spat twice, and then she just kept running.

Brenna squeezed the small pouch tied to her belt and felt the sharpness of the keys inside it. There was the drug store, and the street just beyond it ran straight to the Clinic compound.

The curfew siren blasted around Brenna and she almost fell. An appalled horror surged through her and she started to run again, faster than she'd ever run in her life.

❖

"They'll start a full perimeter search in two minutes, Jesstin." Dana sounded unnaturally calm. "No more."

Jess knew she had allowed Brenna all the time they could spare. They had counted on being inside the building by now, well before the arc lamps illuminating the Clinic's outer walls went to high and flooded the grounds in a harsh glare. Even the most indifferent sentry wouldn't miss three women crouching in the greenery of their refuge. Their only hope was to get inside before the curfew check started.

"Go for the utility doors." Jess fought down a roil of nausea, picturing Brenna captured or hurt, or worse. *I won't leave the City without you.* She didn't need to speak the promise aloud. It was visceral. "We'll get in through the heating ducts. They're right above them. Move with me."

Then they were running, ghosting across the neatly trimmed grass with the Clinic looming large ahead in the darkness, and they were halfway there when Jess saw her. Brenna was sprinting just as fast, coming around the north wall, crossing open ground against all common sense, searching for them wildly.

At the same moment, a steel door opened in the back of the Clinic, and two armed guards stepped out.

Brenna froze.

The guards didn't see her at first. They stood between the Amazons and Brenna, both lighting cigarettes, one of them laughing. Then the high, powerful arc lamps stationed around the compound clicked on, flooding the area with light.

Still running, Jess slapped Dana's shoulder and veered sharply, increasing her speed. For a sick moment, Jess thought she wouldn't reach them in time. The men had both spotted Brenna, and now one of them was lifting his rifle.

"Hey!" the guard shouted, and then Jess plowed into him, knocking him several yards through the air before they both crashed to the ground. She jumped to her feet and whirled, and the second guard cracked his rifle stock hard against the side of her head.

The night spiraled dizzily in Jess's vision and she dropped to her knees, pain pounding through her skull. She heard Brenna cry her name breathlessly, and then felt her arms around her, steadying her in the grass.

Jess heard Dana take down the second guard, and when she could see again, both men were lying senseless on the ground. "We need to get them under cover," she said. The blow to the head had her reeling, but the glaring light around them spurred her to her feet with Brenna's quick support.

Kyla and Dana grabbed one of the unconscious guards, and Brenna helped Jess grip the second man's collar and drag him toward the Clinic wall.

"Jess, down here!" Dana signaled them urgently.

Still half-dazed, Jess followed her, hauling the guard's dead weight around a waist-high wall of concrete and down four steps into the small utility bay. It was empty except for an old oil-soaked engine in one corner and provided adequate shelter from the floodlights.

Jess dropped the man, gasping, and leaned hard on the cool brick wall, hoping her stomach would settle. "Dana, Kyla. Cuff those men and gag them." She didn't know if either guard was alive, and she didn't care. They just needed them safely immobilized for the night.

"Jess? Let me look at you." Brenna's grip was firm on Jess's shoulders, turning her so she could see the bloody cut above her hairline. Jess felt a drop of warm wetness drip down her throat. She lifted Brenna's cool hands from her face and held them, and let relief flood through her.

"I thought you were lost, Bren," Jess said hoarsely.

"Jesstin, I'm so s-sorry." Brenna's eyes were anguished, but she was alive, and she was here. "How bad is your head?"

Jess couldn't answer. She stared at Brenna. She smelled liquor on her breath, on her clothes. Brenna must have seen her shock.

"Jess, I didn't mean to—"

"Tell me later, Brenna." Jess held Brenna's chin and tried to focus on her features through her blurred vision. "The whys of it don't matter now. I just need to know if your mind is clear."

"Yes, I'm clear." Brenna looked up at her pleadingly. "I got rid of most of it."

"And the keys?"

"Right here." Brenna fumbled with the pouch on her belt and drew out a steel ring of long keys.

"Oh, bless you, Brenna, you got them." Kyla grasped Brenna's arm, still breathing hard.

"Over here, guys." Dana had finished tying off a gag around the guard's mouth, and she went to the double utility bay doors and tried the locked handle. She looked over at Jess, and her eyes widened. "You all right, Jesstin?"

"Aye, I'll live." Jess steered Brenna to the doors, palming blood off the side of her forehead. "Try them, Bren."

Brenna grasped a long silver key in both hands, and its tip jittered against the circular lock of the utility door as she tried to insert it. It didn't fit. She selected another, and Jess laid a calming touch on her wrist. This time the key slid home smoothly, and after some effort Brenna was able to turn it. They heard tumblers click.

"Thank Cybele," Kyla whispered and slid past Dana after she pushed the door open and braced it with one arm.

The Clinic's utility room was cavernous and dim, lit only by pairs of jacklights mounted on narrow poles that ran floor to ceiling. Their shadows cast jagged phantoms over the wide expanse of concrete floor.

"Are you sure you're not hurt, Brenna?" Kyla brushed grass off Brenna's shirt, and then stepped back with a look of surprise.

"Brenna's fine, Ky." Jess tried to speak gently. "She did well, she got us in. Now set our path, Bren."

"Okay." Brenna closed her eyes for a moment, visibly centering herself. Then she looked around, her breathing almost under control. "I think it's this way."

"Not over there?" Dana jerked her head toward a set of double doors in the far wall.

"Absolutely not," Brenna said at once. "That exit opens under the Military Unit. The Civilian ward is through here."

"Lead us, adonai." Jess followed Brenna through a maze of steel banks that stored the terminus of the circuitry and wiring of the buildings overhead. Spools of thick cable were stacked to the high ceiling, and they moved soundlessly around them toward the distant reaches of the echoing space.

"Our timing is lucky in one way." Brenna paused, then took Jess's hand and went on. "It's Friday night, the weekend. The Clinic's on minimum staff after curfew, even security just has a skeleton crew."

"That still leaves armed orderlies patrolling the halls." Dana turned in a cautious circle as she walked.

"Yes, but the cells are in lockdown now. When I left work this late, the orderlies were always swilling coffee at their stations." Brenna stopped them by a single featureless steel door, and Jess heard her blow out a sigh. "This is it, Jesstin."

"Good, querida." Jess waited until they met her gaze. "We meet by those back utility doors if we're separated. You all know your purpose?"

"Ky and Brenna hit the drugs, I find a computer." Dana tucked the back of her shirt into her pants briskly. "Jess will stake out the pharmacy and bazooka anything that moves."

"Clear enough." Jess nodded at Brenna, who pushed open the steel door. Jess tensed, half expecting an alarm to shatter the silence, but the peace held as they moved quietly up a short stairway and into the Clinic's Civilian Unit.

❖

All Brenna's senses, physical and psychic, were keyed to screaming tightness. The small amount of whiskey that hadn't been forcefully propelled from her stomach left a light buzzing in her ears, but she thanked whatever goddesses were listening that her step was steady.

She registered the white corridors extending out from the pharmacy and the main security desk like sterile spokes on half a wheel. She inhaled cleansers and disinfectants that stung her sinuses. She didn't think about Matthew or nearly getting her sisters captured. She didn't think about Jess being injured because of her, or of Shann being ill, or Samantha. She focused on the single guard, reading a newspaper, sitting at the desk, his feet up on its curved surface.

They stood against a wall near the outer atrium of the Unit, hidden from the small camera mounted on a ceiling bracket. As Brenna watched, a uniformed orderly appeared by the desk, and she willed them all to be invisible shadows in the dark hall.

"You see what's left of that poet guy in the east wing?" The orderly was talking to the guard as he dropped paperwork on the desk.

"That kid they did the surgery on?" The guard lowered his newspaper, his wheeled chair creaking beneath his weight. "They cut out the part of his brain that made him what, subversive?"

"Yeah, I guess. Guy's no better than a drooling stool. He can still write poems, though. Not very good ones."

"Hell, bad poems aren't illegal, just seditious poems." The guard snapped out his paper again and crossed his booted feet on top of the desk.

"Night, Vargas."

Relieved, Brenna heard the orderly retreat across the lobby. At least there was only one man to deal with. If they stood up, they would be in his direct line of sight, so there was no sneaking up on him. All four of them thundering down the hallway would alert the guard before they could possibly reach him, so one of them had to take him alone.

Brenna realized a silent communication was passing between Dana and Jess. Dana tapped her brow, and then patted her own chest, frowning. She was telling Jess she couldn't sprint down that hallway with an addled head. Jess grimaced, but then nodded agreement that Dana had to take the run.

It was risky. Dana was almost as fast as Jess, but the tile hallway was long, and Brenna could see the pistol holstered on the guard's belt from here. Inspiration struck her, and she touched Jess's wrist. She pointed to herself, remembered the signal for "distraction," and managed to relay it with reasonable accuracy.

Jess's brows lowered in consternation, but Brenna shook her head firmly. This was a better plan. She could see that Jess was clearly reluctant, but she signaled assent. Kyla patted Brenna's back, a nervous wish for good luck.

Brenna clawed her sticky bangs down in her face, and stepped out into the corridor. She strolled toward the security desk, weaving slightly, her hands clasped harmlessly behind her. She hummed tunelessly, relieved to see she didn't know the man.

"Get—" The burly guard looked old enough to retire, but his boots snapped down off the desk with alacrity, and he jumped to his feet. "Who the hell are you?"

"My name's Rebecca, Mr. Karney. Aren't you the charming Mr. Karney I've heard so much about?" Brenna added a light seductive sway to her hips. She had almost reached the desk. She hoped this jerk could smell the whiskey still coming off her.

"Karney's not on Civilian, he's over in Mili—you stop right there!"

"You're not Mr. Karney?" Brenna continued past the desk, looking blearily around as if impressed by her surroundings. At least he hadn't drawn his gun, but she still might feel a Taser bolt rip into her back. "Too bad. I was supposed to meet him here." She turned and smiled as the guard stepped around his station and came toward her. Over his shoulder, she saw Dana take off on a fast and silent run.

"I don't suppose you might be willing to fill in for Mr. Karney tonight?" Brenna pretended to peer at the nametag on the guard's chest. "Mr. Vargas. There's supposed to be a great party at—"

"Look, lady, this is a secure facility." The guard clenched Brenna's upper arm with unnecessary force. "Unless you show me a pass, right now, you won't—"

Brenna never learned what she wouldn't do because Dana's braced elbow plowed into the back of the guard's skull, and she had all she could manage to help slow his fall to the floor.

"Ouch," Dana muttered, clutching her elbow.

Brenna's pulse was still pounding. "Are you okay?"

"Yeah, but that *hurt*."

They rose as Jess and Kyla reached them. Kyla latched quickly onto Dana's arm to see if she was all right. Jess knelt and snatched the guard's heavy set of keys from his belt, then tossed them to Dana.

"Right, we'll store this little lad behind the desk." Jess spoke low and fast. "Dana, check the security monitors and be sure the Unit is quiet, then find the computer. Brenna, Kyla, see to the pharmacy."

Brenna flipped through Nell's keys with fingers that trembled only slightly, following Kyla to the large glass door that was reinforced with wire mesh. There were two locks, and Brenna needed several tries to open them both.

The overhead light went on automatically when the door

swung open, startling Brenna more than it should have.

"Easy, honey."

Brenna returned Kyla's smile gratefully. "Okay, first things first. Grab a few bags of disposable hypodermics, from that drawer over there."

She spun the ring of keys, this time easily selecting one of the small silver ones and unlocking the first cabinet on the left. She took out a small ampule filled with an amber liquid, and when Kyla brought her the syringes, she uncapped the needle and filled one carefully. "Here. Go jam this in that tacky Mr. Vargas's thigh. Make sure he gets all of it. It's a strong sedative. It'll keep him snoring for several hours."

"Happily!" Kyla plucked the syringe from Brenna's hand and spun on her heel.

Brenna had a few nasty moments when she couldn't locate the anti-virals. Kestadine provided no high and was not in demand by addicts, so it wasn't triple-locked within the recesses of the pharmacy. But the stock had been moved to another storage case, and Brenna felt a surge of relief when she found it.

Kyla was beside her again. "Ready, Bren."

"All right. We need both the serum and the vaccine. One cures, the other prevents new illness." Brenna indicated the small vials. "Each vial contains six doses. We need a hundred vials." She crouched and pulled padded canvas bags out of one of several bins below the counter. "Put them in here, one in each dent in the foam. I know these vials look delicate, but they're hard to break. Try not to drop one anyway."

"Don't drop one," Kyla repeated obediently, and went to work.

"Brenna? You have a minute?" Dana was squinting into the ghostly glow of the computer monitor that stood on the counter by the door. Brenna went to her and looked over her shoulder. "Can you tell me again what I'm looking for? Cause I sure ain't seeing it."

"You're in the right place." Brenna covered Dana's hand,

which was on the computer's mouse, and nudged it slightly. Screens of columned text flipped by. "These are the Unit's archives—records of all births and deaths are recorded here. We're looking for mid-October, three years ago. A female birth." She set the cursor over the last heading. "Look under this column, 'Disposition.'"

"That'll tell us what happened to Sammy's kid?" Dana sounded painfully hopeful.

"That'll tell us if it was a live birth." Brenna tried not to sound grim. "If the baby survived, Jenny's sister might be able to learn which Youth Home she was sent to."

Her lips moved in unconscious prayer as she went back to help Kyla. It might be all she could bring home to Shann and Sammy this time, the bare truth about the baby's life or death.

But if Samantha's daughter still lived, they would find her someday. Brenna remembered Matthew's scarred, doomed face, and the pledge settled deep in her marrow.

Their packing was nearly done. Brenna worked beside Kyla as smoothly as she and Shann had worked together in Tristaine's healing lodge. She let Kyla finish the final fastening of the cases and went to find Jess.

She was a tall, motionless shadow outlined by the dead glow of the security monitors, her still profile proof that Jess relied on her own senses more than electronic surveillance. She turned and signaled Brenna that all was still quiet.

"Uh, Bren?" Dana sounded strangled, and Brenna went to her quickly. "Ah, man. I'm so sorry, Brenna, I fucked up."

Brenna stared at the computer screen.

"I don't know what I did," Dana continued. "I was almost there, I'd just started checking October, then everything crashed and this static came up—"

"Shhh." The sound left her lips softly. Dana might be seeing a screen full of static, but Brenna was looking into a beautiful marble basin, filled to the brim with crystal water—but she was seeing it through an odd, erratic shimmering. "Elise?" she whispered.

Dana turned and looked at her, then stepped carefully aside so she could move closer to the monitor. Brenna heard her call softly for Jess, but she didn't look away from the screen. Not until Elise appeared in front of her, seemingly materializing in the pharmacy's solid wall, surrounded by a nimbus of light.

They stared at each other, Brenna struggling to keep Elise's lovely features in focus through that distorting shimmer.

"Whatever potion you've taken has made our connection more tenuous." There was no judgment in Elise's tone, only concern, as a tear wended its way down her face. *"Can you hear me, Brenna?"*

"I hear, Elise." Brenna could feel her adanin behind her, warming her back.

"You must follow me."

Still facing Brenna, Elise's glowing form began to glide backward through the pharmacy wall and into the hub of the Unit.

"Is it the young maid who weeps, Bren?" Jess's breath stirred Brenna's hair.

Brenna nodded, her gaze riveted on Elise's retreating figure. She floated toward the arched entry of the most distant corridor. "Jess, I have to go with her."

"Say again?"

"Just trust me, I have to go with Elise."

"But..." Then Jess seemed to remember that Brenna led them as surely on the spiritual plane as their sisters followed her onto a field of battle. "Aye, Brenna, but I'm coming with you. Dana, keep watch while Kyla finishes our work. Use the guard's keys to get back to the utility bay."

"Brenna!" Elise's silent tone rang with command. *"You and Jesstin will come with me now."*

Brenna knew her sisters couldn't hear that voice, but she

wouldn't think of resisting it. It was too like Shann's at full power. "You two be careful," she whispered to Dana and Kyla. She snatched Jess's hand and pulled her out of the pharmacy.

Elise was visibly walking now, and the lines of her body were clearing in Brenna's sight. She and Jess followed her down the far corridor with the simple faith of children, trusting their Mothers to keep them safe.

CHAPTER ELEVEN

The tile beneath their feet was suddenly cushioned by plush carpeting.

Jess whispered behind her. "Where are we, Bren?"

"This is the visitor's wing. It's almost always empty." Brenna kept her gaze on Elise, who walked several yards ahead of them. She gestured at one of the ornate, widely-spaced doors they passed. "These are all guest suites. They keep them ready for Clinic's funders when they tour the Units."

She could sense Jess's tension like a prickling force field. They were taking a drastic risk by prolonging their time in this odious place, and Brenna was fervently grateful for Jess's trust. She didn't understand yet what Elise needed them to see, but she felt the spectral woman's urgency clearly.

"Oh boy," she whispered suddenly.

"Oh boy?" Jess repeated.

"That corner up ahead. If we turn it, we'll be visible from the other security sta—hold on."

Elise was stopping, waiting before one of the large suite doors. Her dark head turned and she looked toward Jess and Brenna, and then she melted silently through the wood of the closed door.

"Oh, *peachy*." Brenna pulled Jess quickly down the hall to the suite Elise had disappeared into.

"She went in here?" Jess asked.

"She sure did." Brenna flipped swiftly through Nell's ring of keys. "Damn, Jess, we medics never had keys to these private suites. If Elise can't materialize solidly enough in there to turn a lock—"

Apparently someone solid inside could. The round doorknob turned even as they gaped at it, and the door creaked open a few dark inches.

Brenna felt Jess's arm slide in front of her, shielding her so she could go first. Jess looked sharply up and down the hall, then pushed the heavy door further open, and they slipped inside.

The large, simply appointed living room was dimly lit by a single, low-watt lamp in one corner. It was plainly furnished. The sparseness of these quarters was nothing like the lavish comfort of the other suites Brenna remembered seeing in this wing.

Elise was nowhere to be found, and the room was nearly empty, except for the small child who sat cross-legged on the floor against the far wall, her simple white shift pulled down over her knees. She was awake at this late hour, drawing. Scattered sheets of paper littered the floor around her. She contemplated Brenna and Jess with large, solemn eyes under a short cap of auburn hair, frowning. She looked to be about three years old.

Brenna recognized her on sight, as surely as she knew her own face. Her cold fingers covered her lips, stilling the gasp that threatened to escape. Jess turned to her, startled, and then let her move past her toward the little girl. She stopped yards from her, trembling, and knelt on the frayed carpet. Suddenly she had no idea what to say. The child stared at her silently, beneath lowered brows.

"Hello, honey," Brenna whispered finally. "Thanks for opening the door for us."

"You're welcome." The little girl's piping voice was neutral, and she spoke with no childish slurring. She looked up at Jess doubtfully.

"We're not going to hurt you." Brenna tried to sound reassuring. "Are you...is your name Brenna?"

"No." The girl looked puzzled, and she pointed a sticky crayon at her. "Your name is Brenna."

"Who's out there?" A harsh cry sounded from the back of the suite, from one of the bedrooms. "Is that you, Mr. Vargas?"

Jess pulled Brenna quickly to her feet as they heard a low, electrical hum emerge from the dark entrance. Cascades of shock showered through Brenna. She knew Jess had recognized the voice too. Cracked and distorted it might be, but there was no mistaking its familiar menace.

A lavender sleeping gown draped Caster's painfully thin body, which was braced awkwardly in the electric wheelchair that rolled slowly into the meager light. A long shawl was draped over her lap. Her left arm was withered and useless, held in a clenched angle across her bony chest. Ridged scar tissue covered the left side of her face, but her black eyes glittered with the same brilliant, malevolent light.

Caster's good hand jerked on the control of her wheelchair and she came to a dead halt, staring up at them in open astonishment. "Great God in heaven," she exclaimed, her once famously mellifluous voice strained and high. "Why, it's Brenna! And my own dear Jesstin! You've come home!"

Brenna wanted to bolt for the child and carry her bodily out of there, but she couldn't unlock her knees. She had reached her resurrection saturation point for the evening, and her circuits were starting to snap.

Luckily Jess didn't share her paralysis. She went to the intercom unit on the closest wall and removed its wiring with a few well-placed yanks. "We have no business with you, Caster."

"You never call, you never write." Caster somehow made her destroyed voice cloying with sadness. "Now I find you trying to spirit my precious little one out into the night, and you won't stay for a cup of coffee? We have so much to catch up on!"

"She's not yours." Brenna looked down at her old nemesis with a sudden, welcome dispassion. "You don't deserve to breathe the same air as this child."

The small girl was still seated on the floor, rocking slightly and watching them, sucking on two fingers in meditative silence.

"Oh, don't sulk, Brenna." Caster sounded peevish as she

rubbed her atrophied arm fretfully. "I always found your tendency toward sulking most unattractive. You know that air-headed younger sister of yours was a convicted criminal. She couldn't raise this baby. They gave her to me as a consolation prize."

"Gave her to you?" Some part of Brenna was aware of Jess, scouting the room for any other means of sounding an alarm, but she couldn't take her eyes from Caster's scarred, bitter smile.

"That's right," Caster agreed, as if Brenna had somehow expressed sympathy with her outrage. She used her good hand to pull the shawl in her lap closer around her. "After all my years of distinguished service, all my awards, after more innovative scientific work than this Clinic will ever see again, they disposed of me. All my clearance, gone. All my staff, my labs, taken from me. All I could negotiate was this dreary flat and guardianship of this one small, sentimental keepsake, Samantha's poor parentless babe."

Caster gazed greedily at Brenna, and she knew she was savoring her rage. She forced any emotion from her features.

"Where is your family, Caster?"

"Right here, Miss Brenna." Caster smiled brightly with half of her cracked face, and made a jabbing gesture toward the little girl. "You're looking at my family. My loving husband and sons have disowned me! It seems it was much more fun to be related to a famous scientist than a national disgrace."

The wheelchair whirred as Caster turned to Jess. "What was that charming blessing you bestowed upon me once, Jesstin? You predicted my granddaughters will mock my grave, I believe. How prescient you proved, my mighty warrior."

"We've no time for fond memories, Caster." Jess went to the long drapes that hung behind a threadbare sofa. She drew her dagger and cut the thin ropes that would draw them open.

"I have you to thank for my heartrending downfall, Jesstin." Caster's voice lowered and grew more guttural. "You and that heathen tribe of Amazons you love so much. You're the ones who ruined me. Led by your smug pig of a queen, Shanendra. Give her my best, dear, yes? Remind her that I've saved my prettiest set of surgical instruments for her dissection."

"Close your wretched mouth, woman," Jess snapped. "We'll leave you alive, but we're taking the girl."

"Oh no, you most certainly are not." Caster slapped the arm of her wheelchair, then snapped her fingers at the girl. "You come here to me, Elise!"

The room swam around Brenna.

She saw the child climb to her feet with a sigh and trudge over to Caster, her eyes downcast. In the same moment, the adult Elise appeared before her, shining and pure, and then it was just the two of them, facing each other over the brimming basin.

"This woman's very soul is vile, j'heika." Elise's jade eyes *shimmered with tears. "And she curses Tristaine with her every breath."*

"We're taking you with us, Elise." Brenna took her hands. *"I promise you, we won't leave—"*

Brenna's trance was shattered abruptly by the child's shrill cry, and she caught herself against the back of a chair.

Jess had the finely calibrated reflexes of a lynx, but the head injury slowed her. Elise's scream and the Taser Caster had hidden in her shawl erupted in the same second. The wired bolt hissed across the room and struck Jess just below the throat. Brenna watched in horror as she snapped rigid, her back arched, and then fell to her knees.

"Bull's-eye!" Caster cried. "I haven't lost my grasp of human anatomy, Brenna!"

Brenna took three long steps to Caster's wheelchair.

Caster's eyes widened, and she banged the Taser on the wall. "Vargas, Cornell, get in here!" she screamed.

Brenna snatched the Taser away from Caster and clouted her solidly across the face with it. Caster let out a raw shriek, and sagged in her chair. Brenna threw the Taser aside and raced to Jess.

"Jesstin!" Brenna could hear the quiver in her voice over

Caster's moans and Elise's frightened sobs. Jess had crumpled to the floor on her side, and Brenna turned her onto her back with effort. "Talk to me, Jess!"

She flinched as she saw the Taser's dead bolt embedded two inches below the hollow of Jess's throat. She grasped it and pulled it out, wincing at the burn and the holes inflicted by its two sharp darts. Jess's eyes were fluttering whitely, and she didn't respond to Brenna's voice or her desperate grip on her shoulders.

Brenna's heart thundered in her ears, and she struggled to think. There had been too much noise. Guards were bound to respond.

The Clinic's stunners carried heavy charges, nearly 70,000 volts. Even a woman with Jess's exquisite conditioning would be unconscious for long minutes after such a jolt. And Jess was already injured, and the plague was creeping through her blood.

Brenna couldn't carry her. Not Jess and Elise too.

She looked at the little girl crouching on the floor, still crying fretfully, gathering her scattered drawings around her feet.

Shann sounded in Brenna's mind again. "*Of these three queens, one will be blessed with great powers. The final destiny of Amazon Nation lies in her hands. She will prove Tristaine's salvation, or her destruction, for all time.*"

Brenna had to get Elise out of Caster's grasp. She knew it, firmly and at once, and part of her heart died. She bent over Jess, and whispered to her fiercely.

"I'll come back for you, Jesstin. You hear me? I won't leave you."

Caster was listing in her wheelchair, canted to one side from Brenna's ruthless strike across her face. She was conscious, and saliva and blood dribbled from her lips as she glared at Brenna.

Brenna got up and went to Caster, and something cold and cutting nestled around her spine. "I won't leave you either, old woman," she whispered.

She couldn't bear to look back at Jess. She ran to Elise, snatched her up and then bolted for the door.

❖

Brenna muffled the little girl's outraged protests against her breast as she ran hard down the carpeted hallway. Samantha's daughter was a fighter, and she registered her displeasure at this rude handling in no uncertain terms. She gave voice to the screaming in Brenna's heart as she widened the distance between her and Jess.

Shouts sounded behind Brenna, but far behind. Security must have reached Caster's unit. The security alarms would sound any second. She increased her speed.

Brenna ran through the silent hub of the Civilian Unit. The pharmacy was dark, the security desk manned only by the unconscious guard beneath it. Brenna prayed she'd find Kyla and Dana safely outside in the utility bay. She rounded the corner and flew down the small set of stairs, shifting Elise from one arm to the other.

"You're squishing me," the child complained.

"I'm sorry, baby. I'm getting you out of here."

The shouting was coming closer.

Brenna shook one hand free to find the key to the utility room and managed to pull the heavy door open. Crossing the vast length of the cavernous space was a nightmare of darting shadows and her own harsh breathing in her ears. Brenna heard the heavy clopping of boots on the concrete behind her and stretched for one last burst of speed.

Then a dark form rocketed out of the shadows and tackled her pursuer, and Brenna almost fell into Kyla's arms, gasping. Dana struggled with the flailing guard behind them, and finally silenced him by cracking the back of his head against the concrete floor.

"Brenna, where's Jess?" Kyla took the little girl from Brenna. "And who is *this*?"

"Sammy's daughter, Kyla." Brenna rested her hands on her knees, gasping. "I'll explain later."

"We've got to move, Bren." Dana limped to them. "If that armed chimp knows we're here, there's going to be others."

"I know." Brenna straightened, and every cell in her body strained back through the inner reaches of the Clinic toward Jess. "You two need to take the drugs and this child and head for the frontage road. Find Jenny and Eva and the truck. I'm going back for Jess."

"She's captured?" Kyla paled under the weak fluorescent light. "Sweet Gaia, Brenna."

"If we aren't back soon, you might have to leave us." Brenna sounded extraordinarily calm in her own ears, given the tympani of her pulse. "Your priority has to be getting this medicine and this little girl back to the village."

"Brenna, we're not about to sacrifice you. Or Jess." Kyla's rich voice shook. "Tristaine needs you both. You might be our next queen—"

"I'm giving Tristaine her most powerful queen." Brenna nodded at Elise, who had stopped crying long enough to look around the huge room in wonder. "Leave us if you have to, Kyla."

"I'm going with you, Bren." Dana lifted the straps of their two satchels and brought them to Kyla. "It's a lot to carry, Ky, but you can make it. You're short but you're strong."

"I can't ask you to do this, Dana." Brenna feared this sojourn to the City was rapidly becoming the suicide mission Dana had predicted.

"Well, you can't tell me I can't, either." Dana went to the fallen guard and took the pistol from his belt. "You're not the queen of me yet. And Jess is my captain, Bren. I'm not leaving her here."

"Find her, Dana." Kyla shifted to balance the satchel and Elise, and her heart was in her eyes. "Please. All of you come back safe."

"We will." Dana smiled crookedly, then planted a smacking kiss on Kyla's forehead. "Go on, Ky. Hurry now."

They saw Kyla out the back utility doors and watched her creep up the stairs to the Clinic grounds. Brenna hoped fervently that Jenny and Eva were waiting for her. If it was hard for her to watch Kyla disappear into those bright lights, it must have been doubly tough for Dana. She had to pull her back inside.

"Okay." Dana shook herself. "What happened to Jess, Bren?"

"Caster has her." Dana's jaw dropped, but Brenna didn't have time to explain. "We have to find her before she's transferred to the Prison, Dana." She took off for the doors leading back to the Clinic's Civilian Unit, and after a moment she heard Dana follow. Their running footsteps echoed crazily in the high-ceilinged room.

Then Brenna skidded to a halt and stopped Dana.

"What?" Dana looked around quickly. "You hear something?"

"No, I don't hear anything. And I should." Brenna stared at the heavy door to the Unit ahead of them. "The security sirens should be going full blast."

"You're right." Dana swallowed audibly. "What's up with that? Any guesses?"

Brenna shook her head, thinking hard. The guard who discovered Caster should have thrown the general alarm that signaled a security breach in either Unit. Caster...Brenna closed her eyes and shuddered.

"They're not taking Jess to the Prison." Brenna's lips were numb. "Do you still have the guard's keys?"

"Yeah, here." Dana handed over the bristling ring. "Why?"

"Because the keys Nell gave me won't access the Military Unit." Brenna grabbed Dana and pulled her toward the other set of doors, dread sinking into her blood. "Caster stopped the alarm, Dana. She's wanted Jess at her mercy for years, and she's not going to share her until she has to."

❖

The Clinic's Civilian Unit was stark and antiseptic and utilitarian. The Military Unit was all that, but more intensely so. A grim hopelessness permeated the air of its sterile corridors. Brenna could smell rank fear and despair in these halls as distinctly as their stinging chemical stench.

Part of her still refused to believe that she was walking into this horrific scientific charnel house again. The tortures and experiments performed on prisoners in the Civilian Unit paled to what happened here. Witnessing it had almost stripped Brenna's soul. *And Jess will open her eyes and find herself back in this place,* she thought. She groped for Dana's hand.

"Quiet, isn't it?" Dana whispered. They hadn't run into any security.

"Yes. Very." Brenna knew where they were. She paused, then led Dana down another dark wing, staying close to the wall. The overhead fluorescents were at their lowest setting, but Brenna couldn't have forgotten Military's layout if she tried—and she had. She still dreamed about these grim passages. "This way."

They passed a long series of iron doors, each heavily bolted. Jess had been imprisoned for weeks in one of these spartan cells. Brenna's viscera still remembered the icy chill of that bleak chamber.

"I wish we could spring every one of 'em." There was no guard in sight, but Dana still whispered. "Let out the whole damn block. These cells are for political prisoners, right?"

"Dissidents, protestors. Hard core criminals." Brenna peered down another deserted corridor. "I wish we could let them out, too."

She knew without question that there was only one place Caster would take Jess—the gymnasium that had been the site of her clinical trials. When Brenna worked at the Clinic, the large space had served as Caster's laboratory or her torture chamber, depending on the day's protocol. Jess had almost died there.

The doors to the gymnasium were around the next turn, and Brenna forced her legs to move faster. *Caster was disgraced and stripped of her title,* she thought. *Does she still hold enough authority to order Clinic guards to break policy?* The better question was whether Brenna could summon the courage to find out.

"In here." Brenna keyed open a narrow door, and led Dana into a large storeroom, a warren of shelves containing bundled supplies. Except for the windowless double doors in the hallway, this room provided the only entrance to the gym. If Brenna remembered rightly, it opened onto its south wall.

She found the door and waited until she felt Dana's touch on her back. Then Brenna turned the cold steel knob, and light flooded her eyes as she cracked the door open. She stared, and then closed it again almost at once.

"She's there." It was all Brenna could get out past the gorge rising in her throat. She slumped against the wall and lowered her head.

"Brenna?" Dana whispered.

Brenna had absorbed Caster's tableau in one glance, and it still pulsed redly on the back of her eyelids. She registered Caster in her chair and a few guards, but then her attention was riveted by the large, standing wooden frame in the center of the gym floor. Jess was upright, strapped to it by her wrists. She had been beaten—her clothing was torn and there was blood on her face.

Brenna shifted so Dana could inch the door open. After a moment of appalled silence, she closed it again quietly.

"That fucking harpy," Dana snarled, bunching her fist against the door. "Damn the flood for not taking her."

"Dana, what should we do?" In that moment Brenna was desperately grateful for the young warrior beside her. The sight of Jess bleeding had shaken her so badly she couldn't think.

"Caster's in the wheelchair?"

Brenna nodded blindly.

"All right. Her back is to us." Dana sounded calm. "I saw three guards. Two to our left and one behind Jess against the far wall. Is that what you saw?"

"Yeah." Brenna was regaining her composure.

"We don't know if Caster has a weapon, but we know the guards are armed." Dana pulled the pistol out of her belt and checked it. "I've got six bullets. I'm a good shot, Bren, but I need three clear targets. We have to wait until the third guard moves out from behind Jess. Are you hearing this?"

"Yes, I hear." Brenna braced herself to crack open the door again. "I'll take Caster, then help you if I can."

"Jess is still alive, Bren."

"I know." Brenna drew a deep breath and reached for the knob.

❖

"Good morning, sweetheart!" Caster's cracked but cheerful greeting echoed across the gymnasium.

Jess saw fit not to respond. She lifted her throbbing head and screwed her eyes shut against the blinding lights overhead. The last thing she remembered was Caster's living room and seeing Brenna suddenly go still, as if she were hearing other voices.

Brenna. Alarm sluiced through Jess and she stiffened, fighting the painful pull the leather straps exerted on her wrists and shoulders. She twisted in the frame, gasping at a heavy pain in her side, but she couldn't see Brenna anywhere in the room.

"Our Brenna has been trundled off to Prison, Jesstin." Caster had rolled her electric chair a safe distance away from the frame. Her ruined face beamed up at Jess, her lower lip bloody and swollen. "Isn't that right, Mr. Cornell?"

"Yes'm." One of the two guards against the wall shifted, his arms crossed and his hat brim lowered. Jess knew that Caster wanted her to be aware of her backup.

"I've asked that Brenna be housed in the communal cell with the male predators for a few nights, until her sentencing." Caster stroked her paralyzed arm. "You won't see her again, dear."

Jess didn't give Caster's claim much credence. She couldn't bear to, that was certain, but she also knew her wife. Brenna was strong and fast, and she might well have escaped the Clinic. She had to believe that Brenna and the child, and their adanin, were on their way to the hills with the medicine that would save their clan.

Jess decided to make good use of the blood welling in her mouth. She spat at Caster, but hit the polished floorboards a yard from her feet.

"Oh, Jesstin, that's just nasty." Caster plucked at her shawl. "You should know I'd never get close enough to be struck by your venomous Amazon spittle. Is that all you have to say to me, after our many years apart? Don't you even want to ask how I escaped that tacky flood?"

Jess stopped listening. She shuddered as the pain of a dozen blows and kicks reached her. Nothing felt broken, but her head pounded with a terrible ache, and she was dizzy and sick. But the sudden loneliness was worse. In the unnatural brightness of the gym, Jess longed for the green hills of Tristaine with a yearning so deep tears almost rose to her eyes.

"Oh, dear. You're really quite uncomfortable, aren't you?" Caster attempted sympathy. "Mr. Cornell, I told you and your boys to take it easy on this prisoner while bringing her here, didn't I? Pity, the working classes never listen. Not to worry, my delectable warrior. I'll have the pleasure of doctoring you myself when the night's over." Caster lifted her good hand and waggled her fingers in the air. "I still have the dexterity to wield a scalpel! Staunching your wounds might prove the very best part of the evening."

Jess waited, hoping Caster would tire of talking soon and just hurt her. She wanted this over.

"Tomorrow you belong to them, Jesstin." Caster's wheelchair creaked a few inches closer. "In the morning, I'll have to turn you over to those Military cretins who think they run the Clinic. But tonight, it's just the two of us. It took all the money in my sadly depleted coffers to buy these guards for a few hours, but hearing you scream up there will be worth every penny."

"It suits you, Caster." Jess was hoarse, and she had to spit again to clear her mouth of blood. Caster moved her wheelchair back hastily. "The hideous wreck of your face. For the rest of your life, everyone who looks at you will see you truly, your cankered heart."

Caster had been a handsome woman before being mangled by the floodwaters, and now her scarred visage darkened. Jess turned her mind inward and called on Dyan's memory for courage. She pictured Shann's loving smile and promised her queen she would endure what was coming with the strength of an Amazon warrior. She saw Brenna's eyes, large and soft, and almost felt her light touch on her skin.

"The Military might believe your primitive tribe is no longer a threat, Jesstin." Caster's voice now held the icy calm that Jess remembered so well. "But I know better, and I'll convince them. You'll never see Tristaine again, proud savage—but I will, someday soon. From the front seat of the helicopter that drops napalm all over it."

Caster turned her chair sharply, its treads squeaking on the wooden floor. "Now, let's begin our intimate chat! You can start, dear, by telling me what's so important about Samantha's sullen little brat that you risked enduring all *this* for her. Mr. Wilson? Our big battery, please. I'm almost positive our prisoner will require some persuasion."

Jess heard a low creaking behind her, and a third guard pulled a large portable generator up to the right side of the wooden frame. A dozen paddles and clips were connected by wires to its bulky shape.

"Drat. I wish I'd brought that nice chilled sangria I've been saving." Caster smiled up at Jess brightly. "It's getting hot under these lights, Jess, yes? All right, gentlemen, hook her up. I want clips wherever I see blood or a bruise."

A small door in the wall behind Caster exploded outward. Two blurred figures hurtled into the gym, and Jess heard the crack of a pistol as Caster gasped and jerked her chair around. Breath gushed out of Jess's lungs as Brenna came into focus, clubbing Caster so hard with her joined fists that she toppled out of her wheelchair and sprawled on the floor.

Three more shots rang out, and Jess twisted in the straps, blood stinging one eye. The guard by the generator had gotten off a bullet, but it ricocheted high off the wall. She could see Dana now, standing braced and balanced, the pistol gripped in both hands. She had taken down two of the guards with one shot each, and now she fired again, and the third man staggered back and fell.

Jess heard Dana fire one more time, but she didn't see which guard merited a finishing shot, as Brenna reached her.

"Jesstin. Look at me." Brenna struggled to unfasten the heavy buckles on the leather straps binding her wrists. "Say something."

"Good evening, querida." Jess smiled, though it hurt her split lip. "We never got around to saying that."

Brenna let out a breath that was part sob and part laugh. "How badly are you hurt?"

"I can get out of here."

"Jess!" Dana belted the pistol and attacked the buckles on the straps holding Jess's other arm. "Are you sure you can walk? You look pretty rocky."

"Aye, I'm sure. Kyla?"

"She's got the drugs and Elise, Jess, she's waiting for us outside." Brenna grunted as the strap finally gave, and a moment later Dana had Jess's other wrist free.

Jess fully expected her legs to support her and was dismayed when her knees buckled and she sagged into their arms. Cursing, she righted herself, shaking her aching head to clear it.

"Easy, Jess. Just stand here a moment." Brenna examined her quickly.

"Well done, adanin." Jess scanned the now silent gym and the three motionless guards, then looked at Dana. "My thanks to you both."

"Well, you're not exactly rescued yet." Dana wrapped a strong arm around Jess's waist and helped her step down from the frame. "We've got to make tracks fast, sisters."

"Wait." One hand still on Jess's chest, Brenna had turned to stare at Caster, who lay twisted on her side yards away. One of the wheels of her capsized chair, devoid of power, still spun slowly, like a metallic eye, under the glaring lights.

Jess heard Caster's dry sobbing, a ratcheting, gruesome sound. She looked at Brenna and saw that stillness take her and the sudden glaze in her eyes that signaled trance.

"She will never give up."

Brenna heard the adult Elise clearly in her mind and the heavy dread in her tone.

"This woman has made destroying Tristaine her life's mission, j'heika. She will do whatever she must to regain power. Her dark star will rise again. And she will find us."

And then Elise repeated the words she said to Brenna the first time she appeared, when she had thought they were talking about the epidemic.

"Hear me, Brenna. You have seen the face of our enemy. Now act."

"Brenna?" Dana looked down at her belt as Brenna slipped the pistol from it.

"Stay with Jess, Dana. This is mine to do."

Brenna crossed the floor to Caster, and a cool breeze swept her that smelled of fresh pine.

"Br-Brenna." Caster lifted herself, crab-like, on her good elbow. Her macabre face was drenched in tears. She pointed a shaking finger at Brenna as she came closer. "I could have had your sister's baby drowned at birth, Brenna. I spared—Br—*no!*"

Brenna aimed the pistol carefully, squeezed the trigger, and shot Caster between the eyes.

CHAPTER TWELVE

D ana gave one of the double doors to the gym a solid kick, and it swung wide with a crash. After the echoing gun shots, Brenna knew they had to sacrifice stealth for speed. She and Dana half-carried Jess at first, but she regained her footing as they ran down the dark, still deserted corridors.

"Is there any chance in hell nobody heard that racket?" Dana panted.

"Not a chance," Jess answered through clenched teeth, and Brenna knew she was right when they rounded the cellblock. Apparently the battle in Caster's gymnasium had awakened every prisoner in the Unit. Fists were pounding steadily on cell doors in grim celebration of the chaos, and the muted thumping powered them faster toward the outer bay.

Brenna ran close to Jess, trying to assess her injuries in quick glances. There was a frightening amount of blood on her face, most of it from the blow to her head. Her normally graceful gait was mechanical and stiff, and she ran holding her right side.

The sirens hit before they were halfway across the utility room, a deafening wail that almost froze Brenna mid-stride. She grabbed Jess's arm and they hurtled toward the outer doors.

The baying klaxon only grew more strident as they burst out the doors into the utility bay and staggered up the concrete steps onto the light-drenched grounds. Both Units of the Clinic had gone into full lockdown, and the compound would soon be flooded with added security from the adjoining Prison.

"Fence," Jess gasped, and Dana gripped the collar of her torn chambray shirt and helped Brenna haul her toward the south wall of reinforced barbed wire.

Even over the siren Brenna heard the flat report of a rifle, and the bullet's whining trajectory passed perilously close on Dana's side. She started to shout a warning, but then was distracted by the blessed crash of a large green Army truck through the wire fence.

For Brenna, it was like seeing a wheeled goddess roar down from the heavens to snatch her daughters from a cobra's nest. By luck or inspiration, the driver—presumably Eva—executed a nearly perfect churning circle in the grass, and they raced for the truck. Brenna heard more shots now and orders shouted behind them.

The driver's door flew open and Eva leaped out of the cab. She darted to the back of the truck and unlatched its tailgate. Brenna had time to see Jenny inside on one of the steel benches, her arms wrapped around Elise, before she jumped into the bed and turned to help Jess. Eva pushed Jess over the metal lip of the bed and scrambled in after her.

"Kyla?" Brenna heard Dana's breathless voice as she threw herself behind the wheel.

"I'm fine, the satchels are fine, are you guys all right?" From the front seat, Kyla cast an anxious glance through the panel window, and then they all lunged as Dana kicked the accelerator hard. There was a sharp clang as a bullet hit the truck, and Brenna could only pray it struck nothing vital.

Dana plowed the truck back through the sagging fence.

"Turn left," Brenna cried, and tried to brace Jess on the bench as they swerved toward the small park that lay across the street from the Clinic.

"Brenna?" Jenny's teeth were chattering. "Didn't you say the frontage road was the—"

"We circle the park first," Brenna cut in. "I have a promise to keep."

The pagoda at the park's center was as empty as Brenna feared it would be. She lifted the edge of the plastic-sheet window and tossed Nell's keys beneath the pagoda, and sent her friend a final, grateful blessing. "All right, Dana, get us out of here!"

Dana steered them skillfully onto the frontage road, dust roiling up in their wake.

She hit the headlights and the narrow road was illuminated as it sped under them. The ugly screech of the Clinic's sirens began to fade in the distance.

"This will take us around the downtown district." Brenna tried to speak calmly. Elise's eyes were huge, and she had to be terrified. "Dana, look for any street that might lead north, out of the City."

"Kyla, the drugs?" Jess asked.

Kyla was already checking the contents of the padded satchels on her lap. "Nothing's broken, adanin, it's all here! Vials, hypodermics, the lot."

"Bless you, Ky," Jess sighed. Brenna slid her arm around her to steady her as they bounced over an uneven rut in the dirt road.

Eva was looking at Jess closely. "Jess took a bad knock to the head, Brenna."

"Yes, I'm worried about concussion." There was no real light to see by in the rocking bed, but Brenna tried to check Jess's eyes. She slid her hand beneath her hair and cupped the back of her neck, and Brenna's pulse spiked unpleasantly. Jess's fever wasn't high, but she had one. The flu was moving through her blood.

Jess went still beneath her arm, and then she slid off the steel bench and rummaged beneath it.

"Hey, Jess, you need to..." Brenna trailed off as she heard the faint, two-note siren far behind them.

Jess lifted out the rifle and stepped toward the back of the truck. "Brenna, brace me."

Brenna went to her quickly, praying the truck's rocking wouldn't worsen. She gripped Jess's waist, and peered over her shoulder through the opening in the canvas hood. There were two sets of flashing blue and red lights behind them, distant but moving fast.

"We need to get off this road," Jess barked. She slid the barrel of the rifle through the hole in the canvas.

Dana muttered an obscenity and spun the wheel, taking them off the frontage road and down a twisting, paved path that wound through a shabby neighborhood. "Good. We're good, I know where we are." Dana sounded relieved. "Some of my buddies grew up here, I know these streets."

"Take us north as fast as you can." Jess grasped the bunched canvas with one hand and held the rifle steady with the other. "We might see close fighting."

The oncoming sirens were louder now, the two-tone clang marking them as City Police cars. Brenna felt their speed increase.

"Man. This could get a little intense, guys," Dana called. "Hold on."

"Get?" Jenny gasped, holding Elise tightly.

Their Army transport was built more for strength than agility, but Dana guided it skillfully through a maze of ramshackle neighborhoods. She drove at an ungodly speed, but her hands on the wheel were steady and sure. They sped through twisting streets, emptied by the curfew, taking corners at a velocity Brenna wouldn't dare attempt, but Dana handled them with ease. Elise actually giggled at one such swerving jolt.

Brenna remembered this feeling. Twenty years ago, on one of the Youth Home's rare outings, she and Sammy had gone on a ride at a carnival. Their little motorized car had whizzed on tracks through a house of plastic horrors, careening around corners, terrifying them both. Brenna had been far more afraid that they would crash and burn than of any of the hokey phantoms stringed to the ceiling. She had held Sammy on her lap then as Jenny cradled her daughter now.

In spite of all Dana's efforts, the Police cruisers pursuing them edged inexorably closer, following their every turn, and the blue-red lights grew brighter. Then the splash of the leading car's headlights filled the bed.

"Guide my hand, Brenna." Jess was trying to site the rifle. She shook her head hard, and tried again. "Where's its heart?"

"Aim for the center of the front hood." Brenna grasped the rifle's barrel and adjusted it, then Jess fired, the stock hitting her shoulder. The Police car rocked slightly, but kept coming. Jess bolted another bullet in place and fired again, then a third time.

Steam erupted from the speeding cruiser's hood. It lurched, and then spun in a screeching arc before coming to a stop broadside, blocking the street. The second Police car swerved hard to avoid it, but the two heavy vehicles connected with a solid crash Brenna could hear from the truck.

"Excellent, Jess!" Dana pumped her fist.

"Okay, you're sitting down." Brenna took the rifle away from Jess and handed it to Eva, then pushed Jess gently back to the bench.

Moments later they cleared the dark buildings of the shabby subdivision. Dana cranked the wheel, and they rumbled down an incline and onto the wide, dry bed of a shallow ditch.

"Jesstin?" Kyla twisted on her seat. "Speak to me."

"Bumps and bruises, Ky. I'll live." Jess straightened on the bench next to Brenna, holding her right side. "Our path, Dana?"

"I think this old ditch peters out soon, but we're headed toward the hills." Dana kept their course steady on the rough trail, and Brenna felt the City begin to fall away behind them. Even the close, dank air in the covered truck bed seemed to hold more oxygen as they distanced themselves from the Clinic.

"We can pick up the north access road from this direction." Eva slid closer to Jenny and touched her leg. "Thank god those cops didn't hit our gas tank."

"That was a damn fine rescue, you guys." Brenna felt slightly queasy after hours of adrenalin-charged terror. She tried to smile. "Elise? How are you, honey?"

The child just studied her curiously.

"Elise is one brave little girl." Obviously a natural with children, Jenny cradled the small girl easily on her lap. "She's having quite an adventure tonight."

"Whee," Brenna agreed faintly. Her vision had adjusted to the dim light Selene sent through the bed's small windows. She turned to Jess and stared at her for the sheer pleasure of it, soaking in the reality of her presence. Then she touched Jess's head, wincing. "This is going to need stitches, love."

Dana hit a rut in the ditch and they bounced a half foot in the air, coming down with a teeth-rattling thump.

"Sorry," Dana called back hastily.

"Perhaps stitching should wait," Jess suggested. She lifted her arm, and Brenna slid beneath it. She rested her palm on Jess's chest and measured her heartbeat, and gradually her own slowed to a more bearable rhythm.

Caster will never hurt you again. Brenna closed her eyes. *Tristaine is free of her forever.*

Her mind replayed Caster begging for her life, crippled and helpless on the gymnasium floor. Brenna had fought in Tristaine's past battles. She had poisoned a dying soldier and lamed a young policewoman. She had never before looked at a defenseless human being and deliberately taken their life. But she knew if she faced the decision again, her bullet would still shatter Caster's skull. Brenna was a healer capable of killing, and that was part of the humanity Shann said she must accept.

They found the north access road, and Dana maintained a steady speed. Brenna knew they were well out of the City when stars began to emerge in the sky above them, and Tristaine's Seven Sisters glittered again in the heavens. Brenna craned her neck to see them through the small window, and a tight muscle in her chest relaxed for the first time in days.

Then she saw the adult Elise appear there, in the midst of the stars. Her glowing figure stood quietly, her arms at her sides, the basin gone. Her beautiful eyes were clear, loving, and tearless. Elise lifted a hand in benediction, and the truck trundled on through the night, carrying them higher into the hills.

❖

The first rays of dawn ignited the eastern peaks before they made it to the ridge where Vicar and Hakan waited.

"Thank the Goddess, Jesstin." Hakan jumped down off the high boulder where she'd been keeping watch. "Did you find—"

"We have what we came for, adanin, and more." Jess tried not to lean so heavily on Brenna's shoulder. She was grateful when her old friend asked no questions and just herded their party back to their camp.

They made for a bedraggled group. Brenna walked beside her, her arm around her waist, so weary she stumbled every third step. Elise was a rumpled lump sagging in Eva's arms, wan and exhausted.

"You all need rest." Hakan took the satchels from Dana. "I'll find you some breakfast before you bed down."

"We all have more ground to cover before we sleep." Jess drank in the sight of their horses, grazing peacefully in the small pasture next to their holdings. She saw Vicar, wrapped in blankets near the embers of a campfire, sitting up against a fallen log. She limped to her, and lowered herself with a stifled groan to one knee.

"Home from the hunt, Stumpy. Well met." Vicar was pale and her voice rasped, but she clasped Jess's hand tightly. "You look as dainty and pampered as ever."

"We have the Clinic's remedy, Vic." Jess was dismayed by the dark circles beneath her cousin's eyes. "You'll be strong again soon. How are your spirits?"

"I miss my wife." A vulnerable wave softened Vicar's strong features and then faded. "But your ugly mug gives me hope again. Sit down, Jesstin, before you fall on me."

"You're both getting injections, right now." Brenna went to Hakan and unzipped one of the bags.

"Aye, but then we move on." Jess settled onto the ground beside Vicar and accepted the canteen she handed her. "We have to assume they're after us, adanin. Our escape from the Clinic wasn't as blithe as we'd hoped."

"Jenny can ride with me, and Eva with Vicar." Hakan hunkered down on her haunches and stared at Elise. "And I'm sure one of us can carry this wee lass."

"Hakan, Vicar, meet Elise." Kyla's weariness vanished as she smiled at the little girl. "Samantha's daughter."

Hakan grinned, her white teeth flashing against her ebony skin. "Cybele be praised!" She extended a large, gentle finger toward Elise, who grasped it in her small hand and shook it solemnly. "Our queen's granddaughter. Jesstin, it's a miracle."

"Aye, Hakan. One of many." Jess swirled cool water in her mouth, then winced as she swallowed. Her sisters had gathered in a close circle. "Hear me, adanin. We'll be traveling with injured, and a small child. We can't possibly ride at full speed. Hakan." The big warrior was a dark blur to Jess, but when she squinted she was able to focus on her intent gaze.

"I'm sending you ahead, sister, with half the medicine in these bags. Tristaine's master of horse can travel much faster alone. Our clan needs this remedy badly, and as fast as Gaia allows."

Hakan's big hand smoothed across one of the carrying cases. "My Valkyrie's fresh, Jesstin, and so am I. We'll bring these to our lady with the speed of winged Pegasus."

"Watch me, Hakan. You'll need to show Shann." Brenna knelt beside Jess, uncapping one of the hypos and inserting its tip in a vial. "This is one dose." She showed Hakan the amount, and then injected Jess's arm smoothly, the tiny sting melding with her myriad other aches. Brenna's soft sigh stirred Jess's hair before she turned to prepare an injection for Vicar.

Hakan was watching Brenna carefully. "And should some disaster fell me, Jesstin, you'll still carry enough to save us?"

"Aye, we will." Jess shifted against the rough log bracing her back. "Your portion of our stock will cure those already sick. We'll bring enough to prevent anyone else from falling ill. But I warn you, Hakan, Tristaine is in turmoil. I send you not only as courier, but for your strong arm to defend our queen."

"Shann is ill, adanin." Brenna had been checking Vicar's wounded shoulder, but now she looked up to meet Hakan's stricken look. "And there's a rebellion in Tristaine, a faction of women who want to take their children off the mesa to escape the plague. Shann is doing all she can, but she's getting weaker. I'm afraid it might come to bloodshed if we don't get home soon."

Hakan had obviously heard enough. She inserted two fingers between her lips and unleashed a curling whistle. Moments later her large stallion came loping out of the small pasture toward them. "I'll make ready, Jess."

Vicar kicked off her blankets and extended her hand to Dana, and Jess curbed the urge to stop her. Vic looked worse than Jess felt, and that was going some. "Get me up, youngster."

Dana pulled Vicar slowly to her feet. "We'll get the horses, Jess. Let Brenna take a look at you."

"What a fine idea." Brenna sat beside Jess and opened the small bag containing her medical supplies. "I vote for Dana to be queen."

"We have a camp to pack," Jess pointed out.

"Yes, and Jenny and Eva are seeing to that nicely. And Kyla's looking after Elise." Brenna nodded at Kyla, who was fitting Elise with one of her smaller tunics. "We're going to take time for this now, Jesstin, unless you want me stitching you on Hippo's back. What a lovely scar that would make. Let me see your side first."

Jess let her unsnap what was left of her tattered shirt. She heard Brenna draw in a quick breath, and felt her cool fingers touch the heated ache high on her right side.

"This has to be killing you, honey." Brenna palpated the area carefully.

"I can draw even breath, so no ribs are broken."

"I'll wrap them anyway." Brenna brushed Jess's hair off her forehead, a faint line of worry between her brows. "You have a concussion, Jess, you know you shouldn't ride."

Jess smiled down at her. "Not much choice, lass."

Light was flooding their small clearing as morning dawned in full. The distant stench of the City still reached Jess, but at least the disinfectant stink of the Clinic itself was a bad memory again. She rested against the log and tried to ease the tightness in her shoulders.

"Jesstin."

The bleak note in Brenna's voice coaxed Jess's eyes open.

"You wouldn't have taken that blow to the head, if I'd made it to the Clinic in time." Brenna touched the burn below Jess's throat lightly. "You probably wouldn't have this, either."

"Bren, it could have played out a hundred different ways." Jess knew she couldn't absolve her lover with empty words, but she had to try to ease her sadness. "What matters is we're together as the sun rises."

"I'm trying to tell you I'm sorry." Brenna lifted Jess's hand. "Just hear that, okay?"

Jess raised Brenna's fingers to her lips and kissed them. "Aye, Bren. I hear."

They looked up as Hakan's braided head, high over her towering Valkyrie, was outlined by the rising sun.

"I ride for Tristaine, Jesstin." Hakan's touch on her stallion's neck calmed his prancing impatience. One of the canvas bags was lashed securely across the horse's withers. "I'll guard our lady's life as my own."

"Safe travel, adanin." Jess sketched a blessing in the air. "We follow fast."

Hakan spun Valkyrie in a tight circle then raised her hand in farewell to the others as she cantered out of the clearing.

Elise stumbled over to them, watching the retreating horse with wonder. The big beast was a marvel to her, and Jess studied the child with equal fascination. Samantha's lost bairn, alive and safe. Jess loved Brenna's younger blood-sister well, and she would give much to be with her when she returned the child to her mother.

"Go get my pickers." Elise stood in front of them, looking uncertainly from Brenna to Jess. She didn't seem to expect her command would be obeyed. She clenched the soft fabric of Kyla's tunic, which fell almost to her ankles. She turned and pointed back toward the City. "I left them there."

"What are pickers, sweetheart?" Brenna asked.

"Of my real mom. That I drawed of her down there. I hid 'em from *her*." Elise turned from side to side. "*She* wasn't my real mom."

Jess looked at Brenna. They both knew whom the child was referring to.

"No, she wasn't your real mom, honey." Brenna brushed the dust off Elise's forehead gently. "But you're going to meet her real soon. She's going to be so happy to see you."

"Me too!" And Elise smiled for the first time, a dazzling sight. Then she turned and trotted back to Kyla.

"Hakan's right. It's a miracle." Brenna leaned against Jess, as they watched Elise help Kyla pack their food supplies. "I can't believe we're bringing her home. Even when I let myself hope she was alive, I thought it would take years to find her."

"I thank my Mothers for such miracles." Jess pressed Brenna's knuckles to her lips, remembering those sick moments last night when she feared she'd lost her to the City.

Jess shifted against the log and cradled Brenna's face. Her

blond hair lay across her brow in matted clumps, her cheeks were streaked with dust, and she was more beautiful than Jess had ever seen her. She drew her closer and brushed her lips with her own, savoring their warmth.

"Now, lass," Jess murmured, "stitch me and wrap me, and then we ride."

CHAPTER THIRTEEN

Their campfire had burned down to embers, but even this high into the hills the night air was mild. They needed only their lightest furs and blankets to sleep warmly.

Brenna rested against Jess, pleased to know that her training in anatomy was sound, and there were, indeed, six hundred and fifty muscles in the human body. She could confirm this personally now because every individual one of hers ached like hell. Jess's heartbeat was slow and steady against her ear. She lifted her head with an effort and checked Vicar, who slept deeply nearby.

"Well, I have it on the highest authority that Samantha's daughter was placed with a farming family outside the West Borough over a year ago." Jenny slapped shut the pages of a computer printout in disgust, then tossed them into the glowing coals of the fire. The flaring red light illuminated the dirty, exhausted faces around their circle. "My sister is an idiot."

"Not necessarily." Sitting across the fire, Eva smiled at Jenny. "I mean, yes, Gina's an idiot, but that database did tell us something. Elise spent her first two years in a Youth Home. This Caster only had her the last year or so."

The child was curled on a blanket beside Jenny, dead to the world. Brenna looked at her, troubled. She had suffered four full seasons under the care of that twisted psyche. Elise was well nourished and the right size for her age, and there were no signs of physical abuse, but Brenna feared for her emotionally. She didn't know as much about child development as Jenny, but she knew Elise had been mothered by a monster during her most tender and formative stage of inner growth. They could only pray Tristaine's nurturing would heal her.

"This is one tuckered out little girl." Jenny tucked the blanket around Elise's feet. "Kids this age have only two speed settings, full and off. This is off."

"Man, I hope she holds on to that gorgeous hair." Eva smiled down at Elise. "Isn't it beautiful, that shade of honey-red?"

It'll get darker, as she grows up, Brenna thought. *Elise will have chestnut curls like her father.* She contemplated the night sky and the glorious starfield above her.

She had told only Jess about her harrowing encounter with Matthew. Was there any way she could protect Sammy from knowing the devastating reality of his fate?

The mere fact that Matthew was alive was rendered nightmarish by the horror his life had become. Must Sammy learn about his betrayal, and the torture that compelled it, how Caster had maimed the man she loved? That the depths of her young husband's self-hatred had plunged him into drugs, whiskey, anything that would keep Matthew from remembering her face?

Brenna focused on the Seven Sisters and drew comfort from Jess's fingers drifting down her arm. It would do no earthly good for Sammy to know, and she would never have to. Jess would keep her counsel. Neither Dana nor Kyla had asked her yet about the liquor she had consumed, but they would. They had every right. But they would accept Brenna's heartfelt remorse, and her word that, for good reason, she simply could not tell them what happened.

And then I won't have to tell Sammy what happened. Brenna heard her own inner voice again, calm, but firm. *I won't have to tell my little sister how my actions led to even more grievous pain than she knew. Who am I trying to protect?*

Brenna yearned for Shann's counsel as painfully as she craved a soft bed after nights on stony ground. Shann and Jess would help her with this decision.

"Hey, Brenna?" Dana was carefully arranging the supplies in their second case. "Sorry, but you have to explain this to me again. The woman you kept seeing in your vision, that was our little Elise? Some future version of her?"

"I think the Elise I saw in my vision is kind of timeless, no particular age." Brenna turned her head stiffly on Jess's shoulder. "She's Elise's essence, for lack of a better word."

Kyla stretched out beside the fire. "Do you think you'll see her again, Bren?"

Brenna was quiet for a moment. "I think the Elise I saw on the spiritual plane needed our help desperately. Now that Tristaine is free from Caster in our world, I really doubt she'll appear to me again. The purpose of the vision was fulfilled."

"The spirits of Dyan and Camryn returned to us when Tristaine needed them most." Jess's voice was a low rumble in Brenna's ear. She was resting comfortably on the furs, and if her fever hadn't diminished, at least it was no higher. "Once our clan was safe, we said our last goodbyes. We won't see those adanin again in this life."

"Can I just say again that I can't *wait* to see Tristaine?" Eva's kind eyes sparkled behind her glasses. "Vision quests, ghosts popping in and out. Most of it scares the holy crap out of me, but I can't wait."

Soft laughter rippled around their circle.

Brenna returned Jess's drowsy smile, and then looked at Dana with some consternation. "Dana? What are you doing with—whatever it is you have there?"

"Just keeping this cold." Dana lay another slender pack inside the satchel in her lap. "These chemical ice packs last longer than I thought."

"What are you keeping cold?" Brenna sat up with a wince. "Kestadine doesn't need refrigeration." She saw Dana and Kyla exchange smug looks. "Dana? What else, pray tell, did you and Kyla take from the pharmacy?"

"Sperm," they chorused, and grinned at each other happily.

"You stole *sperm?*" Brenna sputtered.

"Well, the Clinic only collects it from prisoners for their stupid genetic experiments, right?" Kyla nudged Brenna eagerly. "This is Shann's policy of incremental change at its best, Bren! We're going to convert the sperm of a hundred Citizens into little baby Amazons."

"And it's not really criminal sperm," Dana added quickly. "You said the Civilian Unit only locks up renegade artists and rabble rousers. We figure these spermies are halfway Amazons already."

Jess laughed, a small, pleasant quake against Brenna's back. "Well done, adanin."

"Okay. I can work with this." Brenna lay down next to Jess again. "Come spring, Tristaine will have a baby boom. Excuse me, a bairn boom."

"I can't *wait,*" Eva said again.

"I'll take first watch, Jess," Dana volunteered. "There's a good lookout..."

Brenna drifted off before Dana finished the sentence.

❖

The glowing orb of Selene had passed her apex when Brenna woke abruptly.

She sat up and looked around in a minor panic. Their campsite was peaceful and still, her sisters curled beneath their furs, the fire crackling again in the center of their circle. Dana had apparently decided to call Kyla to take the next watch. She was crouching beside Brenna, tapping her foot, and the firelight revealed the concern in her expression.

Brenna felt it then, the irregularity of Jess's breathing, the quivering in the long muscles of her arms and legs. She turned quickly and saw the tension in her sleeping lover's bruised face and clenched jaw. Kyla touched Brenna's knee, then rose silently to return to her watch.

"Jesstin." Brenna breathed the name softly and then cupped

the back of her neck to measure her temperature. Relief filled her when she felt no fever. "Honey? Open your eyes, Jess."

Jess came to slowly, a deep breath shuddering through gritted teeth. It took her a moment to focus on Brenna, and that scared her a little.

"Hey." She stroked Jess's waist. "Talk to me, dearest. What's happening to you?"

"Just a dream." Jess swallowed hard.

"Damn," Brenna whispered. She closed her eyes briefly, cursing herself for forgetting the horrible nightmares Jess suffered after escaping from the Clinic the first time. "It must have been terrible, Jess. What did you dream?"

"I'd rather not go back there, Bren. Not right now." Jess let out a long sigh, her aching body relaxing again against the fur beneath them. "Be patient, lass. We both know I'll be fine. I just need to work the poison out of my head for a while."

"I want to help you." Brenna let Jess ease her head back down on her shoulder, and she sagged bonelessly against her. "Please, tell me how."

Jess's hold tightened around her, keeping her safe. "Be right here, querida." Her lips moved in Brenna's hair. "Be here every time I wake up."

"Ah, Jess." Tears rose behind Brenna's closed lids. "Of course I will."

She was cherished by this remarkable, amazing woman. And Brenna didn't know which Goddess to thank for that miracle, so she thanked all of them for the dark warrior in her arms as they both drifted back to sleep.

❖

"Brenna?"

Brenna rubbed her eyes, surprised to find herself upright and awake. Or apparently awake. She blinked and realized she was standing in one of Tristaine's most beautiful gardens, a lavish feast of flowers with origins from a dozen different lands. The air was sunny and quiet, and she sensed no hint of danger.

Then she turned and saw Elise walking toward her and felt a thrill of surprise. This was not the child Elise, but it wasn't her idealized essence, either. This young woman was fully human. There was no spectral white robe, no marble basin. She wore the simple longshirt and leggings of any Amazon. But here, again, in this peaceful garden, Elise wept.

Brenna stepped carefully toward her through the flowers. Elise stumbled slightly, and Brenna took her cold hands in her own. Her niece's green eyes were still achingly beautiful, but they held none of the serene remoteness of her spirit form. They were bloodshot and desolate.

"Brenna," Elise said again, and then lowered her head, unable to go on.

"Take your time, honey. I'm here, I'm listening." Sweet Gaia, Brenna thought, *she does look like a little girl. Like a child who knows she'll never see her mother again.*

And Brenna knew Samantha was dead.

CHAPTER FOURTEEN

E lise's small, fragile body roused a powerful tenderness in Jess, a maternity that was all but foreign to her. She had never felt drawn toward mothering a child, and doubted she ever would, but the forlorn misery of the little girl riding in front of her on Bracken's back tore Jess's heart.

Elise had awakened in tears that morning. She didn't sob; she made no sound at all. Her lower lip pushed out, and her large eyes welled and overflowed. She didn't answer Brenna's gentle questions and didn't respond when she finally heard the terrible words. Brenna hadn't had to say them. It was obvious to everyone watching that Elise already knew her mother was gone.

Jess wanted to have Brenna riding astride Bracken with them. One look at her adonai's stunned features told her how badly she needed physical comfort. Brenna rode stiffly and alone on her bay, her first horse, whose name she had chosen to please her little sister.

But necessity must rule, with Tristaine still in danger. Brenna couldn't carry a child safely on an unseasoned horse, not at the pace they traveled. Eva, a nurse, rode with Vicar, who was still dazed and aching from the bullet wound and the flu. Jenny's arms were clasped around Kyla's waist, her eyes squeezed shut as they cantered through a broad field. Dana's horse carried more of their supplies to free the others to ride double.

Crossing the pass had been nerve shredding and cruelly slow, but they had made it over the narrow passage without disaster. Jess spotted a bright cloth tied to a low branch as they emerged from the cliffs, and she went weak with relief. Hakan had left them assurance that she, too, had crossed safely.

Twilight was falling as they reached the meadow's end, and Jess signaled a halt. Their lathered horses snorted to a stop.

"Our big friends have done well, they've earned their feed." Jess clapped Bracken's damp neck. "I call for a brief rest before we put more leagues behind us."

Soft groans of relief convinced Jess that her adanin needed this respite as much as their horses. They couldn't spare a full night here, but Selene would rise in an hour and light their path toward Tristaine.

"Uh, Jess, someone?" Eva, seated behind Vicar on her roan, was struggling to hold the sagging warrior erect. "We need some help here."

"Jeeze, Vic!" Dana jumped off her horse and ran to help Eva lower Vicar to the ground.

Jess lifted Elise off Bracken's back, wincing at the pain in her side as she handed her down to Kyla. She joined Brenna next to her cousin, her heart thumping queasily in her chest.

Vicar was conscious, pushing weakly against Dana's supporting arms. "Stop, this is bloody embarrassin'."

"Hush, Vic." Brenna checked the wound on the back of her shoulder. It looked to Jess to be healing well.

"She was fine until we pulled up," Eva said quietly. "I think she's just beat."

Dana, who had had more than one nasty brawl with Vicar when she first joined Tristaine, held her now with solicitous care. "When did you give her and Jess our magic juice, Brenna, two days ago? How long does it take to kick in?"

"It's already kicking." Brenna sat back on her heels and appraised Vicar. "It'll be a few days before the kestadine takes full effect, Vic, but your fever's broken. With food and some decent sleep, you'll live to ride again."

Vicar grumbled a petulant war cry that loosened the band of worry around Jess's chest. She felt Brenna's cool hand on her face.

"What about you?" Brenna's expression was oddly wooden,

but the love in her touch was unmistakable. "Your fever's gone too, but you still have to be feeling pretty rotten, Jesstin."

"Aye," Jess admitted easily. "But I'll eat and rest, too."

"Aye, you will." Brenna glanced past Jess, and got to her feet. "I'll be back," she said quietly, and walked away from them, toward a small hill nearby covered with wildflowers.

Jess turned and saw Kyla behind her, holding Elise on her hip. She watched Brenna compassionately. Kyla, too, had loved Samantha deeply.

"Lay camp, adanin." Jess leaned an elbow on her knee and got stiffly to her feet. Jenny patted her arm sympathetically as Jess walked past her, keeping sight of Brenna as she disappeared over the hill.

❖

Some instinct told Jess to allow Brenna her distance until the first storm of weeping had passed.

Jess waited at the top of the hill, her hands clasped tightly behind her, aching with the need to hold her young wife. Brenna sat halfway down the gentle slope, her head buried in crossed arms, her shoulders shaking violently. Finally, after interminable minutes, Jess walked quietly down to join her.

Brenna lifted a trembling hand when Jess settled beside her, not quite ready for touch. Jess filled her lungs with clean mountain air, and asked her Mothers for the wisdom to comfort this woman she loved more than sunlight. She had never doubted her intuition where Brenna was concerned, but then Brenna's heart had never been this cruelly devastated.

"I'm s-sorry." Brenna cleared her throat. "I just couldn't see Elise's face, back there. Sh—she looks so much like Sammy."

"Aye, she does. It's all right, Bren. Take all the time you need."

Brenna nodded dully. For all the life in her features, they could have been seated before the City Clinic gates instead of this beautiful expanse of cliffs and meadows.

"Is it because she wasn't Amazon?" Brenna sounded honestly bewildered. "Is that why Sammy didn't rate Artemis's protection?"

Jess was silent for a moment. She reached for a scarlet wildflower and plucked it, and fingered its tender leaves thoughtfully. "Samantha is well-loved in Tristaine, Brenna. Our Mothers know her kindness, the sweetness of her spirit." She laid the wildflower in Brenna's lap. "Amazon or not, I believe They hold our little sister precious in Their hearts, just as we do."

"She was twenty-four years old, Jess." Brenna showed her the flower, fresh, vibrant with color, but dying even now. She tossed it aside and stood up gracelessly. "Samantha was healthy. She had no chronic medical conditions. If the Goddess who guides Tristaine is picking and choosing the sisters we lose, She had to stretch hard to take Sammy."

Jess made herself stay seated in the high grass as Brenna stumbled away from her.

"Three fucking days?" Brenna searched the craggy mountain peaks, and Jess knew she was addressing invisible Listeners. "She couldn't have lived three days longer to see her daughter? To hold Elise, just once?" She scrubbed her arm across her eyes and put one hand on her hip, fighting for composure, then turned to Jess.

"We put Samantha through hell, Jesstin. She had a family, she had work she loved, and then Amazon Nation fell on her life. Like an axe. And she gave us..." Brenna had to pause again. "Sammy gave us Elise. She gave Tristaine a queen. Don't you think that should merit one tiny, bloody shred of Gaia's mercy?"

"Aye, I do." Jess got to her feet and closed the distance between them. Brenna let her come, but the heartbreak evident in every line of her body almost winded Jess. "I don't know why Sammy was taken from us, Bren. The injustice of her suffering galls my spirit, too. We can't change her sad fate, but one thing we can do for Sam. And we will."

Jess took Brenna's hands. "We'll see that her baby is raised cherished and free, in the heart of a loving clan. You risked your life to give your Sammy a wonderful gift, lass. You saved her child from prison, and delivered her to sisters who will nurture and guide her, all her days. Samantha's joy in this must be immense."

Tears welled in Brenna's eyes again, and she let Jess take her in her arms at last. Jess cradled her, and then held her up as she sobbed, her own tears blending with Brenna's.

It gradually occurred to Jess that a light rain had begun to fall. She heard it, but she didn't feel it, and she scanned the cloudless skies, puzzled. Then she realized the hillside beyond their private embrace was dry. The fresh rain fell in a small, perfect ring around her and Brenna, not touching them, just gently encircling their grief.

She turned Brenna's head on her shoulder, so she could see the bright drops showering around them. "We're not alone in weeping for Samantha, adonai."

They held each other until the rain stopped, and stars began to appear in the darkening heavens.

❖

"Jesstin! Elise is gone!"

Dana's shout galvanized Jess, and she grabbed Brenna's hand and powered up the hill, ignoring the ache in her side.

"What happened, Dana?" Fear sharpened Brenna's tone.

"We were laying camp." Dana spoke rapidly. "She was there, and then she wasn't."

Jess's mind sorted quickly through what she remembered of the surrounding terrain. "How long gone?"

"No more than ten minutes, Jess." Dana nodded back toward their camp. "Eva's staying with Vicar. Jenny and Kyla are searching the meadow."

"Then we'll take the forest beyond the pasture," Jess said. "Spread out, but stay in each other's sight."

They moved quickly through the deepening twilight, the stars emerging in isolated pinpricks overhead. It was dim and treacherous light to search by, and Jess called on her other senses to detect any sign of Elise. She cursed the lingering fogginess that afflicted her thinking and slowed her reflexes. Soon the trees surrounded them, still sparse this close to the cliffs.

"Call her, Bren."

"Elise!" Brenna's cry was strident, and Jess knew she was imagining the child confronting a bear or toppling into a swift stream. She shared those visions. Jess shuddered at the thought of telling Shann, mere days after she lost her younger daughter, that she had let harm come to this little girl.

"Elise, honey, sing out!" Brenna managed to project a less anxious tone, and Jess listened intently for a response. She heard nothing but the faint song of a nightbird on a high branch.

Jess could see Dana weaving through the trees several yards ahead, and Brenna turning in place off to her right. Then she realized she could see Brenna more clearly with every passing second, and she came to a startled halt. Jess held out her palms, and they filled with silver light. A luminous glow washed down from the sky on all three of them, growing steadily brighter.

Brenna turned and pointed to the northern heavens, and Jess sighted the source of the eerie illumination. The Seven Sisters pulsed overhead with a fierce intensity, like sparking pinwheels in the blue-gray sky. Even as Jess watched, their light gathered and narrowed, and became a pure beam pointing above their heads. The beam disappeared behind a thick bank of trees just ahead.

Jess whistled sharply, and they broke into a run.

She heard a high-pitched yapping sound before she broke through the trees and saw the child. Elise was sitting in a large patch of wildflowers, brightly illuminated by the silver light, her small hand extended to a prancing wolf pup. Jess read the danger in a heartbeat and kept running, forcing more speed from her aching legs.

The pup was young, perhaps not even weaned. Its mother would be close by, with the rest of its pack. Elise was obviously enchanted by the dancing little creature and ignored Brenna's breathless call.

A ferocious growling prickled the nape of Jess's neck, and a large, full-chested gray wolf streaked into the far side of the clearing. Elise saw it, and her small body froze, hand still outstretched.

The charging she-wolf was targeting directly on Elise, and Jess realized it would come down to a simple footrace. Running flat-out, she despaired of reaching the child in time, but Dana was racing ahead of her, already drawing her dagger from her belt.

Half-crazed for the safety of her pup, the wolf never hesitated. It launched toward Elise's throat, and Dana smacked solidly into its body in mid-flight. Warrior and beast crashed into the grass only two feet from the child.

"Brenna!" Jess snapped. "There'll be others! Get the girl!"

Dana's scream chilled Jess, and she saw the wolf's powerful jaws clamped on her upper arm. The animal's churning hindquarters almost knocked Jess off her feet, but she was able to twist and swipe her dagger over its haunch. The wolf released Dana, snarling, and backed a few feet to face both its prey.

"Jesstin!" Brenna had swept Elise into her arms. She pointed toward two more gray wolves loping in on their left.

"Hold!" Jess reached out to stop Dana. The she-wolf was still crouching, set to leap, but it hadn't moved. Its silver hackles were raised, and it growled gutturally through bared, pointed teeth. Its pup was several yards behind it, cowering in the grass.

"Jess?" Dana gasped.

"Hold, Dana." Jess risked a glance at Brenna, who stood behind them, carrying Elise. The two new wolves had stopped several yards away, bathed in the constellation's strange light. Wolves on the hunt were known to attack a lone child, but they rarely confronted humans unless cornered. For a long moment, the only sounds in the clearing were the she-wolf's low growl and Elise's sobbing, and then both faded to silence.

The strange tableau held an eerie quality that resonated in the part of Jess's mind that harbored portents and prophecies. She couldn't guess the pup's gender, but all of the adult wolves were female, unusual in itself. Their gold eyes seemed locked on Brenna and Elise, even the crouching she-wolf, who slowly rose from its aggressive stance.

Her eyes on the wolves, Jess put a hand on Dana's arm, and touched sticky blood. "Back away," she said quietly.

They moved slowly and as one through the high grass, distancing themselves gradually from the motionless pack. The she-wolves watched them silently, and a shiver moved up Jess's back. The beasts' gazes remained centered on Brenna and Elise. As they reached the thick bank of alders and pines, the wolves turned and trotted back into the forest.

The ghostly illumination of Tristaine's starfield faded and left them deep in shadows.

❖

Jess raised her fingers to sound an all-clear whistle, and Brenna shielded Elise's ear with one hand. The child had stopped crying and sat in her arms listlessly, her head on Brenna's breast. She talked softly to her niece as they trudged back to camp.

Brenna remembered Samantha at this age vividly, though she had been only a few years older. When they were taken to the Youth Home, Sammy had clung to her the way her daughter did now. She slept for months curled next to her big sister. Brenna kissed the top of Elise's head, then forced Samantha out of her mind. "Dana? You've got some nasty bites on that arm."

"You're telling me." Dana examined her shoulder, frowning darkly. "Dang, another inch and that flea-infested cur would have chomped right into my glyph."

"She's able to lift it, Bren." Jess was still breathing hard after the brief climb, and her forehead gleamed with sweat. "How's Sammy's lass?"

"Good question. Hey, little girl." Brenna nudged Elise gently, and she lifted her head. "Did you get hurt, honey?"

Elise shook her head, and snuck two fingers into her mouth. "Go get the puppy."

Brenna had to smile. "There are lots of dogs in Tristaine, sweetheart. Lots of puppies to play with."

"They were my friends," Elise said. "The wolfs."

Brenna looked at Jess, startled. She wouldn't have expected Elise to even recognize the animals as wolves.

"I've never seen a pack focus like that, Bren." Jess was catching her breath as they entered the camp. "Dana and I attacked them, but they never took their eyes off the two of you."

"Somehow," Brenna murmured, gazing at Elise, "I don't think they were looking at me."

"Oh, hallelujah!" Eva was grinning broadly, her hands on her hips. "Vicar was right about that whistle, our escaped waif looks fine."

"She is. Just a bit shaken." Brenna smiled wanly at Eva, and let her take Elise. "Vic, how are you?"

"I've rallied, Brenna." Vicar lifted herself on one elbow.

Kyla and Jenny ran out of the meadow, their faces flushed with color.

"Great catch, you guys!" Kyla went to Eva and Elise and stroked the little girl's head. "Where did you go, wee one?"

"Is everybody okay?" Jenny panted. "What was that crazy light in the sky?"

"A guiding signal from our Mothers." Jess was lowering herself stiffly onto a folded blanket. "We wouldn't have found Elise in time without it."

"Dana, let's take care of your arm." Brenna went to her pack to take out her satchel of medical supplies and almost walked into Kyla as she pushed past her to reach Dana.

"Demon's bile. What happened?" Kyla lifted Dana's arm gingerly and stared at the two sets of bloody bite marks.

"Our Elise ran into a wolf pack," Jess said. "Dana tackled a charging she-wolf in full flight. It was an amazing feat, adanin."

Brenna smiled at Jess, knowing she had deliberately voiced this praise when others could hear it.

"Well done, youngster." Vicar gave Dana a gruff nod of approval.

"Shucks." Dana shivered visibly. "I'm still spooked by how close it was."

"Look, you did a wonderful thing, and that's great." Kyla was still examining Dana's arm. "But these bites are still bleeding, Dana." She flicked Brenna a glance that held real fear. "Is there any chance these wolves were rabid?"

"Nah, Jess said they were normal." Dana smiled. "Just looking after their young, like us."

"Kyla?" Brenna got one of their canteens and brought it to Kyla. "I want to get Elise settled. Would you wash out those punctures? I'll be right there."

"Sure, of course." Kyla tugged Dana gently to the campfire and sat cross-legged on the grass beside her.

Eva and Jenny had gotten Elise seated on a fur, but she was fretful and whining and looked far from ready for sleep. Brenna went to Dana's pack and pulled out their rolled map of the City. She selected a slim chunk of cold charcoal near their fire, and brought them to the little girl. She spread out the blank side of the parchment in front of her.

"Here, honey. Could you draw us a picture of the wolf puppy?"

"Okay." Elise accepted the charcoal and peered at it curiously. "He had blue eyes."

Coming down off their latest adrenaline-fueled escape, the Amazons prepared efficiently for sleep. Brenna checked Vicar and

Jess, then doctored Dana's arm and let Kyla take over bandaging it. Selene was fully visible above the trees by the time Brenna lay down beside Jess.

Elise had switched off halfway through her drawing and lay curled on the fur, still clenching the charcoal stick. Eva and Jenny had settled near her, both of them yawning widely. Jenny lifted herself on her elbows and sought out Brenna. There was a question in her eyes, and Brenna read the friendly compassion in Jenny's gaze as if she'd known the woman for years. Brenna smiled assurance that she was all right.

Kyla and Dana were talking quietly together beside the fire. Their tones were hushed, but their words still carried in the still night air.

"Just don't let these get infected." Kyla was tying off the last bandage around Dana's arm, the strips gleaming white against her tanned skin. "I really hate it when you're hurt, Dana. You need to take better care of yourself. See? You're still shivering."

Brenna lifted her head from Jess's shoulder and saw Dana seated next to Kyla, counting slowly on her fingers.

"Nah, I'm all right. I've just been sitting still too long." There was a hollow note in Dana's voice. "When I'm not moving, I start to count them up again."

"Count who, honey?" Kyla slid closer to Dana and slipped her arm around her waist.

"The people I killed on this mission. Four or five, maybe. I don't know if the men I shot in the Clinic are dead. I may have killed one of those guards before we got in." Dana was watching the flames. "I keep remembering knifing that kid in the gut."

"Oh, baby." Kyla stroked Dana's back. "That must be so hard."

"It's weird not knowing the exact number." In the firelight, Dana looked years younger, open and unguarded as she gazed at Kyla. "This shouldn't bug me, right? I mean, they were all clean kills."

"It's probably going to bug you all your life, Dana. And I thank Gaia you have the conscience for that." Kyla touched Dana's face. "Our Grandmothers honor your bravery in defending Tristaine, sweetie, but they cherish your noble heart even more, and so do I."

The wonder rising in Dana's eyes was intended for Kyla alone, and Brenna lowered her head to Jess's shoulder again and tried to relax. She listened to Jess's steady breathing. She wanted her home and safely bedded in their cabin, now, tonight.

"Sixteen." Jess's voice was a low rumble in her ear.

"Sixteen?" Brenna murmured. "And you're supposed to be asleep, Jess."

"The number of Tristaine's enemies I'd killed, when I was Dana's age." Jess sounded drowsy. "I used to shake sometimes, too."

You still shake sometimes, love, after a battle. Brenna kissed Jess's shoulder. *You're our clan's perfect warrior, Jesstin, with all the burdens that honor entails.* "You'll never take joy in killing, Jess. The Army didn't teach Dana that a true warrior must revere life. She's learned that from you."

"As I learned it from Dyan." Jess shifted beneath her. "We're almost home, lass. Sleep, now."

Across the campfire, Brenna saw Dana and Kyla draw closer to each other. They hesitated, their lips inches apart, and then Dana kissed her. Their first kiss was tentative, and then their mouths melded again, soft and lingering. Brenna smiled, and closed her eyes.

She prayed she'd find a vision of Tristaine in her sleep. She needed to know how Shann fared, and how serious the rebellion in the village had grown. But Brenna knew while her psyche was out searching the heavens, she would listen desperately for one loved voice.

Sammy? Are you out there? Tears welled behind Brenna's closed lids. *Come and tell me you're all right. Please.*

CHAPTER FIFTEEN

The yearning for home grew stronger in Jess as they neared the mesa, and she knew the sisters riding with her shared that pull. Even their horses sensed the welcome of Tristaine's stables, and they broke into a weary lope after they crested the last forested rise that led to the mesa. Twilight had faded to full dark, but they needed no illumination to follow this well-loved path.

"Jess!" Brenna urged her horse alongside Bracken. "There's trouble."

Jess took in the distant sheen in Brenna's eyes. She reined in and signaled the others to stop. "What do you see, Bren?"

"It's what I'm hearing." Brenna turned her head slightly, with a look of intense listening. "Women's voices. Shouting. Lots of anger and fear."

Jess began to signal formation, but then a distant sound reached her, too. Not the cries of women, but the faint clapping of horses' hooves through the underbrush.

"Jesstin?" Vicar called from the rear of their pack.

"Aye, Vic, I hear."

"They're running, Jess." Brenna's eyes were filled with dread. "They've left the mesa."

Jess whistled sharply, and Bracken exploded into a full gallop with one nudge of her knees.

The trees were still dense this side of the mesa, and Jess gave Bracken his head to weave through them. She ducked to avoid low-slung branches, part of her focus trained on the adanin riding in quick formation behind her. Jess heard a metallic creaking ahead, around a closely studded stand of maples.

The Amazons fleeing the mesa had taken a wagon, drawn by two horses. Its wooden bed held half a dozen children of various ages, their frightened faces flashing by Jess as she urged Bracken faster. Besides the two women driving the wagon, Jess saw three mounted warriors riding escort, and a low rage kindled in her gut. She whistled complex instructions to her cadre to surround their targets, and to fight without harm.

Startled faces turned toward them as they broke through the trees. One of the drivers lashed the horses and the wagon lurched, careening through the thick brush. Jess feared the cretins would dump their fragile cargo if they hit a rut. The warriors rode close by the wagon, and Jess pointed Bracken toward the one in the lead.

Cries of alarm rang out, and the high, fearful screams of the children, and she knew this had to end quickly. Jess drew aside the lead warrior, gathered herself, and leaped off Bracken's back. She knocked the woman sideways off her horse, and they smacked the ground with a teeth-rattling impact. Jess dismissed the pain coursing through her and twisted on top of the warrior's flailing body.

She knew this Amazon's face, and her smell. Perry's adonai considered fresh mint a protective charm, and she always wore a sachet of crushed leaves around her neck. Jess swiveled and pinned her to the ground, but not easily. Her strength was flagging, and it would be a close match if this came to blows.

Seeing their escort fall had broken the nerve of the wagon's drivers, and they let Kyla and Brenna grab their horses' bridles and slow them to a stop. Jess saw, with some relief, that the other two warriors had not so flagrantly forsaken their vows that they drew arms on their guild's leaders at first sight. They sat rigidly on their horses, under Dana's close watch and Vicar's notched bow. Jenny held Elise while Eva climbed into the wagon's bed to check the young.

Jess sensed a flurry of movement beneath her and reacted, answering Perry's jabbing knee by pounding her own into her gut. Breath gushed out of Perry's lungs and she tried to bend double, but Jess straight-armed her flat again.

"Don't vex me, Amazon," Jess hissed. "You disgrace your glyph by defying our queen's law."

"Jesstin, the sickness is everywhere!" One of the warriors was Kadisha, the mother of twin daughters. "The City remedy Hakan brought us doesn't work!"

"I'm breathing proof it works, you witless dunce!" Vicar spat, still sighting her arrow carefully on the warrior's leg.

"Hear me, Perry." Jess had seen the furtive glances the other women sent Perry's way, and knew she was the leader of this ill-advised plot. "We will do what we must to turn this wagon back toward Tristaine. If you insist on letting these little ones see their mothers injured or killed, let's have it done."

"Jesstin." Perry was still gasping from the blow to her gut. "I tried to reason with Shann—"

"Silence, woman." Jess shoved Perry down again and drew her dagger in one swift motion. "You can argue this betrayal to your guild and the Council. Your only choice now is to fight us or sur—"

"Please, Jesstin." The third warrior, Kaden, broke in. "You know we honor you—"

Jess whipped her dagger into whistling flight, and its tip thudded deep into a branch just inches from Kaden's wide left eye. Jess realized she should have considered the possibility that her concussed aim would be off, but she was too angry now for regrets.

"Don't talk to me about honor, warrior. You abandoned our queen at Tristaine's darkest hour. You shame Dyan's memory." Jess got to her feet and hauled Perry up with her, suppressing any hint of the grinding effort involved. The night air was quiet except for the harsh breathing of their horses. Even the children were silent as Perry and Jess faced each other.

Jess eyed her evenly. "Will you stand down, adanin?"

Perry was struggling to compose her features. She glanced

over her shoulder toward the wagon, and then met Jess's gaze. "We'll go back with you, Jess."

"Wise decision." Jess couldn't look at her anymore. She liked Perry, and respected her, and that made the sting personal. That warriors under Jess's guidance had joined this rebellion galled her deeply. "You warriors, into the wagon. Dana, gather their horses."

"You heard her, bait." Vicar nudged Kadisha none too gently with her foot. "Move."

Jess rested her hands on her knees and pulled in a deep breath. She felt Brenna's light touch on her back.

"That fall did me absolutely no good," Jess complained, before Brenna could say it. She straightened stiffly. "The bairns are all right?"

"Yes, they're fine." Brenna looked her over quickly. "You sure you're okay?"

"Aye, Bren."

"Jess, I'm still hearing them."

Jess saw that Brenna's shoulders had lost none of their tension. "The screams in the village, lass?"

"I need to be there, Jesstin." The dreamy cast had left Brenna's features, and her gaze was direct and sharp. "I'm riding ahead."

Jess realized Brenna was not asking her permission. She spoke with a sure certainty that brought Shann strongly to mind. Jess gave the hand signal that acknowledged an order from an Amazon queen. "Aye, Brenna, I hear. We'll follow you fast."

❖

Brenna pulled herself onto Hippo's back and urged her to a gallop. The little bay seemed startled that her gentle rider's touch suddenly held such command, but she obeyed gamely. They cantered up the rising path that led to the top of the mesa only minutes later.

After one stunned look at Tristaine's village square, Brenna just kept riding. It seemed half the clan had gathered there, carrying blazing torches, an angry mob incarnate. She nudged her horse into the midst of the roiling women, trying to pick out individual voices from the shouts cutting the air.

"Let us see Shann!" An invisible cry sounded behind Brenna. "If this City drug can save us, why hasn't it cured our lady?"

Small pockets of Amazons clustered together, arguing furiously. Brenna saw Bethany and Martine in one such group, their faces flushed with anger.

"My grandmother took that potion two days ago, and she's no better!" Jaisa, one of the weaver's guild, stood on a log bench, tears streaming down her face. "Let our mothers take their children out, it's their only chance!"

"Our lady's rule is clear, sisters!" Oisin jumped onto another bench and raised her hands for silence. "No one leaves the mcsa. Hakan tells us that Shann will address us in the morning. Our lady must rest tonight—"

"Our lady is too weak to leave her bed!" Bethany spun on Oisin. "Shann might be dying, warrior! This miracle drug she promised us is worthless." Someone cried in agreement, and Bethany lifted her fist. "We've lost seventy Amazons, sisters! How many more must die before you let us take our young out of this pestilence!"

"Brenna!" Sarah was making her way toward her, brandishing a cane to clear her path. She slapped her gnarled hand over Brenna's. "Thanks kindly for finally getting your lily-white butt back here, girl."

Brenna saw the genuine relief and affection in her elder's eyes. "It's good to see you, grandmother. But this is an ugly welcome."

"Isn't this the snotrag-sorriest mess you ever saw?" Sarah spat on the ground as shouting rose around them again. Brenna leaned down to hear her. "Hakan got here yesterday morning with the City's brew. She's with Shann in her lodge."

Brenna's chest tightened. "How's our lady, Sarah?"

"Knocked flat off her feet with grief, youngster." Sarah's wrinkled face softened. "Brenna. Have you heard?"

"Yes, I know Sammy's gone."

The old warrior nodded and patted Brenna's hand again. "Shanendra took a bad turn for the worse, but she's got that drug in her now. Seeing your face will do her a damn good turn. But first..."

"First we have butts to kick, lily-white and otherwise." Brenna smiled grimly. "Stay close, Sarah."

"I'll be right here, lady." Sarah stepped back and smacked her cane in her palm smartly, and Brenna turned Hippo toward the center of the village square.

Other voices called her name now, as more women sighted her. Brenna clicked Hippo to a trot, and she didn't pull up when she reached a snarl of arguing Amazons. They scattered from her path with yelps of alarm, and Brenna kept riding.

The rugged stone block that rested in the center of the village marked holy ground in the eyes of every Amazon who dwelled there. It sanctified the spot where once rested the diabolic altar of a deranged and demonic queen. The sculpted rock now served as a monument to the warriors lost in the battle that vanquished her. Brenna lifted one leg over Hippo's back and stepped nimbly onto its flat, chiseled surface.

She heard more than one gasp break out among the milling women as she faced them, and heads turned her way from every corner of the square. Touching the altar was no sacrilege—many women in the clan had draped themselves on its rough length, prostrate in grief, more than once. But something in the easy command of Brenna's stance on the stone claimed it as her royal pulpit.

The noise and clamor abated slowly, but then Brenna was in no hurry to speak. She saw that Jess had arrived and was riding Bracken around the outskirts of the crowd, studying it with diamond-sharp eyes. Sarah and Aria were watching Brenna, their postures tense and ready.

Brenna's breathing was even, her pulse slow and measured. She waited for silence with the same certainty that filled her when she tended Tristaine's wounded. Jess had sensed it, the strange confidence that filled her now, and so had Sarah. Whoever Brenna might be tomorrow morning, tonight she was an Amazon queen.

The warrior Jackson, holding a blazing torch, stood in the inner ring of women around the stone. Brenna extended her hand, and Jackson stepped forward and tossed her the torch. She caught it easily and lifted it, bathing the monument in a red-gold light.

"Adanin, hear me!" Brenna shouted the words—not in anger, but to reach every ear. "I stand on a shrine raised to honor our Amazon dead. The warriors remembered here died defending Tristaine, and their courage and sacrifice are sacred to us. Now we face another battle, no less deadly than the one that killed our valiant sisters. And we must attack our enemy with equal courage."

"We hear, Brenna!"

Brenna heard Shasa's cry, and continued. "We've asked for your patience as our healers fight this plague, but patience isn't enough. We must draw upon all the courage that courses through Amazon blood to hold faith with each other now. We *must* fight this battle as a united clan."

"Brenna!" Bethany stepped between two women. "We've lost enough dear blood to this nightmare. The youngest in our clan are—"

"The children of Amazons," Brenna finished. "And just as worthy of respect as all our adanin, Bethany. Their bravery is needed as well, to preserve our family." She stared at Bethany, and found compassion for her. "I've lost dear blood in this battle too, sister. I understand your fears, and share them. But listen well."

Brenna turned in a slow circle on the stone, taking in the faces around her. "The remedy we brought from the City *will* work. We're seeing it happen. But this drug does not bring an instant cure. The ill among us will regain strength slowly, over several days. And it will not save all. We may still lose those most gravely sick before we wake from this shared nightmare."

An uneasy rustling moved through the crowd. Brenna sought out Jess among the shifting figures, keeping watch near the edge of the throng. Jess looked at her with simple pride, affirming Brenna's faith in their clan. She was following Shann's teaching—tell Amazons the whole truth, and trust them to follow their Mothers' lights.

The mob was loosening, groups of women separating, all focused on one face.

"Our healers now have enough medicine to protect all our sisters, including our young, from falling ill with this flu. Aria?" Brenna lifted the torch, and saw the voluptuous Councilor move into its light, her smile as welcome as a warm bath. "Help our adanin move in shifts to the healing lodge. See that all who still need this remedy receive it before they sleep."

"It'll be done, Brenna." Aria winked at her, a signal of approval and thanks.

"We have ill who need tending." Brenna addressed the quiet crowd, her tone gentle now. "And the caretakers who have nursed them for days are exhausted. Those of you who are strong, offer our sisters respite, and care for their charges while they rest. Oisin, Jackson. Build a storyfire here, so the rest of our clan can gather and share comfort and hope."

Brenna waited, and heard no more murmurs of protest. She released a long breath. "We meet here again in the morning to hear our queen's address. May the Goddess protect your sleep, adanin."

"And yours, lady." The traditional response was called by several voices.

Brenna tossed the torch back to Jackson and stepped lightly and without ceremony off the stone block. Several women drifted nearer to speak to her, but Brenna moved past them with a quick touch and whispered apologies.

"Well done, lass." Jess's warm hands enfolded her own.

"Where's Elise, Jess?"

"She's with Kyla." Jess slipped her arm around Brenna's waist and led her toward the lodges that surrounded the village square.

"Dyan smiles proud on you tonight, Jesstin." Siirah, one of Jess's warriors, clapped Jess on the back as they passed. "You and your adanin rode true for Tristaine."

"Aye, Jess," another voice called, "our thanks to you all!"

A small but warming chorus followed them as they walked down the tree-lined trail that led to Shann's personal dwelling. Kyla waited at its steps, holding a sleeping Elise, and her eyes glowed when she saw Brenna.

"I heard every word, honey, and you were wonderful. You spoke as our lady, Bren."

"And now I need to speak *to* our lady." Brenna smiled at Kyla, and held out her arms for Elise. The child didn't wake as she was eased into Brenna's embrace. Jess put a steadying hand to her back as they went up the steps and entered the lodge that housed Tristaine's queen.

For a royal palace, its two rooms were remarkably simple and tidy. The log walls were all but covered with childish drawings from the clan's young. The only lavish appointments were the small, beautiful sculptures and paintings given to Shann by her sisters, not in tribute, but out of affection. The larger outer room held a fieldstone fireplace, a thick bear pelt rug, and several cushioned benches and chairs for the comfort of guests.

Brenna could already hear Shann, frighteningly hoarse, from the smaller room that served as her sleeping chamber.

"Hakan, Dana, stand down. Please remember I outrank you both."

Brenna stood in the doorway, and for a moment she was

unable to move, shocked by her mother's appearance. Shann looked as though she had lost ten pounds she couldn't afford, and her skin was dry and sallow. She stood shakily upright by her bed, clothed in a simple robe, pulling a shawl around her shoulders.

"I'm going to the square to tell them all to go the bloody hell to bed," Shann insisted, "and then I'll return here to my own. It will take all of five minutes."

Shann turned and saw them, then, Brenna and Jess and Elise. Her shaking stopped, and she stood very still.

"This is your granddaughter, lady." Brenna stroked the girl's soft hair. "Her name is Elise."

Shann's red-rimmed eyes flew to Brenna and then fastened on the sleeping child.

"You need to sit down, Shann." Hakan's large hand was both deferential and firm on Shann's elbow, and this time the queen didn't protest. She sat very carefully on her bed, then leaned back against the thick sheaf of furs that bolstered its head.

In the few steps it took Brenna to reach her side, a myriad of expressions fled across Shann's pale features. Brenna lowered Elise into her waiting arms.

Shann stared down at the child's face in open wonder. Brenna felt Kyla squeeze her hand as she joined her and Jess. With Hakan and Dana hovering near the bed, the small chamber should have felt crowded, but there seemed a vast and warm expanse surrounding the reclining queen and the child she cradled on her lap.

Elise stirred and rubbed her eyes with her fist. She blinked up at Shann.

"Hello, little one." Shann's whisper was tender and calm. "I'm your grandmother. My name is Shann."

"Oh..." Brenna could barely hear Elise. She seemed to study Shann for a moment, and then patted her face with her small hand. "Oh, good." Elise laid her head on Shann's breast with a tired sigh and burst into tears.

The child's sisters stood around her, sharing her grief. Shann rocked Elise as she sobbed, letting her tears flow as long as they would. Brenna's own eyes welled, but she saw the love and gratitude in Shann's expression clearly enough to imprint on her heart.

Three blood-bonded queens wept together that night, for the loss of a woman they would always hold dear. But Elise's spirit had shed her fill of tears, and another day was coming—a dawn all their clan could greet with renewed hope.

"My dear Elise." Shann rested her face in the child's hair and closed her eyes. "Welcome to Tristaine."

❖

Hours later, Brenna lay beside Jess and stared at the low fire that flickered in the hearth of their small cabin.

Sammy had always needed some kind of nightlight when she was little. The dormitories of the Youth Home were notoriously dark and ominous after lights-out, and Brenna had to be creative about arranging a little forbidden illumination. A small flashlight beneath their blankets worked for years once Brenna learned where she could filch batteries. Now the flames in the hearth bathed the bed she shared with Jess in a soft glow and offered the same comfort.

Jess was dozing, finally. Brenna lifted her head and stared down at her still profile, outlined by the moonlight that fell through the window. Jess's rugged features were relaxed in sleep, her brow was smooth, and her firm breasts lifted in deep, even cadence.

The mild weather allowed them to sleep without wraps, but this night they would have curled naked together had Tristaine been buried beneath blizzard snows. Brenna brushed the tips of her fingers down the side of Jess's face. She lay close against her, one leg slung across her thighs.

She lifted herself on one elbow and tried to see the bruises on Jess's ribs, but the red shadows cast by the flames were too deep. She drew her finger across the colorful glyph that capped the smooth swell of Jess's shoulder, and then over the faint scar on her collarbone, a remnant of the clash with Botesh. Her lover's powerful body was a living history of Tristaine's battles. So many scars, faded now against Jess's bronzed skin, so many times she had spilled blood for her clan.

Jess stirred beneath her touch, not in response, but in the first grip of dark dreams. Her forehead creased, and Brenna felt the long muscles in her legs begin to tighten. She nearly shook her awake, but then hesitated and continued her ministrations. Her lips moved across the darkness on Jess's side, and then coasted down to a thunderhead bruise emerging on her hip. Her breath warmed Jess's skin as she traveled, and the shivering in her long form began to ease.

"Gaia grant me a thousand awakenings like this." She could hear Jess's smile in her drowsy alto.

Brenna kissed her way up Jess's side, ending with a light brushing of her lips across her cool brow.

"Why are you awake?" Jess mumbled.

"Just hanging out with our Mothers." Brenna rested her head on Jess's chest. "Thanking them for answering my prayer, again."

"Ah, please give them my best." Jess stretched beneath her, cautiously. "We all owe our Mothers thanks for preserving Tristaine."

"I pray they'll preserve you, Jesstin. Every time." Brenna stroked Jess's muscled arm. "I watched you fight City soldiers and street punks and Clinic guards, and you're still here. You caught a killing flu, and you're still here. Being able to sleep beside you, whole and healing, at the end of the day is all I really ask of the Universe."

"And my Brenna is back."

Brenna could see Jess's smile this time. "What do you mean? Where have I been?"

"Claiming your rightful throne as a ruler of Amazons. It was amazing, Bren. You changed before my eyes tonight."

"Did I get any taller?" Brenna asked hopefully.

"I'm serious, querida." Jess kissed the top of her head. "Shann is right, you have it—the blessing of royalty our Mothers grant the queens who guide Tristaine. You've shown flashes of it before. I saw it in full flower tonight. We all did."

"The blessing of royalty?" Brenna wondered if she could ever see it that way.

"And the strength to bear its burdens." Jess wound her arms around Brenna, and a pleasant, creeping warmth filled her. "And we'll always have nights like this, adonai, to lay those burdens down."

Brenna melted against Jess and let out a sigh, a small wind that blew the lingering mists of battle and fear and loss from her mind. She watched the scarlet firelight flicker over the sculpted planes of Jess's body. She looked weary beyond measure, but a gleaming heat was rising in her eyes. She lifted her head and brushed her lips against Brenna's.

Their kiss deepened, and grew long and rich. The tips of Jess's fingers tickled over Brenna's bare breasts, finding her nipples and stroking them to taut peaks, so suddenly sensitive a hard shiver coursed through her.

Brenna closed her hand over Jess's. "Lie still." Jess growled some reply, but Brenna insisted, pressing her back against the furs. "No, Jesstin. You lie still now. You were right, I am back, and we're going to get acquainted again."

Their lips met, slow and sweet, and Brenna's fingers tangled in the wildness of Jess's dark hair.

"You've taken care of all of us since this plague started," Brenna whispered. "It's time you let someone look after you."

Jess rested her head against the folded fur and closed her eyes in acceptance, and Brenna began to strum her strong body like a breathing harp. Her fingers played over Jess's firm breasts, coaxing her dark nipples erect as she sucked lightly on the smooth skin of her throat.

She heard Jess's guttural moan of pleasure and moved lower, stroking the flat planes of her lover's belly. She lipped each nipple wetly, taking her time, drawing on her intimate knowledge of the best ways to pleasure this body she loved so much.

I guess I can't really claim I despise power, can I, Brenna thought, *because I'm powerful now, and I relish every moment of it.*

Jess's arms, strong enough to chop kindling from dawn to dusk when she was healthy, lay still at her sides, thrumming with a fine tension inspired by Brenna's skillful caresses. Her fingers drifted down to Jess's powerful legs, and delved into the soft folds between them. Jess hissed with pleasure, and Brenna had to lay her hand at the base of her throat again to keep her lying flat.

Her fingers moved with exquisite care, circling Jess's wetness, exploring deeper. This was the simplest of the many ways one woman made love to another, and Brenna's favorite way of loving Jess. She was able to track her rising passion by watching that sweet tension tighten her austere features.

"If I never command another Amazon in my life," Brenna whispered, "I'll still rule here, Jesstin." Jess's breathing hitched as Brenna stroked her relentlessly higher. "You've given me lasting reign over one warrior's heart...and you will submit to your queen."

Jess arched hard, and rode Brenna's churning fingers to a long and shuddering climax. Brenna caught her breath, awed as always by the wild, feral quality of Jess's rugged beauty when pleasure took her. She held her as her trembling began to ease, and she relaxed in stages, finally sagging back against the furs in sated exhaustion.

Brenna smoothed Jess's hair off her forehead. "Sleep, adonai," she whispered.

"My love." The corner of Jess's mouth lifted as she began to sink into sleep. "My j'heika."

CHAPTER SIXTEEN

Several days passed before Shann was strong enough to see her younger daughter laid to rest.

Her Council stepped in as the proficient backup to the throne they were intended to be. As the queen's second, Jess held traditional authority over all aspects of clan life until Shann could rule again. Given the nature of their enemy, Jess chose to defer many decisions to Brenna. Had Tristaine been under physical attack, Jess would have commanded their response, but she knew a healer's wisdom was needed to raise arms against this invisible foe.

The kestadine was administered quickly and efficiently, and few of their sisters suffered adverse reactions. Brenna organized shifts of healers to visit each lodge and monitor the recovery of the ill. The plague began to turn its last corner. There were no more reports of new cases, and fevers that had burned frighteningly high finally broke, allowing sufferers cool and restorative sleep.

Jess permitted no one but herself to handle the painful arrangements of funeral rites. Tristaine lost nearly eighty souls to the flu, twelve of them infants and young children. There were heartbreaking losses of the strong and vital as well—nineteen of Jess's warriors died, slain in their prime by an unseen and implacable enemy. Every guild in the clan lost women they loved.

The morning they were to say goodbye to Samantha had not yet dawned when Shann's Council gathered in the lush green park at the center of the village. The stars were still visible overhead, but they had begun to fade. Amazon funerals tended to be held at sunrise or sunset, those two periods of celestial transition when the curtains between worlds were most translucent.

Aria passed mugs brimming with a fragrant, potent tea that chased the last of the mist from Jess's mind. She had recovered rapidly from her illness, at least physically. Her stamina wasn't back to par yet, but Jess's body made sense to her again. The urge to move was returning to her, the itch to race through the pastures below their mesa for the simple pleasure of it.

Jess sat cross-legged in the grass, close to Brenna, who was leaning back on her hands, scanning the pale stars overhead. Shann had not yet called her Council to order, and the seven women sat in a close circle around the small, crackling fire, talking quietly. They had shared each other's company like this only weeks ago, but Jess took as much comfort in this reunion as if a full season had passed.

Shann and Kyla were deep in hushed conversation, their hands joined on Shann's lap. Their lady looked a decade older, and while her vitality was returning slowly, the new strands of gray in Shann's hair would remain, testament to her grief for her lost sisters.

Dana kept her voice low, as befit the predawn stillness, but her gestures were sweeping and elaborate. She sat between Aria and Sarah, who listened avidly to her report of their escape from the City. Sarah rocked back and snorted appreciative laughter, and tousled Dana's shaggy hair.

"I think Shann's strong enough now, Jess." Brenna leaned gently against Jess. "She can take Elise tonight."

"Good." Jess smiled. "That'll speed our lady's healing like no remedy on earth."

"Yes, and her granddaughter's, too."

Like all the clan's young, Elise would be nurtured by a whole tribe of mothers. One lodge, usually the biological parent's, served as an infant's primary home, providing the secure foundation all young ones needed. But many Amazons clamored to share child-raising duties, and Elise would grow and thrive under the loving watch of several of her elder sisters.

As Brenna and Jess had had to focus all their waking hours

since their return on serving Tristaine's needs, Elise had stayed a few nights with Dana and Kyla, and the rest in the affectionate care of Eva and Jenny. Their two new sisters were sheltered in a comfortable cabin kept ready for the clan's guests until they could help in the construction of their private lodge.

"Shann was robbed of the chance to mother us, Sammy and me." Brenna folded her arms around her knees. "She was intended to raise this child, Jess, this special young girl. Shann will teach Elise to cherish her clan, and to serve it in every way she can. She'll raise her to be a wise queen, and Tristaine will flourish under Elise's guidance."

Jess stared at her. "Is this prophecy, Bren?"

"Nope." Brenna had not smiled often in recent days, but she did then. "This is common sense, honey. I know my mom."

"And so we're met." Shann's warm voice drew them, still slightly hoarse, but rich again with both affection and assurance. Shann smiled at her women, letting the silence linger, and a collective sigh moved through them. "Our clan has traveled a dark and perilous path since I last looked on your dear faces, adanin. My thanks to our Mothers that you're all safely home again."

"And a few kudos to our grand dames up there for bringing you through your illness, Shanendra." Aria rested her hand on Shann's hair. "This clan is in deep grief, but we have our queen strong and steady at the helm again."

"So many," Brenna murmured. "Seventy-nine sisters gone."

"Yes." Shann cupped her hands around her mug of tea as if to warm them. "But we could have lost four times that number, Brenna. The plan you and Jesstin devised was courageous and sound, and it worked. You and the sisters who rode with you saved hundreds of lives."

"And you brought us Samantha's beautiful little daughter." Aria's large eyes were warm with compassion.

"And sperm," Dana added proudly.

Sarah cackled and slapped Dana's leg.

"Ah, yes, the sperm." Shann smiled sweetly at the heavens. "Brenna, meet with me soon to devise some way of storing our stolen specimens long-term. Everyone will want to claim their shot at motherhood at once, and I refuse to have two hundred Amazons going into labor in the same week."

"Wow. You're right, lady." Kyla grinned, and Jess's heart lifted at the fresh happiness in her eyes, a welcome glimpse of Kyla's younger self. It had livened all of them, the thought of welcoming new souls to Tristaine. "We'll have to have at least a zillion meetings to plan for all this, you guys. Our mothers' guild is going to triple in size!"

"Now, there's a grim notion." Sarah lit her pipe, scowling, the firelight gleaming off her bald head. "Those cretins were a hotbed of maternal stupidity through this siege, lady. What should we do with Bethany and her ilk?"

Shann refilled Aria's mug and her own before she replied. "Bethany and Perry and several others galvanized the dissent in our clan. They were following their own lights, but they were dangerously blind to reason."

"In the City, they'd be locked away for life," Dana said soberly. "Any kind of political rebellion means a Prison sentence down there."

"Hell," Sarah grumbled, "even a moral sewer like the City has good ideas now and again."

"Oh hush, you old crank." Aria tossed a pinecone at Sarah's foot. "Lady, what are you pondering in that judicious mind of yours? You look troubled."

"Just thoughtful, sweet girl." Shann searched the gradually lightening sky. "Tristaine follows the system of government Lady Artemis bequeathed to us centuries ago, but our monarchy is a difficult legacy, adanin—rife with risk of abuse. Bethany's crime was defying her queen—refusing to obey my sovereign command. We must never condemn an Amazon for challenging authority without careful consideration."

"But Shann, do you really doubt the wisdom of your decision?" Brenna looked puzzled. "Because medically, practically, ethically—every way I can imagine, forbidding anyone to leave our mesa was the right call."

"It was," Shann nodded, "and my heart rests easy there. But I rely on my Council to hold the frightening power of my crown in check, in this and all things. Are we in agreement in this matter?"

Jess studied each face in their circle. Brenna was watching Shann with a thoughtful expression, and it occurred to Jess that Elise was not the only queen Shann was preparing for Tristaine's crown. "We are, lady. Those who violated your rule endangered our clan, and they must answer for it."

Shann folded her hands in her lap. "All right, we're in accord. The leaders of the dissent will be required to serve Tristaine's guilds to atone for their choices. The physically strong will put in extra hours cleaning Hakan's stables after their regular day's work is finished. The others will toil for our weavers and healers. They must perform these added labors daily until Tristaine's first snowfall in the coming season."

"Old Bethany is tough and stringy as a mountain goat, she can handle mucking out the stables." Sarah looked cheered at the prospect. "Lady, order Hakan to load our horses' feed with extra bran!"

They heard it then, the unique swirl of birdsong that signaled the rising of the sun. Moments later the first rays of dawn bathed their circle in gold light, and Jess took Brenna's hand.

"It's time to say our farewells to Samantha, dear ones." Shann held Brenna's gaze for a long, private moment. "Our Mothers have chosen a beautiful morning to welcome our little sister to the stars."

❖

Amazons chose different paths to the spirit realm, according to their natures.

Warriors were often cremated, to launch their spirits heavenward with the same fiery passion that infused their spirits. Many in the artists' guild rested on pallets in the limbs of high trees, returning to the elements in the free open air and the rustling music of wind through leaves.

Samantha had not chosen a guild, but she had taken great pleasure in the restful beauty of Tristaine's gardens and orchards. She would be laid to rest as many of their growers preferred, nestled in the fertile earth that sustained their clan.

Her body had been lovingly prepared and wrapped in a shroud of white linen, barely visible beneath the thick carpet of wildflowers strewn over the pallet on which it lay. Samantha would be buried near their most lush and brilliant flowerbed, a short distance away up a gently sloping hill.

Women were gathering around the bier now, and more were joining them. This farewell would have been well attended even if Samantha had not been the daughter of a queen. Brenna clasped hands with one Amazon after another to hear their condolences and realized her younger sister had touched even more hearts than she knew.

"Brenna?" Jenny patted her arm, and Brenna turned to embrace her with a grateful sigh.

"Hello, Jen. It's good to see you."

"Eva's on her—ah, Eva's here." Jenny smiled as her partner joined them, balancing Elise on one hip.

"Good morning, Elise." Brenna's throat tightened as she kissed her niece's cheek. "How are you, sweetie?"

"Morning, fine," Elise replied. She found a smile for Brenna, but her little face was wan.

"She didn't feel like breakfast this morning," Eva said. Then she gulped and stepped back as Shann approached them. "Oh. Hello, your—highness."

"Good morning, Eva, Jenny. Thank you for being here."

Shann smiled at them warmly, and touched Elise's face. "Adanin, I believe we're ready."

"Shann, Oisin and Jackson can carry your chair." Brenna was still a little concerned about Shann's pallor. "There's no need for you to walk up there."

"It's not far, Brenna." Shann gazed at the bier. "I don't need carrying. I want to walk my daughter home."

Elise patted Eva's breast. "Put me down."

Eva threw a questioning look at Brenna, then lowered Elise to the ground. The little girl looked up at Shann solemnly, ready to walk her mother home. Shann and Brenna took her hands.

Samantha's last journey began. She was lifted to the shoulders of the four Amazons selected for that honor, including Dana and Jess. Kyla stood immediately behind her cortege. She turned and waited for Shann's nod, and then looked at Brenna, and sketched a sign of love and comfort in the air with her fingers.

Sammy had been mesmerized the first time she heard Kyla sing. Beautiful even when she was a girl, Kyla's voice was full-throated and glorious now. The melody she sang as they began their walk to the gardens was one of Tristaine's oldest dirges, a song so moving its first notes invited the natural release of tears.

Brenna made no effort to restrain her own. She was blinded, but she didn't need to see clearly to follow this familiar path, holding Elise's small hand. The crowd made its way up the grassy hill, Kyla's mournful song giving poignant voice to their grief.

When its last notes dwindled, an expectant hush fell over the women following Samantha's bier. Brenna brushed her hand across her eyes and saw a few smiles break out on the faces around her. Amazon funerals began in sorrow, but they also celebrated the woman lost to the clan.

"Do you remember when Sammy learned to ride?" Dana's call sounded first. She threw a glance back at the throng, grinning. "It took her about five seconds. Hell, she taught *me* how to stay on a horse! Remember when we raced to the canyon, lady? Sammy out rode some of our best!"

There was laughter, and several shouts of agreement.

"Our little sister helped me spin my yarn, many a time." An older voice rose somewhere off to Brenna's left. "She sat at my feet and listened to my stories by the hour. Her sweet face is before me still, lady, and always will be."

Someone else called out praise for Samantha's bravery during their battle with the demon queen, and Brenna smiled through her tears. Sammy would be the first to admit that through the battle with the demon queen, she was either throwing up or trying not to faint with terror. But she'd stayed beside Brenna through those long, terrible nights, and it warmed her to hear her sister's courage praised. Another Amazon drew more soft laughter by recalling Sammy's lavish love for the clan's many dogs.

Kyla began singing again as they crested the hill, and a dazzling carpet of colorful flowers opened before them. This time her song held no grief, just a melodic appreciation for the gift Samantha's life had been to her friends. The fond stories continued as the women gathered at the south end of the flower field, and the towering oak tree that would keep watch over the new grave.

"Here." Elise let go of Shann's and Brenna's hands, and rummaged in her shirt. She withdrew a neatly folded sheet of parchment, and opened it carefully.

Brenna crouched beside Elise. "What is it, honey?"

"It's for my mom." Elise handed her the sheet. "See?"

Elise would probably never grow to be one of Tristaine's great artists. Hardly the work of a prodigy, her drawing held all the crudity of a three-year-old's scrawl. But it was Sammy's face. She was there, in the primitive quirk of line and curve, and the very roughness of the sketch brought her smile to life. Elise had never laid eyes on her mother, but somehow she had rendered her image with loving faithfulness.

Brenna couldn't speak. She handed Shann the parchment, and the queen studied it for a long moment. Her fingers trembled slightly.

"Do you like it?" Elise's brows puckered with worry.

"Oh, Elise. Sweet girl." Shann released a long breath. "It's beautiful. Just like our Sammy."

"It's for my mom," Elise said again. She sounded apologetic. "But I can drawer you one if you want. So we won't forget."

"I would like that very much," Shann told her. She gave the drawing back to Elise.

The gathering around the oak tree stood quietly now. They watched the small girl go to her mother's bier, the parchment balanced in her hands. She laid it carefully on the wildflowers covering the pallet and placed stems on its edges to hold it in place.

"Here," Elise whispered. She spoke a few more words too softly for Brenna to hear, a private message intended only for her mother.

A light breeze stirred the high grass, and the field of bright blossoms bowed in gentle waves. Brenna closed her eyes and opened her senses, hoping again for any faint sign of Samantha in the mystic ethers beyond this world. She waited, but all she heard was the scattered birdsong of Tristaine's gardens.

When she opened her eyes, Shann was standing before the bier, her hands resting on Elise's shoulders. She was, in the same heartbeat, an Amazon queen and a mother whose child died in her arms. Her fingers sifted through Elise's fine auburn hair, the same shade as Samantha's at that age.

"I named her Joanna." Shann's voice was as low and intimate as a lullaby. "She graced my life for less than a year before the City took her. Before I lost her to the terrible system her father and I, and many others, were trying to fight."

A murmur ran through the women, honoring their queen's memory of that long-ago devastation.

"I couldn't protect my baby from the horrors of a Youth Home," Shann continued. "I wasn't there to teach her to look beyond the oppressive fear of the City, to better and kinder ways of seeing the world. But someone was there." She sought out

Brenna. "My eldest, my Rebecca. She watched over her little sister through the bleakest childhood imaginable, and helped her grow into an honorable and loving young woman."

Brenna's vision blurred again. She felt Jess's strong hands cup her shoulders, and she leaned back against her gratefully.

"All our blessings on your journey, Samantha." Shann's gaze moved to the jagged peaks beyond their mesa. Elise peered up at her grandmother's face, then looked toward the mountains too. "Wherever your spirit travels, Tristaine will always shelter you. You will find an eternal and loving family waiting for you here. And as surely as I know Gaia lives, I know Her kindness will allow our reunion one day." Shann lowered her head. "Sleep well, my Sammy. I'll see you in the morning."

Jess's arms enfolded Brenna's waist. Brenna closed her eyes and prepared herself to say her own private goodbye.

Find happiness, little sister. It's there for you, somewhere out there, and you so richly deserve it. Find friendship. Find love. And, Sammy, please, find me again. I'll search for you forever.

Kyla's last song, an ethereal aria, enveloped them in a beauty that held melancholy and solace in equal measures. Above them, high in the limbs of the oak, a solitary wren sang its own benediction, and Brenna turned into Jess's waiting arms.

❖

"It's good to feel your strength returning, Jesstin." Shann walked arm in arm with Jess through the gold light of late afternoon. The weather had been sweetly mild in the three days since Samantha's funeral, but there was a bare hint of crispness in the air, a harbinger of the turning season. "Brenna had to threaten to tie you to your bed to get you to rest, but it seems your uncanny resilience has won out at last."

Jess murmured agreement, searching the wide pasture of waving grass for Brenna and Elise.

"Of course, I'm assuming Brenna ties you to the bed with some regularity, in any case."

"*Lady.*" Jess stopped abruptly.

"Just seeing if you were listening, adanin." Shann pressed Jess's arm, obviously pleased with herself. "Forgive me if I offended your chivalrous sensibilities."

"Forgive any scandalous reference to your daughter, lady." Jess lowered her voice. "But I do tie better knots."

"Well, that's fine," Shann said quickly. "Have our two little sisters deserted us again?"

Jess grinned and turned to look back down their path. Kyla and Dana had fallen some distance behind. They were trying to walk with their faces cemented together. Dana was quite a bit taller than Kyla, so keeping their lips locked made for rather stumbling progress.

"You'd think they were trying to best the sperm," Jess sighed.

Shann glanced behind her and laughed softly. "They're not alone, dear one. Tristaine is seeing the dawn of a great surge of romantic energy, and we're all the better for it. It's the irresistible call of life after so much loss. You've felt it, Jess."

"Aye, I have." Jess spotted Brenna and Elise down at the bottom of the pasture, small figures at this distance. "I do."

Shann looked at Jess appraisingly. "You're stronger now in many ways, Jesstin. The City demons that haunted you were vicious, and you faced them with great courage. You led your adanin through terrible dangers bravely and well, and proved again that my Dyan's faith in you was wisdom itself."

"Thank you, lady." Jess smiled at her queen. "You were right. An Amazon's terrors are better borne with her sisters at her back."

Jess reached behind her in time to plant a hand on Dana's chest and prevent her and Kyla from walking into them.

"Whoops! Sorry." Dana didn't look particularly contrite.

Kyla adjusted her hair quickly. "Are they here, lady?"

"Yes, we've found them." Shann nodded toward the lower end of the pasture. "They look quite content and I'm sorry to disturb them, but it's time Elise had her nap."

And Brenna hers, Jess thought, with pleased anticipation. Shann was right. She and Brenna had both been touched by the rising desire that swept so many in their clan in recent nights.

Brenna's hair was a gold gleam in the distance. She sat gracefully and still in the high grass, Elise in her lap. Neither of them had seen their sisters watching them from the small rise. They were focused on the prancing antics of a small speckled puppy that danced in circles around them.

"Animals will always befriend Elise, just as they did her mother." Shann's smile was wistful. "I don't need to share my kin's second sight to know she has that blessing."

"This child has many blessings." Jess slipped her arm around Kyla's shoulders, and kissed the top of her head.

"Yeah, in her teachers alone." Dana shaded her eyes. "Shann will show Elise how to be a queen, and Brenna will let her in on all the mysteries of the spirit world."

"That teaching has already started." Kyla leaned against Jess. "Look at them, down there. Elise is listening to our seer like she's revealing the marvels of the universe. I wonder what sacred secrets of the mystic realms Brenna's telling her?"

❖

"What did she call the toy?" Elise asked.

"She named him Hippo."

"Like your horse!"

"Just like my horse." Brenna brushed a strand of grass from Elise's hair.

"I won't name you Hippo." Elise scratched the upturned belly of the blissful puppy sprawled by her foot. "You're too little."

"You'll think of a good name." Brenna glanced up and saw the far-off women watching them. "Look, our sisters are here. You about ready for your nap, honey?"

"Tell me the story about the can...the canrival, again? With you and my mom and the scary cars?"

"I sure will, once you're tucked in." A languid warmth filled Brenna. She could feel Jess's gaze on her face like the soft brushing of her lips across her skin. She kissed the top of Elise's head. "Come on, little one. Let's go home."

About the Author

Cate Culpepper is a 2005 Golden Crown Literary Award winner in the Sci-Fi/Fantasy category. She is the author of the *Tristaine* series, which includes *Tristaine: The Clinic, Battle for Tristaine, Tristaine Rises,* and *Queens of Tristaine.*

Cate lives in the Pacific Northwest, where she supervises a transitional living program for homeless young gay adults. She's currently at work on a new novel, *Fireside*, set in present day, but peopled by Amazons nonetheless.

She can be reached at Klancy7@aol.com.

Books Available From Bold Strokes Books

Queens of Tristaine: Tristaine Book Four by Cate Culpepper. When a deadly plague stalks the Amazons of Tristaine, two warrior lovers must return to the place of their nightmares to find a cure. (978-1-933110-97-4)

The Crown of Valencia by Catherine Friend. Ex-lovers can really mess up your life...even, as Kate discovers, if they've traveled back to the 11th century! (978-1-933110-96-7)

Mine by Georgia Beers. What happens when you've already given your heart and love finds you again? Courtney McAllister is about to find out. (978-1-933110-95-0)

House of Clouds by KI Thompson. A sweeping saga of an impassioned romance between a Northern spy and a Southern sympathizer, set amidst the upheaval of a nation under siege. (978-1-933110-94-3)

Winds of Fortune by Radclyffe. Provincetown local Deo Camara agrees to rehab Dr. Nita Burgoyne's historic home, but she never said anything about mending her heart. (978-1-933110-93-6)

Focus of Desire by Kim Baldwin. Isabel Sterling is surprised when she wins a photography contest, but no more than photographer Natasha Kashnikova. Their promo tour becomes a ticket to romance. (978-1-933110-92-9)

Blind Leap by Diane and Jacob Anderson-Minshall. A Golden Gate Bridge suicide becomes suspect when a filmmaker's camera shows a different story. Yoshi Yakamota and the Blind Eye Detective Agency uncover evidence that could be worth killing for. (978-1-933110-91-2)

Wall of Silence, 2nd ed. by Gabrielle Goldsby. Life takes a dangerous turn when jaded police detective Foster Everett meets Riley Medeiros, a woman who isn't afraid to discover the truth no matter the cost. (978-1-933110-90-5)

Mistress of the Runes by Andrews & Austin. Passion ignites between two women with ties to ancient secrets, contemporary mysteries, and a shared quest for the meaning of life. (978-1-933110-89-9)

Sheridan's Fate by Gun Brooke. A dynamic, erotic romance between physical therapist Lark Mitchell and businesswoman Sheridan Ward set in the scorching hot days and humid, steamy nights of San Antonio. (978-1-933110-88-2)

Vulture's Kiss by Justine Saracen. Archeologist Valerie Foret, heir to a terrifying task, returns in a powerful desert adventure set in Egypt and Jerusalem. (978-1-933110-87-5)

Rising Storm by JLee Meyer. The sequel to *First Instinct* takes our heroines on a dangerous journey instead of the honeymoon they'd planned. (978-1-933110-86-8)

Not Single Enough by Grace Lennox. A funny, sexy modern romance about two lonely women who bond over the unexpected and fall in love along the way. (978-1-933110-85-1)

Such a Pretty Face by Gabrielle Goldsby. A sexy, sometimes humorous, sometimes biting contemporary romance that gently exposes the damage to heart and soul when we fail to look beneath the surface for what truly matters. (978-1-933110-84-4)

Second Season by Ali Vali. A romance set in New Orleans amidst betrayal, Hurricane Katrina, and the new beginnings hardship and heartbreak sometimes make possible. (978-1-933110-83-7)

Hearts Aflame by Ronica Black. A poignant, erotic romance between a hard-driving businesswoman and a solitary vet. Packed with adventure and set in the harsh beauty of the Arizona countryside. (978-1-933110-82-0)

Red Light by JD Glass. Tori forges her path as an EMT in the New York City 911 system while discovering what matters most to herself and the woman she loves. (978-1-933110-81-3)

Honor Under Siege by Radclyffe. Secret Service agent Cameron Roberts struggles to protect her lover while searching for a traitor who just may be another woman with a claim on her heart. (978-1-933110-80-6)

Dark Valentine by Jennifer Fulton. Danger and desire fuel a high stakes cat-and-mouse game when an attorney and an endangered witness team up to thwart a killer. (978-1-933110-79-0)

Sequestered Hearts by Erin Dutton. A popular artist suddenly goes into seclusion; a reluctant reporter wants to know why; and a heart locked away yearns to be set free. (978-1-933110-78-3)

Erotic Interludes 5: *Road Games* eds. Radclyffe and Stacia Seaman. Adventure, "sport," and sex on the road—hot stories of travel adventures and games of seduction. (978-1-933110-77-6)

The Spanish Pearl by Catherine Friend. On a trip to Spain, Kate Vincent is accidentally transported back in time...an epic saga spiced with humor, lust, and danger. (978-1-933110-76-9)

Lady Knight by L-J Baker. Loyalty and honour clash with love and ambition in a medieval world of magic when female knight Riannon meets Lady Eleanor. (978-1-933110-75-2)

Dark Dreamer by Jennifer Fulton. Best-selling horror author, Rowe Devlin falls under the spell of psychic Phoebe Temple. A Dark Vista romance. (978-1-933110-74-5)

Come and Get Me by Julie Cannon. Elliott Foster isn't used to pursuing women, but alluring attorney Lauren Collier makes her change her mind. (978-1-933110-73-8)

Blind Curves by Diane and Jacob Anderson-Minshall. Private eye Yoshi Yakamota comes to the aid of her ex-lover Velvet Erickson in the first Blind Eye mystery. (978-1-933110-72-1)

Dynasty of Rogues by Jane Fletcher. It's hate at first sight for Ranger Riki Sadiq and her new patrol corporal, Tanya Coppelli—except for their undeniable attraction. (978-1-933110-71-4)

Running With the Wind by Nell Stark. Sailing instructor Corrie Marsten has signed off on love until she meets Quinn Davies—one woman she can't ignore. (978-1-933110-70-7)

More than Paradise by Jennifer Fulton. Two women battle danger, risk all, and find in one another an unexpected ally and an unforgettable love. (978-1-933110-69-1)

Flight Risk by Kim Baldwin. For Blayne Keller, being in the wrong place at the wrong time just might turn out to be the best thing that ever happened to her. (978-1-933110-68-4)

Rebel's Quest, Supreme Constellations Book Two by Gun Brooke. On a world torn by war, two women discover a love that defies all boundaries. (978-1-933110-67-7)

Punk and Zen by JD Glass. Angst, sex, love, rock. Trace, Candace, Francesca...Samantha. Losing control—and finding the truth within. BSB Victory Editions. (1-933110-66-X)

Stellium in Scorpio by Andrews & Austin. The passionate reuniting of two powerful women on the glitzy Las Vegas Strip where everything is an illusion and love is a gamble. (1-933110-65-1)

When Dreams Tremble by Radclyffe. Two women whose lives turned out far differently than they'd once imagined discover that sometimes the shape of the future can only be found in the past. (1-933110-64-3)

The Devil Unleashed by Ali Vali. As the heat of violence rises, so does the passion. A Casey Family crime saga. (1-933110-61-9)

Burning Dreams by Susan Smith. The chronicle of the challenges faced by a young drag king and an older woman who share a love "outside the bounds." (1-933110-62-7)

Fresh Tracks by Georgia Beers. Seven women, seven days. A lot can happen when old friends, lovers, and a new girl in town get together in the mountains. (1-933110-63-5)

The Empress and the Acolyte by Jane Fletcher. Jemeryl and Tevi fight to protect the very fabric of their world: time. Lyremouth Chronicles Book Three. (1-933110-60-0)

First Instinct by JLee Meyer. When high-stakes security fraud leads to murder, one woman flees for her life while another risks her heart to protect her. (1-933110-59-7)

Erotic Interludes 4: *Extreme Passions* ed. by Radclyffe and Stacia Seaman. Thirty of today's hottest erotica writers set the pages aflame with love, lust, and steamy liaisons. (1-933110-58-9)

Storms of Change by Radclyffe. In the continuing saga of the Provincetown Tales, duty and love are at odds as Reese and Tory face their greatest challenge. (1-933110-57-0)

Unexpected Ties by Gina L. Dartt. With death before dessert, Kate Shannon and Nikki Harris are swept up in another tale of danger and romance. (1-933110-56-2)

Sleep of Reason by Rose Beecham. While Detective Jude Devine searches for a lost boy, her rocky relationship with Dr. Mercy Westmoreland gets a lot harder. (1-933110-53-8)

Passion's Bright Fury by Radclyffe. Passion strikes without warning when a trauma surgeon and a filmmaker become reluctant allies. (1-933110-54-6)

Broken Wings by L-J Baker. When Rye Woods meets beautiful dryad Flora Withe, her libido, as hidden as her wings, reawakens along with her heart. (1-933110-55-4)

Combust the Sun by Andrews & Austin. A Richfield and Rivers mystery set in L.A. Murder among the stars. (1-933110-52-X)

Of Drag Kings and the Wheel of Fate by Susan Smith. A blind date in a drag club leads to an unlikely romance. (1-933110-51-1)

Tristaine Rises: Tristaine Book Three by Cate Culpepper. Brenna, Jesstin, and the Amazons of Tristaine face their greatest challenge for survival. (1-933110-50-3)

Too Close to Touch by Georgia Beers. Kylie O'Brien believes in true love and is willing to wait for it, even though Gretchen, her new boss, is off-limits. (1-933110-47-3)

100th Generation by Justine Saracen. Ancient curses, modern-day villains, and an intriguing woman lead archeologist Valerie Foret on the adventure of her life. (1-933110-48-1)

Battle for Tristaine: Tristaine Book Two by Cate Culpepper. While Brenna struggles to find her place in the clan, Tristaine is threatened with destruction. Second in the Tristaine series. (1-933110-49-X)

The Traitor and the Chalice by Jane Fletcher. Tevi and Jemeryl risk all in the race to uncover a traitor. The Lyremouth Chronicles Book Two. (1-933110-43-0)

Promising Hearts by Radclyffe. Dr. Vance Phelps arrives in New Hope, Montana, with no hope of happiness—until she meets Mae. (1-933110-44-9)

Carly's Sound by Ali Vali. Poppy Valente and Julia Johnson form a bond of friendship that becomes something far more. A poignant romance about love and renewal. (1-933110-45-7)

Unexpected Sparks by Gina L. Dartt. Kate Shannon's attraction to much younger Nikki Harris is complication enough without a fatal fire that Kate can't ignore. (1-933110-46-5)

Whitewater Rendezvous by Kim Baldwin. Two women on a wilderness kayak adventure discover that true love may be nothing at all like they imagined. (1-933110-38-4)

Erotic Interludes 3: *Lessons in Love* ed. by Radclyffe and Stacia Seaman. Sign on for a class in love…the best lesbian erotica writers take us to "school." (1-9331100-39-2)

Punk Like Me by JD Glass. Twenty-one-year-old Nina has a way with the girls, and she doesn't always play by the rules. (1-933110-40-6)

Coffee Sonata by Gun Brooke. Four women whose lives unexpectedly intersect in a small town by the sea share one thing in common—they all have secrets. (1-933110-41-4)

The Clinic: Tristaine Book One by Cate Culpepper. Brenna, a prison medic, finds herself drawn to Jesstin, a warrior reputed to be descended from ancient Amazons. (1-933110-42-2)

Forever Found by JLee Meyer. Can time, tragedy, and shattered trust destroy a love that seemed destined? Chance reunites childhood friends separated by tragedy. (1-933110-37-6)

Sword of the Guardian by Merry Shannon. Princess Shasta's bold new bodyguard has a secret that could change both of their lives. *He* is actually a *she*. (1-933110-36-8)

Wild Abandon by Ronica Black. Dr. Chandler Brogan and Officer Sarah Monroe are drawn together by their common obsessions—sex, speed, and danger. (1-933110-35-X)

Turn Back Time by Radclyffe. Pearce Rifkin and Wynter Thompson have nothing in common but a shared passion for surgery—and unexpected attraction. (1-933110-34-1)

Chance by Grace Lennox. A sexy, funny, touching story of two women who, in finding themselves, also find one another. (1-933110-31-7)

The Exile and the Sorcerer by Jane Fletcher. First in the Lyremouth Chronicles. Tevi and a shy young sorcerer face monsters, magic, and the challenge of loving. (1-933110-32-5)

A Matter of Trust by Radclyffe. When what should be just business turns into much more, two women struggle to trust the unexpected. (1-933110-33-3)

Sweet Creek by Lee Lynch. A celebration of the enduring nature of love, friendship, and community in the heart-warming lesbian community of Waterfall Falls. (1-933110-29-5)

The Devil Inside by Ali Vali. The head of a New Orleans crime organization falls for a woman who turns her world upside down. (1-933110-30-9)

Grave Silence by Rose Beecham. Detective Jude Devine's investigation of ritual murders is complicated by her torrid affair with pathologist Dr. Mercy Westmoreland. (1-933110-25-2)

Honor Reclaimed by Radclyffe. Secret Service Agent Cameron Roberts and Blair Powell close ranks to find the would-be assassins who nearly claimed Blair's life. (1-933110-18-X)

Honor Bound by Radclyffe. Secret Service Agent Cameron Roberts and Blair Powell face political intrigue, a clandestine threat to Blair's safety, and the seemingly irreconcilable differences that force them ever farther apart. (1-933110-20-1)

Innocent Hearts by Radclyffe. In a wild and unforgiving land, two women learn about love, passion, and the wonders of the heart. (1-933110-21-X)

The Temple at Landfall by Jane Fletcher. An imprinter, one of Celaeno's most revered servants of the Goddess, is also a prisoner to the faith—until a Ranger frees her by claiming her heart. The Celaeno series. (1-933110-27-9)

Protector of the Realm, Supreme Constellations Book One by Gun Brooke. A space adventure filled with suspense and a daring intergalactic romance. (1-933110-26-0)

Force of Nature by Kim Baldwin. From tornados to forest fires, the forces of nature conspire to bring Gable McCoy and Erin Richards close to danger, and closer to each other. (1-933110-23-6)

In Too Deep by Ronica Black. Undercover homicide cop Erin McKenzie tracks a femme fatale who just might be a real killer...with love and danger hot on her heels. (1-933110-17-1)

Erotic Interludes 2: *Stolen Moments* ed. by Radclyffe and Stacia Seaman. Love on the run, in the office, in the shadows...Fast, furious, and almost too hot to handle. (1-933110-16-3)

Course of Action by Gun Brooke. Actress Carolyn Black desperately wants the starring role in an upcoming film produced by Annelie Peterson. Just how far will she go for the dream part of a lifetime? (1-933110-22-8)

Rangers at Roadsend by Jane Fletcher. Sergeant Chip Coppelli has learned to spot trouble coming, and that is exactly what she sees in her new recruit, Katryn Nagata. The Celaeno series. (1-933110-28-7)

Justice Served by Radclyffe. Lieutenant Rebecca Frye and her lover, Dr. Catherine Rawlings, embark on a deadly game of hide-and-seek with an underworld kingpin who traffics in human souls. (1-933110-15-5)

Distant Shores, Silent Thunder by Radclyffe. Dr. Tory King—along with the women who love her—is forced to examine the boundaries of love, friendship, and the ties that transcend time. (1-933110-08-2)

Hunter's Pursuit by Kim Baldwin. A raging blizzard, a mountain hideaway, and a killer-for-hire set a scene for disaster—or desire—when Katarzyna Demetrious rescues a beautiful stranger. (1-933110-09-0)

The Walls of Westernfort by Jane Fletcher. All Temple Guard Natasha Ionadis wants is to serve the Goddess—until she falls in love with one of the rebels she is sworn to destroy. The Celaeno series. (1-933110-24-4)

Erotic Interludes: *Change Of Pace* by Radclyffe. Twenty-five hot-wired encounters guaranteed to spark more than just your imagination. Erotica as you've always dreamed of it. (1-933110-07-4)

Honor Guards by Radclyffe. In a wild flight for their lives, the president's daughter and those who are sworn to protect her wage a desperate struggle for survival. (1-933110-01-5)

Fated Love by Radclyffe. Amidst the chaos and drama of a busy emergency room, two women must contend not only with the fragile nature of life, but also with the irresistible forces of fate. (1-933110-05-8)

Justice in the Shadows by Radclyffe. In a shadow world of secrets and lies, Detective Sergeant Rebecca Frye and her lover, Dr. Catherine Rawlings, join forces in the elusive search for justice. (1-933110-03-1)